SLOW HAND

SLOW HAND

Women Writing Erotica

Edited by

MICHELE SLUNG

HarperCollins*Publishers*

FIRST EDITION

Designed by Alma Hochhauser Orenstein

Library of Congress Cataloging-in-Publication Data

Slow hand : women writing erotica / Michele Slung. — 1st ed.
      p.   cm.
ISBN 0-06-016598-7
    1. Erotic stories, American. 2. Women — Sexual behavior — Fiction. 3. Short stories, American — Women authors. I. Slung, Michele B., 1947– .
PS648.E7S56 1992
813'.01083538 — dc20   91-58375

92 93 94 95 96 ❖/RRD 10 9 8 7 6 5 4 3 2 1

This one is Trin's, with love

And therewithal Criseyde anoon he kistè;
Of which, certeyn, she feltè no dis-easè.
And thus seyde he: 'Now woldè God I wistè,
Mine hertè sweetè, how I yow might pleasè.

FROM *TROILUS AND CRISEYDE*, BY GEOFFREY CHAUCER

I want to write a book of erotic short stories.

MADONNA, QUOTED IN THE *WASHINGTON POST*

CONTENTS

❧❧❧❧❧❧❧

Introduction   xiii

IN THE PRICK OF TIME   1
by **Susan Dooley**

LEAPER   11
by **Jenny Diski**

DROUGHT   27
by **Wendy Law-Yone**

OH, BROTHER   41
by **Bea Wilder**

NINETY-THREE MILLION MILES AWAY   51
by **Barbara Gowdy**

THE SHAME GIRL   71
by **Carolyn Banks**

THE FOOTPATH OF PINK ROSES   81
by **Carol Lazare**

THE WAGER   91
by **Sara Davidson**

THE STORY OF NO   99
by **Lisa Tuttle**

REASONS NOT TO GO TO FORT LAUDERDALE   115
by **Liz Clarke**

BLESSED IMMORTAL SELF: HOW THE JEWELS
SHONE ON YOUR SKIN!   131
by **Susan Swan**

BLUE FEATHERS   139
by **Anne Rhyd**

THE AMERICAN WOMAN IN THE
CHINESE HAT   149
by **Carole Maso**

WINDOWS   157
by **Idious Buguise**

THE MANGO TREE   163
by **Sabina Faye**

EROS IN OVERTIME   177
by **Kay Kemp**

ANECDOTE   183
by **Catherine S.**

TREATS   193
by **Rebecca Battle**

TOO TALL FOR GRACE   201
by **Susan J. Leonardi**

About the Authors   223

INTRODUCTION

❧❧❧❧❧❧❧

It seems worthwhile to me to establish from the start that prior to beginning this project I had not previously considered myself an expert on sex or sexy stories, any more than is any average, curious reader holding what is now the finished book. However, as with art, I do know, unequivocally, what *doesn't* work for me and so, trusting my experience and judgment as a skilled editor, I set about fashioning a collection of erotic imaginings that *does*.

More than anything else, I have wanted, in choosing the very varied selections you will encounter here, to elicit the same kind of recognition that *all* women I know felt when a decade ago they first heard the Pointer Sisters song—female anthem, really—that inspired this book's title. The idea, in case you missed it back then and aren't still humming along, was to find a lover willing to "spend some time," one with "an easy touch" who'd put a higher value on teasing anticipation and gradual sensation than on mechanically grinding body parts. Frankly, even hearing a few bars of "Slow Hand" on the car radio, while stalled in traffic, was enough to induce a pleasant shiver or two, and I don't for a single moment think I'm alone in this reaction.

Naturally, then, I confess it was a surprise and a fairly severe disappointment when recently I learned that a pair of male songwriters had actually written this brilliant answer to Freud's famous question, "What does a woman want?" But, taking stock of what's positive (as is my frequent habit), I'll just point out that it was the Pointer Sisters, bless their hearts, who did, after all, sing those amazing lyrics with such fabulously convincing oomph. And, thankfully, it is *their* identification with it that stays with us—even if they're not collecting *all* the royalties.

At any rate, "Foreplay, and lots of it" was the musical message the father of analysis didn't live to hear, and it came at the start of a decade when quick, easy self-gratification seemed, for just a while there, to be every person's right. Mind you, we're not talking about the sixties, which was the (actually, only partly) permissive era of my own youth and sexual coming-of-age, but about the eighties, when, at the same time, the unyielding and ghastly nature of the AIDS virus began to make itself known. In many ways, then, this was a hostile climate for romance—or perhaps not, it's hard to say. On the one hand, there was the need to consider more carefully one's sexual partners and what one chose to do with them, perhaps, indeed, to spend more time in sensual play and touch. And on the other, there was the specter of sexually associated disease and death, along with grim predictions of the widening spread of AIDS, to act as an anaphrodisiac for generations of men and women well into the twenty-first century.

Still, it seems to me that at the moment when the Pointer Sisters sang this song and put it into the ears of women young and old—then and now, now as then—a line was drawn and many of us crossed it. To make sex sexy is surely one fine goal; to make it sensual is, I believe, an even finer one. And to be erotically *aware* is to understand that there is knowable human reality behind that fateful moment in Greek mythology when the sage Tiresias, truthfully replying and blinded for his pains, told the disputatious gods that women are capable of receiving nine times more pleasure than men from the act of love.

Thus, I think it's no coincidence that erotic writing by women writers for woman readers seemed to come into its own in the 1980s, following that seductive affirmation of our own perceptions about our *need* for seduction delivered in "Slow Hand." (Male readers, to be sure, are welcome in these precincts, although one man of my acquaintance, given an early glimpse of a story I'd accepted, commented carefully, "Well, it doesn't turn me on, but it's certainly instructive." In fact, what more can I hope for?) Building upon the success of earlier books by Nancy Friday and Erica Jong and the phenomenon of Anaïs Nin's posthumously published *Delta of Venus*, Lonnie Barbach, herself author of the influential self-pleasuring manual *For Yourself* and other works in the field of sexuality, led the way with her collections, *Pleasures* and *Erotic Interludes*. But she was not alone: there was also the Kensington Ladies Erotica Society of San Francisco, as well as the writers/editors Susie Bright, Tee Corinne, Terry Woodrow, Laura Chester, and others still.

These books were eagerly bought by women, perhaps first as novelties and later as necessities. What seemed crucial about them, simply stated, was their opening up to women an area of human experience heretofore dominated—like nearly every-thing else—by male principles. As with the consciousness-rais-ing evenings of an earlier epoch and the myriad support groups now so ubiquitous, this new wave of women's erotic writing offered the embrace of acceptance: we are like you, you are like us—and self-consciousness at least be *damned*, if not wholly dis-pelled.

When it was initially suggested to me that I attempt to edit such a collection of original erotic writing myself, I wasn't at all sure what I thought—or what I felt. I was not, you see, in any sense, a student of the literature; my own personal mental library of erotic writing was no more and no less than the stock repository of a person of my generation: mainly the naughty bits in Harold Robbins and Grace Metalious, Jacqueline Susann and J. P. Donleavy. Molly Bloom's soliloquy worked best when read aloud by that ardent English professor whose mission was to try and make us amateur Joyceans, and a copy of *Fanny Hill*, of course, was generously circulated by its owner around my dormitory. I also discovered *The Story of O* on a bookshelf one late-sixties night while babysitting for some faculty brats, and I will now confess to having utterly forgotten the little tykes' existence by the time their parents returned home, so engrossed was I.

Yet, upon examining the memories of erotica's impact on those tender sensibilities that once were mine, I did have a surprising moment when I realized that, in fact, the sexiest reading experience I could recall was one I'd all but forgotten: Chaucer's *Troilus and Criseyde*. And in Middle English, no less. It was the same spring that everyone, myself included, was devouring *Portnoy's Complaint*. But, to tell you the truth, Philip Roth is no Chaucer, and the melting sensation between my legs as I formed each difficult archaic word aloud, stanza by slow stanza, and awaited the eponymous lovers' much-delayed consummation, was a splendid antidote to Roth's *haut*-contemporary neurotic carnality.

Anyway, back in the present, at my editor's suggestion, in order to make up my mind about taking on the project, I began to browse in the more recent compilations of women's erotica. Quite soon, not surprisingly, my own synapses of personal recognition were firing madly: I was hooked. But, intrigued as I was by my own strong skin responses to many of the stories I read, what affected me more was my delight at how these works broke free of the tyranny of physical beauty and the desirability of youth which figured, crushingly, as elements in most of the sexy writing I'd previously known. That is to say, whether these new stories functioned as teasing turn-ons, or as evocations of tenderness, or as explorations of the boundaries of passion, or whether they ventured into the adjoining territories of betrayal, jealousy, loneliness, rejection, insecurity, they always kept clearly in the foreground *real* women—not nymphets or sex goddesses, not unblemished starlets or virginal misses, but women with both bodies and histories that were not free of imperfections.

Remembering all those times when unwashed hair, or a

recalcitrant pimple, or an unwished-for five pounds seemed to stand between me and the enjoyment I might take from a kiss, and always sensing the unfairness of it, but accepting it, nonetheless, as the set of rules from which to operate, I appreciated at once the sea change these stories represented. To see beyond the envelope—the flesh—that contains us, to the message inside ("my sexual self may not be exactly who I *look* like") is what, in an ideal world, we'd naturally expect from our lovers, or potential lovers, yet gaining such intuitive sympathy, such tolerance, is still an elusive goal for most of us.

Erotica being written by women today (and including all the stories in this book) distinguishes itself not only by its equal-opportunity treatment of the issues of age or physical attractiveness, of course. But that was the first thing that struck me about it, and I sensed it as one of the more important elements of the greater power being returned to women: not to have our sexuality be about things that are (often) beyond our control and not to have our sexual selves dictated or defined by others. In the male-female sexual relationship, at any rate, the mutuality of acceptance has until now been almost as rarely observed *in theory*, even, as it has been in practice. (For most of history, for example, women's bellies were admired as beauteous symbols of fecundity, yet today paunchy guys are given society's carte blanche to nag voluptuous girlfriends who rarely find it a two-way street. And how many women are allowed, or are willing, to turn their gray hairs into a sexual asset, as so-called distinguished gents may do?)

In this collection there are stories by many sorts of women; I know what very few of them look like. There are contributions by women barely out of their teens and those by women past their half-century mark. Quite a few of the pieces are about seductions of one sort or another, but others are about love, and there are some about lust. A few deal with the secrets we keep, as well as those we don't. Some of the stories are about characters who are strangers to each other, while others feature familiar lovers known all too well. One or two selections are angry, and a couple are startling. What they have in common, though, is the impression of honesty they leave, whether the mood is realism or fantasy or some area in between. And, for me, what's so truly wonderful is that all I had to do was *ask*, in order to summon most of these stories into being.

The contributors selected also represent a fairly good cross section of women: American, Canadian, English, Asian, straight, gay, bisexual, urban and rural, teachers and journalists, novelists and poets, actresses and athletes, students and mothers, women divorced, separated, and single. But I did not start out with a pretested recipe that called for including a teaspoon of this kind of person or a half-cup of that kind. There were, however, some very general guidelines with which I approached individual women, and also networks of women, both here and abroad asking them to give it a try. What I said was this:

"The stories can be long or short. They can be about heterosexual or lesbian sex, about old women or young, middle-, or teenaged, about couples, groups, or solitary pleasure. They can also be true, or based upon true-to-life experience, or even upon such experience as you might have preferred it, with a few adjustments for fantasy. The main goal, as I see it, is that the stories, each and every one, tickle my senses, make me feel sensuous or sensual, sexier, in fact, for having read them."

If my mailman had only known! But once the stacks he left at my door started getting higher, it was hard not to notice with what alacrity many women — most of them strangers to me — took to the task. Even more rewarding was the way a great number of my correspondents warmly thanked me for allowing them the opportunity to try this New Thing: being given an invitation, that is, unexpected license, to examine their sexual attitudes or express their sexual preferences or fantasies or to explore an erotic memory long stored away. "I don't know if it's any good, but I'm having fun," one woman wrote me back. (Her story was later accepted.) Said another, "I send it to show I tried, but I also had fun doing it so you needn't feel bad about sending it back." (This one made it into the finished book, too.)

Similar sentiments, with "fun" the word most frequently used, were echoed by women thousands of miles apart, and quite a few, as well, stated their belief that such a project was an all-too-needed antidote to the "fearful, conservative" mood with which we were closing the century. "A lot of us have been writing, or dying to write, more erotically for some time now," another contributor informed me, and, indeed, of the nineteen selections, half are by women for whom this was not their "first time."

Anyway, drawing upon the enveloping camaraderie I soon began to feel, I'd like to point out once again that women, by and large, *do* know what they want in the way of erotic stimulation and satisfaction; it's only feeling strong and confident enough to express it and *then* getting someone to pay attention that's the problem! For my part, I've tried to keep all earnestness and moralizing at bay, for to listen is to learn, and to hear these disparate voices is to realize that there is not—that there *cannot* be—one politically or aesthetically correct single way to inhabit fully our female sexual selves. Ever. But, with more and more women revealing what they want, be it a slower hand or a quicker one, we will increasingly be able to check our own instincts against those of other women and gain strength in the process ... and, perhaps, better orgasms, as well.

In this book, as I've intimated, I gave the writers no formulas to follow, no party line to adhere to; at the same time, I recognize a very real responsibility to acknowledge that the need for "safe sex" exists at every level throughout our society today. (Make that civilization: there is nowhere to run.) But I could not bring myself, even in the face of this appalling knowledge, to edit a cautionary safe-sex passage into each and every story. I am not the surgeon-general, and while fiction can indeed be influential as well as be a type of drug, its effect cannot be monitored nor should its content be regulated. While it is potentially informative, it is also a place of refuge, and I firmly believe it simply need not be connected to *absolute* reality at every juncture. Perhaps I can ask you, then, to consider the erotica you find here to be "interactive" and to imagine a condom in every relevant scene.

In conclusion, I want to quote the late Bruce Chatwin, English novelist, essayist, and adventurer extraordinaire, who once wrote the following: "Descriptions of the sexual act are as boring as descriptions of landscape seen from the air—and as flat: whereas Flaubert's description of Emma Bovary's room in a *hôtel de passe* in Rouen before and after, but not *during* the sexual act is surely the most erotic passage in modern literature." There is room for disagreement here, naturally, but if you believe you yourself to be of a similarly inclined disposition and prefer the fade-to-black school of erotic entertainment, be aware that the stories in this collection—which you surely must already suspect—are frankly carnal, full of explicit language, deeds, and thoughts of the sort that some people may term "pornographic" ("intended primarily to arouse sexual desire," according to my Webster's) and others dismiss as "dirty."

This may please some and offend others, but my main hope is that readers new to the audacious genre of women's erotica—readers *both* female and male—who pick up *Slow Hand* out of curiosity will enjoy and appreciate the sensual/sexual explorations they encounter here. All responses are legitimate, backgrounds and natures differing as they do, yet I can't help but hope that the book I've assembled will turn out to be the best kind of seducer. Whether for those who step forward eagerly to embrace it, knowing already that they will like what they find, or for those less certain but willing to allow themselves be caught up in its compelling rhythm and its surprises, *Slow Hand* exists to reflect the needs and desires of its audience.

SLOW HAND

IN THE PRICK OF TIME

❖❖❖❖❖❖❖

By Susan Dooley

We admire some stories for the dazzle of their artifice; others, however, may win our hearts with their naturalness. Susan Dooley's "In the Prick of Time" embodies, I think, everything that is splendid about being a Grown-Up Woman, yet it reminds us also that we are the sum of our experiences, that our sensuality can grow and flourish only if we accept and nurture it.

"Too fat."

The mirror was an old one, its oak frame holding glass that was wavy and dappled with dark spots. It could distort image, she thought, just as earlier she had muttered about how her jeans had shrunk in the wash.

"Too fat," this time she sighed and accepted it.

"Just right." He had come up behind her in the bathroom where she stood, her body still wet from the shower. He put his arms around her and nuzzled his face into her neck. She watched in the mirror as he slid one hand up her body and cupped her breast. He played with her nipple, running a finger back and forth until the flesh hardened beneath his hand. Then he moved until he was between her and the mirror. She watched as the back of his head ducked forward and felt the slight pressure as his mouth began a soft sucking at her breast.

The man in the mirror curved his hand over her hip. His fingers pressed in for a minute and then continued on until he had shoved his hand between her legs. She could feel his tongue teasing the inside of her mouth, and she felt a warmth and an urgency even as she watched, detached, the two strangers who slid awkwardly to the floor and began to press themselves together in the shifting light.

She could no longer see the mirror. There was only the pressure of him, hip to hip, tongue to tongue, as he pushed himself inside of her.

The telephone rang.

She tried to ignore it, but both of them had gone still, waiting for it to stop. The noise had broken their connection, and though they rocked together for a minute more, she felt him ebbing away.

Mary raised herself on an elbow. In the wavy glass she saw two people who had passed their moment of passion. The woman had wet hair. The man had on his shoes.

"What are you writing?"

"An erotic memoir," she said, turning around and placing the flat of her hand on the front of his jeans. She felt him move at her touch, and she smiled up at him. "I'm going to call it *In the Prick of Time.*"

She was sitting at the long pine table, having cleared a small space between a stack of books and a large gray cat, and was writing out the grocery list. He put one hand on her shoulder and leaned forward to read what she had written.

"Oatmeal?" he asked. "I thought this was supposed to be erotic."

"Well, it's not the *most* erotic thing I could think of," she conceded, wiggling her eyebrows in what she hoped was a Groucho Marx leer. "But once a long time ago I stood and watched a pot of oatmeal boil for ten minutes. It was a very sensual experience. Voluptuous. It sort of ..." She was remembering that time when she had eaten oatmeal six days a week, saving all her money to have one glorious meal on the seventh, and of how she had often gotten mesmerized by the sight of the bubbling oatmeal. "It sort of erupts at you. Oatmeal has orgasms."

"You must have been a very cheap date," he said, going to the refrigerator to see what other erotic treats were on offer.

"Do you remember oleo orgies?" he asked, having found a piece of lemon pound cake.

"Did you ever go to one?" She put her pen down and turned expectantly—the magician about to pull a rabbit out of his past.

"Once in Ohio when I was in graduate school. It wasn't oleo. It was some vegetable oil in a bottle, and we all got a little drunk and then smoked pot for courage. Then we took off our clothes. Except Nancy. We were still married then, and she insisted on keeping her underpants on. Everyone else looked innocent. Nancy in her underpants looked like a very dirty girl.

"We sat in a circle, willy nilly, except you couldn't sit next to the person you came with.

"The man giving the party went around the circle, pouring out handsful of oil. He made it a priestly act. We began rubbing the oil on each other. I was sitting next to a woman with incredible breasts and a beautiful tan. I put my head in her lap so I could look up and watch the light gleam on her skin. She leaned over to rub oil on my chest and I caught her breast in my mouth to suck it. It tasted strange—almonds, vanilla—I can't remember except that made it even more erotic.

"She didn't seem to mind, but she didn't seem aroused either. She kept rubbing me with oil in a very efficient fashion, and all around us everyone was doing the same thing. Suddenly I started to laugh. I felt like a leg of lamb.

"Everyone else began to laugh too, and the girl whose lap I was on would give these great hee-haws and my head would bounce up and down. It was silly, but at the same time it was very erotic."

"What ever happened to her?" Mary asked. Her voice had gone cool.

"To who?" asked Paul.

"The woman you were bouncing about on."

He looked at her curiously. "I have no idea. I never even knew her name."

He got up. "I'm going into town. Do you want anything? Oatmeal?" He bent over and rubbed his chin against the top of her head and was gone.

She heard the rough cough of the car's motor and watched Paul back the old station wagon out of the driveway. When she was sure he was gone, she pulled a fresh piece of paper off the pad and wrote his name.

"Paul."

She tried to think what it was exactly that made her want him. Rationally, there were only so many spots the hand could touch, so many places the tongue could lick, and that made fucking finite in its possibilities.

Why was it that somehow lovers were not?

She folded the paper with Paul's name and set it aside. Then she began again:

"Herbert."

An erotic memoir should begin at the beginning. In the prick of time, when that first tentative tickle had come from the unlikely Herbert, a leering red-haired boy of eleven who had pushed his way through the children on the school bus to sit beside her. He had squeezed himself over onto her side of the cracked leather seat as the bus made its familiar and halting way down the highway, extruding children at each stop like some demon machine that had had its fill and now was belching out the leftovers.

Herbert had never actually put his hands on her. But he had leaned on her, and he had *looked* at her. It was frightening. It was exciting. Not like Jimmy Mason who had chased her through the orchard and knocked her to the ground to deliver a hasty kiss, his lips slamming to a halt on her cheek. The way Herbert had shoved and bumped her had made warmth start between her legs and roll up her body until she could feel the heat turning her face red. It was uncomfortable. She hoped he wouldn't stop.

"Carole."

Carole had been her best friend in grade school. When the weather was too wet for the nuns to scatter the schoolchildren onto the playground, they would gather them together, march them into the auditorium, and show them a religious film. The ones that weren't about the Virgin Mary hovering over some foreign meadow starred pretty nuns and handsome priests— none of them had warty cheeks like Sister Octavia or the smooth hairless skin of Sister Joyce, whose eyes had been popped naked into a face that lacked both lashes and brows. Mostly the movie priests were Irish and adorable. Not like Father O'Toole, the arrogant pastor who strode each week into every classroom to bellow damnation at any child who had been seen talking to a Protestant.

She and Carole sat next to each other in the dark, while a wavy shaft of light cast pictures on the screen. The big, bare room smelled of chalk and wet socks, and above the faint hum of the projector you could hear the constant rustle of children forced to sit still. The darkness, the muffled noise, the shadows of people you no longer knew turned the barren room into a private place.

For the first half of the film, Mary would trace a delicate line up and down the soft skin on Carole's arm. When they changed to the second reel, it would be Mary's turn. She would stare entranced at the screen while Carole's fingertips returned the delicate, feathery stroking.

That wasn't really erotic, Mary admitted. Not like Herbert. But Mary decided that sensual also had a place on her list. She left Carole's name on it.

"Mr. Maxwell."

Mr. Maxwell was an older man in his twenties. When Mary was sixteen, he had hired her older sister, Helen, as a file clerk. Whenever she went to pick up Helen, Mr. Maxwell would call Mary into his office and flirt with her. One day he had leaned over and run his finger up her leg.

Mary pretended not to notice, but after that, whenever Mary came to get Helen, Mr. Maxwell invited her to come into his office. Sometimes he asked Helen to work overtime, and while she busied herself outside, trotting back and forth down the hallway with full file folders, Mr. Maxwell asked Mary about her boyfriends and tipped himself forward in his chair so that, as he talked, he could run his fingers lightly up and down, up and down her leg.

"Wesley Sutcliffe."

She still thought of him occasionally when she saw the moon lying low, pouring light onto water as it had at that beach party the year she was thirteen. She had barely known Wesley, but when everyone had gone for a final swim, he had waded through the water and picked her up. Holding her wet body against his chest, he had carried her up the moon's line of light, walking into the darkness of the sea. The silky, clinging wetness of her bathing suit was all that was between her breasts and his chest, and her nipples had hardened at the touch of his skin. He had carried her farther and farther into the silver light until at last they vanished in the moon.

The phone again. A neighbor was calling to give warning. The raspberries were going by. If Mary wanted any, she must pick them now.

There was enough of a breeze to keep the bugs away, but also enough to send her notes skating off the kitchen table and across the floor. And out the window. And into the hands of a neighbor child who would later ask, "Mommy, what does 'fuck' mean?" She picked up a brass candlestick and placed it firmly on the papers before taking a basket and heading for the raspberry patch.

She picked for an hour. Someone was practicing the piano—"In the Good Old Summertime"—and the ponderous notes came to her over the buzz of bees. It was all the summers that ever were, and Mary began to miss the moment even as it was happening. Next January, pulling up close to the wood-stove, she would be able to close her eyes and remember the clean feel of sun and the pleasure of licking a finger smeared

red with raspberry juice. A mosquito danced across her back, and she straightened up to swat it. Drops of sweat slid down between her breasts.

How nice it would be to strip off her blouse, to unhook her bra and let the breeze lick the sweat from her skin.

She reached absentmindedly toward a dark red raspberry, but stopped at the sight of a small white worm humping and sliding its way down the cane. Mary brushed it off, decided she had picked enough, then saw one more ripe berry, then two just a few steps farther on.

"Picking raspberries is like orgasms," she said to Paul later that evening as they lay in bed together.

"You think everything is like orgasms," said Paul, who had only been half listening to her account of the raspberry patch. He had been smooching around her body, planting sweet, silly kisses on her elbow, her wrist, licking the place where her waist lowered itself onto her hips.

"I always think if I wait a minute there'll be a better one. Sometimes I don't want to come."

"We all think that," said Paul complacently. "Prolonging the pleasure. It's why eighteen-year-old boys aren't all they're cracked up to be."

Paul was fifty-two. Much better than an eighteen-year-old, Mary agreed. Although now that she thought about it ...

"I've never been to bed with an eighteen-year-old," she said. "By the time I lost my virginity I was too old for someone eighteen. What were you like then?"

"Fast," said Paul. "It didn't occur to me to try to please a woman. It was me who was pleased just to have one; I didn't dare take any time for fear she might get away. Hop on, vrooom, hop off. Poor woman."

"Poor woman," Mary agreed, feeling the pleasure of his weight as he slid on top of her, rubbing himself against her inner thigh before pressing inside of her and beginning to move slowly back and forth, finishing at last what had started their day.

❊ ❊ ❊

Obsessed was too strong a word, but Mary admitted she had spent a lot of time the last few days adding names to her erotic memoir. Partly it was because Paul had fastened on it. Whenever he saw her writing, he tried to look over her shoulder, pretending to believe it was a shopping list. All his insecurities had snugged down into her past. She rather liked the past he gave her, all glamor and carelessness. The real one had been much more painful.

She, in her turn, had no fear of his past. She shied at his future. She kept herself ready for the day he would announce that being together had become more difficult than being apart.

She knew that for both of them, these were protection myths, like the Indian legends of creation. You were ready with a cover, a story which would explain how strange and terrible things that could not happen sometimes did.

"Tim."

Her first lover. She had been devastated at his loss. It had never occurred to her that one would go to bed with a man and *not* marry him and live happily ever after. She had. They had not. It had been sex, but had it been erotic? She was too full of trying to please him, her mind poking itself into everything, wondering if it was all right to do this. And what he would think of her if she did that. Never in the few years they were together had she relaxed in bed and listened to him with her skin. But the first man you ever fucked, surely he had to be in your erotic memoir.

Erotic was not just a hand on your body, or she would have been swept away by the strange man who came up to her at a dinner party, gave an enchanting smile, and reached out and cupped his hands around her breasts. The Masons' secret handshake, or was he Mr. Magoo? It had been as erotic as watching a nurse plump up a pillow. Erotic wasn't the motion, or the mechanics, it was what had gone before, even if before was only a brief connection. It was the connection that counted. The mind knew not to be wary and allowed the flesh to have its say.

❊   ❊   ❊

The phone. It was Paul.

"Are you busy, or would you like to go on a picnic?" he asked.

She met him at the town wharf, passing him the picnic basket and taking his hand. She rocked for a moment on the edge of the dock, so that she could say before she stepped into the boat, "If you were the kind of man who looked up a woman's skirt, you'd notice I don't have on underpants."

She jumped lightly into the boat, dropping safely down amid the piles of slickers, sweaters, boots, and lines.

"Aha!" he gave her a quick grin, but he was coiling the painter as he talked and she knew better than to pursue the conversation. He drifted off when they were on the water, his mind going ahead in search of rock or wind.

They ate on the shore and then walked the edge of the island. In the distance they could hear the bleating of an island ewe, anxiously calling back a wandering lamb. They walked to the top of the hill, past low bushes of sheep laurel, whose brilliant pink flowers looked innocent and enticing. "It's also called lambkill," Paul said, poking at a bush with his toe. "It doesn't seem to have hurt this batch." Another mother with her two lambs scampered off in front of them.

"They probably don't eat it unless there's nothing else," Mary said, her eyes straining ahead to pick out the gray sheep from the gray rocks that jutted out of the meadow. At the top of the hill they stood for a minute, looking down on the ocean below. Then Paul lay on his back, and she leaned on one elbow above him. His shirt was open, and she walked her fingers across his chest, lightly like a spider. She kissed the place where his neck hollowed into his shoulder and then ran her fingers around the edge of his mouth.

"You are erotic," she said. "You are the last entry on my list."

"Sure I am," he said, lost again in his vision of her past. "Number 27."

"227," she corrected him. "Do you take me for a slacker?"

He smiled and unbuttoned her blouse. He pulled the sleeves

carefully down off her shoulders, and then, impatient, he gave a yank so that the whole thing dangled around her waist. He unfastened her bra and pulled her breasts free.

"I think I'll just take you."

His own pants were off, and he put his hands under her skirt. She raised her hips, and he pulled the skirt up, a clutter of clothing wrapped around her waist, her top and bottom bare. He put his fingers in his mouth, moistening them with his tongue as she watched him, then he leaned over and kissed her, putting his wet fingers between her legs.

His lips touched hers, his tongue sliding softly into her mouth so that as she inhaled she breathed him deep down inside her. His tongue in her mouth, the hardness of him pushing in between her legs, the spirit of him sliding deeper and deeper into her life.

AUTHOR'S NOTE

I've read a great many mediocre novels where the author was desperate to present sex in a shocking light—jamming people into clothes closets, conference rooms, and company. Sex in odd places and sex with odd groupings seemed to me to be like aerobics, something people do when the flab sets in. Thinking about it, I decided it was not simply flesh on flesh that awakens desire; it is the pasts that people bring to each other and the hope with which they merge.

LEAPER

❧❧❧❧❧❧❧

By Jenny Diski

In contrast to the sensuous ease of the familiar, presented with such spirited warmth by Susan Dooley, other stories in this book, of which "Leaper" is one, take a look at chance encounters. It is quite clear to me from the many submissions I read, though in itself hardly a new idea, that the element of "unknowingness" —of unfamiliarity with another body or its history— can strongly enhance the erotic quotient of a sexual episode, whether real or imagined. But Jenny Diski and every other writer selected for this collection who has taken the sexy-stranger theme has made it her own.

Known for her daring, Diski here examines the coming together of two people whose needs and vulnerabilities match up for only a very brief moment.

He phoned at completely the wrong time, my lover. "Write me a story. A man and a woman, fucking. Keep it short and dirty."

"Fuck you," I said. "If you want a story, speak to my agent. The going rate is five hundred pounds a thousand words. If you want a fuck, speak to me. The going rate is ... what is the going rate?"

"Do as you're told," he said, just the tiniest bit menacing.

"Fuck you," I said and put the phone down.

I'd spent the morning struggling with a never-to-be-published story and was sunk in a kind of slime of incapacity. What I lack is confidence. Much good it does to know what's lacking. I've written quite a lot: short stories and articles for magazines, most of them published. Looked at from the outside, the writing's going quite well. I've made a small but significant reputation with a number of editors, and it's only a matter of time now, before I attempt The Novel that will, I hope, fulfill the promise I've shown.

If that sounds like an efficient piece of PR, it is, because I know, in that place where you really *know* things, that I can't write at all. That fact, that I have produced decent stuff to murmurs of quiet appreciation, doesn't affect this knowledge I have about myself. Something to do with my childhood, I suppose. Anyway, although things turn out more or less all right in the end, it doesn't change anything, and I face every blank piece of paper in a state of panic. This time, I know for sure, they'll find me out.

Things could be worse. That bone-deep knowledge of my own inability doesn't, as it might, pervade my entire life. Not any more. At least it's contained in the writing department, realizing, I suppose, that there is where I've decided I can live. I see this now as part of my internal structure; just as there is a language center in the brain, so I have a worry center which fills with anxiety and has to find something to worry about. It used to attach itself to anything available: money, sex, shopping, the daily news, the condition of my flat. For no reason connected with anything that was happening, anxiety would erupt. Suddenly, it would occur to me that there was dry rot under the floorboards, or perhaps, since I didn't know one from the other, it was damp rot; and the gnawing worry would infest the day. No matter what sensible things I told myself, that it probably wasn't true, or, if it was, so what, or I could do something about it, the ache would thrum away, coloring the day with anxiety.

The damp/dry rot was *desperate* all of a sudden, festering and rotting the fabric of my flat. I would go about my business, efficiently enough, but accompanied always in some small space inside me by my fears. By the following morning, the certain knowledge of rotting floorboards beneath my feet would have faded, but something else would take its place, filling up the worry gap before I had a chance to be relieved. A bank statement would arrive, and now the money situation, no different from the situation a day or a week before, would be terrifying, and I'd spend every free moment listing and relisting my income and outgoings, coming up each time with the same answer, forgetting almost what the problem was, but knowing there was some solution it was essential to arrive at. Sometimes, it made life very difficult to live.

All the time, even in the midst of the panics, I knew it to be free-floating anxiety, its source a well of terror in me that had nothing to do with my chosen concerns. But this information wasn't much help. And sometimes, exhausted by it all, I wanted someone around who would tell me none of it was real, and take away from me the problems that seemed, now and then, to threaten my sanity. But, in fact, I managed, and things have improved. The anxiety is contained.

Now, as I say, since I decided that writing is the only route I've got through life, the worry had latched on to that, like a cattle tick, and gains sustenance from my fears.

What I've learned about this is to ignore it. Most of the time, I write through a miasma of terror, and something decent comes out the other end. I don't know how. I think of it as "The Process" and leave it at that. It's like swimming in mud; not pleasant, but you get to the other side if you just keep going.

Usually, I can live with the discomfort. Why should things be easy? But occasionally I get exhausted by it, with having to contain my insecurity and generate enough energy to just bloody well get on with it. And still, sometimes, I wish someone else were here to do it for me.

I imagine the conversation with this paragon who will devote his energy to keeping me at it.

"I can't do this. I can't write," I wail, a formless heap.

"Of course you can." The voice is practical, not comforting, even a bit impatient. What about all the things you've written? You did them, and they were all right. Now, do it again."

"I can't," I howl angrily. "I don't know how those other things happened. They weren't anything to do with me. *This* is the real thing, and I can't do it."

"Well, you're just going to have to try harder, aren't you?"

That's what I'm after. Not soggy comfort, but a hard line. A brusque assumption that I can and will do it, that I don't have any choice. And that, I suppose, is what I do for myself most of the time. But, as I say, sometimes it's hard to make that other voice, and I wish someone else were here to help. Which is foolish, I know, and I get over and on with it. But it doesn't help one bit when Dan calls to play games in the mud I feel I'm drowning in. It doesn't make me feel — I don't know — valued.

I decided it was a good moment to take some exercise. Sometimes I can disperse the panic by working up a physical sweat. I go to a gym just past the local underground station.

As I approached the station, trying to contain my annoyance at Dan by promising it a monumental expenditure of energy on the work-out bench, I noticed that something was going on. Too many people on the street for a weekday afternoon; the bus queue a long, rush-hour line; and small, static groups outside the station itself, standing around in *that* way, signaling an event. An ambulance waited throbbing in the road, traffic building up as cars skirted carefully and curiously around it, its back doors open, red blankets folded neatly on the beds. The entrance to the station, normally a corridor of warm air, a dark gloomy cave into which travelers disappeared, was closed, heavy iron gates pulled across, and behind them, a handful of uniformed figures milled about. Two middle-aged men sat in pale silence on the stone step in front of the gates, neither of them looking as if this was their normal way of being on the street.

I allowed myself the luxury of imagining an electrical fault, an unattended carrier bag, a heart attack, even, while I walked through the small crowd and beyond the locked gates toward the gym. Where, no longer needing willed ignorance to get past the spot uninvolved, I gave my brain permission to interpret the signs.

There had been a leaper. Some poor but efficient sod had jumped under a passing train.

It's the drivers that call them leapers. My ex, who likes to know this kind of technical, inside information, met an underground driver in a pub who told him. Also, that leapers are a bit of a blessing among the lads, since any driver it happens to is given two days compassionate leave, with pay. It always sounded to me like front-line bravado, the brutality of the stomach-sick medical student, the ho-ho-ho of the intolerable. Anyway, "leaper" had stuck with us as a generic term for this particular kind of no-kidding suicide, and that was the word I thought.

I exercised viciously on the sloping bench, jerking the pulleys with muscles that surprised me, so that the weights clanked noisily when they came to rest, and the sliding bench screeched as it rolled up and down the gradient. But no matter how hard I pushed and pumped at the weights, I couldn't drown out the conversation. Two other women had stopped exercising and were standing at the window that looked out on to the station.

"What a terrible thing to do."

Right, that's the word, "terrible," I thought.

"Why do you think it's taking them so long to bring the body out?"

Jesus Christ, think about it. Think hard.

"You know, my sister was on a train when someone jumped in front of it. They don't let you out. *And* he wasn't killed, the bloke. Not outright. She had to sit there and listen to these awful screams. He screamed and screamed, apparently. She says she won't ever forget it. Can you imagine?"

Can't blame him, can you? A voice was probably all the poor bastard had left.

"Terrible. Terrible. Such a terrible thing to do."

I kept my end of the conversation silent and worked on grimly at the bench.

But the conversation continued.

"I suppose we shouldn't be ... but killing yourself like that, you'd have to really mean it. I can't imagine what it must be like to feel so ..."

"No. How could anyone imagine it. The poor driver ..."

When I'd finished my routine I sat in the sauna for as long as I could stand, trying to sweat it all away. Which wasn't long, saunas being intolerable. A Swedish Protestant plot, I think, a stab at hell-on-earth, a dire warning of the discomforts to come. Unsuccessful, actually, since it makes hellfire attractive by comparison.

Out in the daylight, dehydrated and aching, I looked to my left, in the direction of my flat, on the far side of the underground. Small groups of people still stood outside the station, some in shock, others merely showing a passing interest, a few professionals looking as if this was all in a day's work, some of them succeeding better than others. The ambulance throbbed and waited. I turned right and sat at one of the tables outside the cafe on the other side of the gym.

Recuperate a bit, I decided. You don't have to walk back through and over that drama until you've had a cup of coffee. Sometimes, I'm good to myself.

The woman sat down at my table a few moments later.

It doesn't seem to make much sense, but there's a difference between tables inside a cafe and those on the street. Inside, unless everywhere else is taken, it's very unlikely that anyone will ask to share a table that is already occupied. It's a virtual act of aggression, the mark of men on the make and the mildly mad. But it's different in the open. Even if there are empty tables elsewhere, it's an easy, insignificant act to sit with a complete stranger. It must be that people feel they can escape more easily where there are no walls to contain them. And the bright daylit street seems to exclude the likelihood of whatever it is we fear. Streets are everybody's. Indoors, in the darker interior of the cafe, the table becomes defensible space, and the approach of another a threat.

I mean to say that I wasn't made uncomfortable by the woman's approach, nor did her presence impinge until she spoke.

She was tall, well-built, and sleek, in her elegant middle age, with a face that was all bone structure, and dark spherical glasses. Smooth, dark hair, cut to a heavy, architectural bob, and the clothes tailored (and not in England) to match her perfectly manicured fingernails. Not English. Diane, I was to learn, but think it with a Mediterranean accent: Dee-ahn.

She sat at the table, facing the station in silence for a little while, and then lit a long, dark cigarette.

"Are you watching or avoiding walking over it?" she asked, releasing smoke as she spoke and moving her head slightly to indicate the underground.

"Both, I suppose."

"It will ruin your day if you watch the stretcher come out."

"It's not much of a day, anyway. And a worse one for him or her down there. Or better."

She shrugged lightly.

"Yes. Or no. Her. I understand it was a woman."

There was a quality of utter detachment about her, as though she looked out on the world and saw, but was untouched by it. Everything—her clothes, makeup, the way she sat poised and posed in her chair—looked deliberate, and yet, it was all so well done that nothing seemed artificial. I hadn't seen her eyes under the sunglasses, but I knew they would be steady whether they looked at me across the table or at the scene along the road. Now she lifted the glasses away from her face and looked me over, running her eyes up and down my body in a slow sweep. Her cool, emerald appraisal was electrifying; the air filled with the static of possibilities.

"Does it excite you, the death down there?"

I took one of her mysterious cigarettes and leaned forward to catch the light she offered. I'm a believer in balance, a serious work-out requires nicotine as ballast.

"I'm thrilled. It astonishes me. I'm bowled over with admiration." Her brow creased in a question. "At the certainty that's been acted on," I explained. "I like a person who knows what they want and leaves no room for indecision or an accident of salvation."

"But what if it were a whim?" she queried. Her deep eyes were amused beneath their steady gaze. "A momentary thing? Irretrievable once acted on?"

I shook my head briskly.

"That's a thought the living use to comfort themselves. *He didn't really mean it.* So that the next time we stand on a station platform we don't have to choose between getting on the train or throwing ourselves under it. We wouldn't mean it, we tell ourselves, we'd be sorry afterward. What afterward? The only thing to be sure of is that we wouldn't be sorry afterward. In any case, what makes a momentary whim less true than the thought we've continued to have for twenty years because we haven't bothered to change it?"

She sat back in her chair, resting the coffee cup lightly on her silk shirt.

"The only thing that's true now is the physical end of a life," she said quietly.

I heard my voice clipped, angry.

"Is anything more important in a life?"

"No," she agreed calmly. But you are a romantic. You will be angry at being told so, but it's true. The fact is that to kill yourself in such a way is childish and aggressive. And stupid, for the corpse down there cannot reap the benefits. Look at the disruption that has been caused. Trains are held up all along the line, people are made late for appointments. Perhaps some of them are important. The traffic is slowed down, and passersby going about their everyday business are drawn in, they cannot avoid being aware of what has happened beneath their feet. Now they feel foolish and petty to be buying a bunch of flowers and a quarter pound of cheese. So much power, so much effect."

But there was no real anger in her voice. It remained distant and melodic. Even a little pedagogical. She continued.

"It makes people think thoughts they do not have to have.

That person a few moments ago was living, they think, I might have passed her on my way to the grocer. Was alive, is dead. Only moments in between. A matter of a moment one way or another, they say to themselves. As I am alive now, this moment. What is to become of me? What right has someone ending their own life to impose such thoughts on others who may not choose to have them?"

This conversation pleased me. I liked her matter-of-fact, practical assessment of the anonymous death. There was a hardness in her voice that made me listen. And it was a relief to hear those things said. She echoed the thoughts I hadn't allowed myself to have, describing exactly my resistance to walking back over the scene.

I think about death a lot, in a general sort of way. I have a tendency to see it as heroic, a feat. I know we can't help dying, but it's such a serious and solitary thing. Death seems to me to ennoble the most frivolous and incompetent of lives. And voluntary death awes me with its absolute refusal to tolerate the intolerable. I admire the cold calculation, the rejection of a life of fear and panic in favor of decision.

But as I walked past the underground station on my way to the gym, what I had actually thought was: "I can't stand this."

I couldn't bear the idea of that person's misery as she walked along the street, moments before me, and the terror she felt as she stood on the edge of the platform waiting for the incoming train. I hated her for making her pain and her death so evident and imposing it on me. It angered and frightened me that she had advertised her safely anonymous unhappiness and required me to imagine that appalling death beneath my feet.

The truth was that I'd had precisely the same thoughts that underlay the conversation I contemptuously dismissed between the women standing by the window. But wouldn't permit myself to say aloud. I couldn't bring myself to admit the common thoughts, banal, true, automatic, human, inevitable, that were being spoken carefully so that the unease could be dispersed by the sound of the words. I prefer to let those thoughts, pointless as I know they are, roll around in the silence between world-weary shrugs. I want them to stay hanging in the air, recognized by their absence. I am, I must admit, ashamed to be on the side of the living.

The woman sitting opposite me with her brisk tones and coolly interested eyes voiced my real thoughts and made them seem acceptable. She spoke knowingly, in the manner of a distant observer, of the uncomfortable effects of death on our doorstep. And always her eyes held me in their gaze, faintly humorous, as if commenting, though not unkindly, on my self-deceit.

I heard myself say, "I'm trying to write something. But I can't. I just can't do it."

And held my breath, horrified to hear the words out there in the world, but certain, now that they were said, that she could give me the right answer. I hadn't thought of that harsh, reassuring voice of my imagination belonging to a woman; it hadn't occurred to me, but it didn't seem to make much difference now that I saw it was.

She stubbed out her cigarette with a sudden urgency, as if she had been waiting for a signal and now, having received it, could get on. Putting her glasses back, she smiled, but so slightly it was hardly there.

"Do you have to be somewhere?"

With you, I thought.

"No, not really."

"Then why don't we go back to my flat and have a drink? I live just around the corner. It's too depressing sitting here. Why don't we turn our back on this melodrama? Refuse to allow it any power."

She gathered her black leather bag from the table and stood, inviting me to join her.

"My name is Diane."

We crossed the road at the traffic lights in front of the cafe, and she led me to a street directly opposite the station. If we had turned to look in the other direction, we would still have been able to see the entrance to the underground. But neither of us did.

The flat was as well-manicured as her fingernails. She made me a drink.

"So you find death exciting?" she said, handing me a large Scotch.

"I suppose so."

"And does going home with a strange woman excite you, too?"

"Yes, that also excites me."

She smiled.

"Death has a way of sharpening our desires. It makes us want to eat good food or listen to a sublime piece of music. Or make love. To lie in someone's arms and feel warm flesh respond to our touch. Death is very sensual, don't you think? The dead have a secret we can't grasp. The secrecy of sex is as near as the living can ever get to it."

Did I say she was beautiful? Apart from all those other things, she was beautiful. Her face was a carved frame for the long, green eyes that looked and looked. Her body was beginning to show its age, loosened a little, but full, ripe, and round. I haven't ever rejected the idea of women as lovers, but the event had never occurred.

She undressed me slowly, looking carefully at my body and then checking back with my face. Whatever she saw in it seemed to give her permission not to hurry. When she had finished her slow examination she took off her own clothes, just as leisurely, giving me as much time for taking her in as she had given herself. Then she took me in her arms with as much passion as Dan would show, but it was different. Not his fast, harsh, funny fuck, but a long, slow pleasuring, a drawing out of desire. It was a lesson in timelessness. By the time she led me to the bed she had woven a veil around us with her intricate caresses that seemed to exclude the light. She made the world contract to a capsule containing only the two of us on the white expanse of her bed. And I knew that that was what we were there for: to create that veil that confused time and light.

All the time, the green eyes watched with the same humor and detachment I'd seen at the cafe. But I didn't mind. It exhilarated me that she was in control, building my excitement with careful touches and stroking, checking my response as she increased or decreased the pressure of her elegant fingers and beautiful mouth. Then she took my hand and guided me toward her pleasure. And all of it was more than sensual delight, it was also a promise that she could respond to my *cri.* That she could give me the energy and certainty that I couldn't find for myself. Everything she did corresponded to that person in my head who seemed too weary now to help.

I lay naked in her arms, waiting. There was no urgency. I drifted in and out of sleep listening to the buzz of traffic in the distance, content with the memory of the tone of her voice and the touch of her hands. I knew nothing about her beyond her name and the style in which she lived. But that, along with her capacity to guide me through desire, was enough information, and I had no real curiosity then about her past. Now that I was sated, it was my solved future that interested me. She would, I knew, encourage and insist I work, understand my necessity, wrap my insecurities in a blanket of her strength. At that moment I thought I had everything. Found, at last, the solution to the panic that threatened to swamp me. I remember the quality of that moment, even now. It was, I think, the first and only time I really felt that everything was going to be all right.

"So you write?"

Her voice was languid and deep, the scent of sex seeped into her low murmur.

"What do you write?"

I lay pillowed in the angle between her arm and breast, smelling the sharp mix of expensive perfume and satisfied desire.

"Stories, articles," I told her, whispering. "I think soon a novel."

I held my breath at the power of the moment, those seconds before one's life comes right.

"You must show them to me," she said and stroked my hair gently. "I'm sure they must be very good."

And the moment was gone.

I sat up and looked about the room. The afternoon sun poured in through the long windows, washing the beige tones of the furnishings with a warm pink. But I was cold. I wondered for a second if they had brought the stretcher up.

"You met me two hours ago, you can't possibly know whether I can write or not."

I was as confused by my chilly reply as I suppose she was. She sat up beside me and rubbed the side of her face against my hair.

"Well, then, you must show me, so I can judge. I'd like to see the story you're working on at the moment. The one you're having trouble with. We'll have dinner tonight, and you can bring it."

I swung my legs out of the bed and stood up.

"I don't show unfinished work. Unfinished work is nothing."

"Then perhaps something you've completed. Bring that so I can see what you do."

She lay back in bed, and I began to dress. Everything, suddenly, had slipped from my grasp, and I watched as reality wrenched at my fantasy of reassurance and tore it to shreds.

"I don't want to talk about my work," I heard myself say. "It's not something anyone else can be involved in. You have to do it alone, or it's not yours."

And this, also was something I knew bone-deep but had forgotten in the surprise of death and sex and comfort. There is no alternative to the panic and the fear, because it is the panic and fear—and the isolation—that *are* the writing. The desperation created the necessity that made me write. I fed on it.

I was only ever half a romantic, the rest of me, the part that keeps on going, knows how things are and would not swap the final satisfaction of a finished piece for the easy comfort of that voice in my head. I had forgotten that voices in the real world have bodies and intentions of their own—and flats and furnishings and make dinner, and need.

I looked at her lying on the bed. She looked to me tired, terribly weary, worn, but her green eyes shone bright and hard still.

"All right," she watched me tie the laces on my shoes. "Dinner without your work. We must get to know each other better. When you're ready I may be able to help you. I have contacts. I can help in various ways. But tonight, just dinner."

She didn't want to be alone, I realized, although there was

nothing of that in the tone of her voice which remained cool and steady. And not just tonight. I wondered, at last, about her life.

"Do you live here alone?"

"Yes. I do now. There was someone living here with me, but she's gone."

Her voice was so vague it was impossible to place this information in time. She could have been talking of decades or moments. I felt as if one of us was no longer in the room.

"I must go," I said, turning to the door. "I've got to get back to work. I don't know about tonight. It depends on how the work goes. Shall I ring you later on?"

She reached for a cigarette. The phone rang as she drew on the flame from her lighter, but she made no attempt to answer it.

"Yes, call me later," she said airily and lay back on the bed watching the smoke spiral through the light beams. The phone continued to make its mechanical bird call.

"Your phone ..."

"I'm not going to answer it."

"But it might be imp—"

"I know what it's about."

She got out of bed, slipped on a faded silk kimono, and moved away from the phone to stand and look out of the window. There was nothing to see except the houses across the road. The phone went on ringing.

"It sounds important."

She inhaled deeply on her cigarette and turned her head slightly in the direction we had walked. From this angle, the station was out of view.

"They will have found this address on Helen. She must have had a letter or something in her jacket, because she didn't take her bag with her."

She turned and glanced at the chair by the door where a tan shoulder bag lay open.

"I suppose they're calling to find out if a relative lives here. They'll be wanting to inform her next of kin."

She spoke more to herself than me, her cool unchanging

voice almost inaudible beneath the insistent squeal of the telephone.

"Are you sure you won't come to dinner this evening?"

She looked at me questioningly, her face an impassive sculpture of angles and planes.

"You lived here with Helen?"

The room for all its elegance was a desert, suddenly, an empty cold place being worn away by time.

"Helen lived here for two years. She left this afternoon. She wasn't a happy girl. I tried to look after her, she needed to be taken care of. But some people just won't be helped."

The telephone stopped ringing as she spoke. We both stared at it for a moment. The silence was shattering.

"I must go," I said. "I'm sorry but I can't stay."

She smiled.

"We must meet again soon. I would very much like to read your work."

But I was already closing the door behind me.

AUTHOR'S NOTE

Levi-Strauss has said, about totemic animals, that "animals are good to think with." I feel the same about sexual writing: sex is good to think with. Although it goes against the current of Freudian thought we seem to be stuck with in this century, I don't believe that anything is *about* sex, but that sex is *about* something. It is, if you like, a metaphor, for how we are as human beings in the social world. So writing about people doing sex, having sexual encounters, is a way of discussing something else about individuals and their relations with others. It's as if sex were a child's playground, an available space we all use both for pleasure, and for working out our other obsessions, fears, and desires. Sexual desire and its fulfillment is, of course, pleasure, but I don't believe it is only that. At least, I hope not, because it wouldn't be nearly as interesting to write about.

This particular story came out of my passing my local underground one day under the circumstances described. The rest, with its mix of death, sex, and insecurity, came from God-knowswhere, as the rest usually does.

DROUGHT

❧❧❧❧❧❧❧

By Wendy Law-Yone

Wendy Law-Yone herself comments on the (for her) natural juxtaposition of the erotic and the exotic; in this synergy was the inspiration for a unique creation, a sexual coming-of-age story that takes "what if?" for its spur and then proceeds single-mindedly to describe an answer. Bold, clever, and also, ultimately, wise, "Drought" is a fable that will be difficult for any reader to forget.

It was wartime, with its crazy misplaced fears—a time when suddenly it wasn't the bloodshed I dreaded as much as drought.

Maybe it was the Red Reservoir incident that sparked these new threats. In the north, where the fighting was fiercest, the rebels had run amok and wiped out an entire European compound, hacking up the bodies of the whites and throwing the parts into the private reservoir until the water turned red. It must have been the rumors that followed—rumors about poisoned wells and severed water lines—that brought on my nightmares about a water crisis.

But as though in a rush to make the nightmares come true, I became wasteful, not sparing, with water—especially once Auntie was gone and I was left alone with him. Amazing, how quickly I took to stripping and washing him as I pleased, using up water heedlessly. And to think how scared I'd been at first: scared to touch, even to look at him.

A white man! In those days—the early days of the Liberation—we all knew what they were doing to the whites on the mainland. We'd all heard about the Red Reservoir. Things were different, of course, on our island, where no one seemed to feel strongly about whites, or about much else. Still, the war had spread to other islands in the archipelago, and some said it was just a matter of time before we too would be caught up in it.

But I was afraid for another reason. I couldn't cast off the uneasy sense that I'd somehow caused an accident to happen.

Because I'd seen it happen. Standing on the veranda that morning, I had watched the plane go down. I didn't know it was a plane, then. It looked like a hawk, diving and disappearing in a flash from its straight-arrow course. The crash was that silent and graceful and swift. In the split moment before the sudden dive, I foresaw the whole thing. *Fall!* I'd said to myself even. And—just like that—the hawk had fallen.

I gave it no more thought until hours later, when they brought the survivor to our bungalow. It was only then that I put it all together. That hawk had been a small plane plunging headlong somewhere into the rubber plantations.

They carried him in on a makeshift bamboo stretcher. Our bungalow was on the hill overlooking the *kampong*, the village, below. From the veranda I could see the small procession snake up along the path that led from the plantations past the *kampong*—and through the gates at the foot of the hill.

"He fell out of the sky!" one of the *kampong* boys was shouting. "Like a god!"

They set him down underneath the monsoon-flower tree. He might well have been a god—large and dead to the world, but radiant. The tree was in full flower—a sign that the monsoons were close—and gold blossoms hung in clusters above him like ceremonial lanterns. His hair was gold too, though

darker than the flowers; very thick and straight. A slight breeze
plowed this way and that, revealing bits of scalp that looked as
tender as wounds. He was wearing a short-sleeved khaki
jacket—the kind with many pockets—and khaki shorts. In the
glow of the flowering lanterns he shimmered all over as though
dusted with mica or powdered glass.

I felt unworthy, staring at such radiance.

The man in charge of the rescue—a fast-talking Chinaman—explained things to Auntie, who was playing deaf. Her
face was clenched; it was her ploy when things got difficult.
And here was a difficult situation suddenly—an accident
involving a white man at a time when whites were being
slaughtered in the north. Not to mention all her other worries
about the war.

The Chinaman was almost shouting, annoyed at having to
repeat himself. The man lying unconscious on the stretcher was
someone important, he kept saying. An adviser. He had flown in
to help out the local militia. The Chinaman seemed to be imply-
ing that it was our duty—Auntie's and mine—to take him in. I
understood why. I was the only half-caste in the area, the only
blood relation to the stranger, so to speak. Naturally, they'd
bring the European to our bungalow and expect us to lodge him.

"Bring him inside; you can leave him here," Auntie said at
last, pointing her chin at me to indicate I should show them the
way. I knew from the chin that she blamed me for this burden.

The men picked up the stretcher and followed me inside. I
led them to my room. I turned down the thin blanket covering
the thin mattress, and as they half-lifted, half-tilted him onto it,
the jolting thought crossed my mind that maybe this was my
father, come in search of me—although in the next instant I
knew of course it couldn't be.

When the men had left, Auntie stood in the doorway, keeping her distance, while I looked the stranger over. A discolored
swelling at the side of a knee and a cut at the temple above the
right ear—the source of dried blood along one cheek—seemed
to be the worst of his visible wounds.

Auntie felt I should try to wake him. This required my
touching him. I put my palm down on the slight frown creasing

his brow. How dark and dull the back of my hand appeared next to the pale gleam of his hair! I shook his shoulders and even slapped his cheeks. "Harder," Auntie said, quite spitefully I thought. I shook harder but couldn't bring myself to slap harder. Every smack left a stripe on his skin. Some time later, he did move an arm and a leg as though in the course of normal sleep—and by the time the doctor came, there were other small improvements: he stirred, he twitched, he turned from side to side in a delirium, he even opened his eyes for brief periods; and when I lifted his head to feed him the first spoonful of rice porridge, he swallowed. But mostly he slept.

The doctor was an old Moslem with a limp and a wheeze. With the war going on, doctors were scarce and getting pressed into service even in the islands. This old man had made the hike from the southern end and looked ready to pass out from the exertion. He put one hand on the patient's chest, tapped it with his other hand, bent the patient's elbows and knees, stuck a thermometer under his armpit, pried his eyelids apart. (Once more I was struck by the expensive color of those eyes, the color of a ring I'd seen on a Chinese merchant. A pale sapphire.)

"Coma," the doctor pronounced at last, scratching absently at the mold on his stethoscope.

"Coma?" Auntie said. "But he wakes up sometimes. He even takes soft rice."

"Sort of coma," the old man said. He handed Auntie a bottle of Gripe Water, usually prescribed for baby's wind. When she asked about the dosage, he hedged. "As needed," he said. "But not too often." He went down the stairs uncertainly, clutching the stair rail with something like panic.

In the beginning it was Auntie who decided what had to be done. *Give him a spoonful of coconut juice. Now wait. Now try a spoonful of rice. Now turn him on his side. Fold the rubber sheet under him. Now turn him back this way. Unfold the sheet from behind. Get the cloth and the basin.* She looked on squeamishly while giving the orders. But she wouldn't touch him.

And why should she? For as long as I could remember, she'd spoken of white men as an unsavory breed. They were bullies, always taking, always wanting more; they were liars, saying one thing, meaning quite another, telling the truth only if the truth was what it took to get them their way. And they were smelly.

In fact there was only one European she had known up close: my father. But the mark he left was enough to stain a race, apparently.

The thing he'd done was to leave my mother pregnant with me, forcing her into service with his lies. Lies about taking her back with him to a place called Antwerp, then—as he took off, solo—more lies about sending for her later, after he was settled.

My mother was not an island girl. Her home was on the mainland, in the dry zone, where her father worked in the oil fields run by Dutchmen like my father. It was only after my father went away that she came to this island—where Auntie, her sister, lived—to have her baby.

I was not yet weaned when she left me in a wicker basket on the floor one full-moon night to drown herself in the sea.

But along with Auntie's rancor I sensed a grudging pride in my half-white origins. "Mixed!" she crowed, when anyone remarked on my volume of curly hair. And the books were another concession. It was only English and Dutch that she wanted me to read.

It wasn't the first time I'd had an invalid on my hands. It was less than two years before that Auntie's father, Old Papu, had required around-the-clock care in the last bedridden months of his life. I had the night shift then (Auntie having collapsed for the day) and had got used to the bedpan and other unpleasant intimacies.

But this one was different. Even in his wakeful states, he wasn't alert enough to cooperate except to open his mouth for feedings or move his limbs for changings. Nor was feeding him always successful. Auntie's close watch didn't make things any easier. And just sponging him was an ordeal that put me in a sweat, though I was generally on my own for that—Auntie didn't care to supervise.

But things did get easier with practice. I learned what to do about the messes (I'd even rigged a sort of loincloth that made the cleanup easier); and I became more adept at feeding and sponging.

The spongings were partial and routine at that point. And necessary. Despite the promise of the monsoon-flower trees, the rains still hadn't arrived and the heat festered and itched like a boil about to burst. Inside, even with all the windows open, the occasional cross breeze blew in a hot vapor that caused the floorboards to steam. Outside, the heat hit you with a force that took the breath away.

I was beginning to understand what Auntie meant about the European body odor. Strong and sour, it smelled like fermenting palm toddy. Even if you liked the smell of toddy, as I did, it wasn't something you could let run rampant.

The hotter it got, the more spongings were called for. By the time Auntie left for her monthly shop on the mainland, the rains were long overdue and the heat had become so intolerable that I was relieved to be able to swab him off at will, unobserved, with a frequency that might have alarmed her.

In truth I could hardly wait for her to leave. No sooner had she caught the ferry than I got down to business. I filled the zinc basin with warm water and brought it, with the washcloth, to his bedside. Early on, I had taken off his clothes—the khaki shorts and shirt—and replaced them with one of Papu's old sarongs, leaving it loose, like a sheet, around his middle. It made the cleaning and changing easier. I took the sarong off now and saw for the first time what he looked like, lying there on the rubber sheet, stripped utterly naked.

Huge. And very hairy. Tangled skeins of gold thread covered his chest, belly, arms, and legs; the threads were darker in the armpits and darkest at the crotch, forming a thick nest there, around the most startling part of his body. Unlike Old Papu's privates, shriveled and discolored all over like fruit gone bad, his seemed to blossom firm and ripe, with a good healthy color to the skin: thick through the scrotum but so fine on the penis that the veins showed up like lines drawn in ink.

A thorough soap and scrub was what I had planned. Auntie was gone, I was alone, and it was safe. But just standing over his exposed body, free to inspect any and all parts to satisfaction—just taking that secret liberty put me in a state. What if he came to, and his blue eyes were to shed their confusion and turn like searchlights on me?

I gave him the sponging; I even took care not to avoid the nest. But I didn't linger; I went about it as always—briskly, hardly looking, almost entirely by feel.

Auntie was to have returned on the last ferry late that evening. When the boat arrived, letting off its few passengers, and she wasn't among them, I knew something serious had happened. With the war getting closer—now we could hear the crackle of gunfire across the waves—she'd been overly anxious about leaving me even for the day. She would hardly have wanted me to spend the night alone.

I went home to wait. I thought of going down to the *kampong,* but soon it was dark and I was afraid—though not because I felt unsafe. No one in the *kampong* would have touched me—not even the older boys who came back to visit from their mainland jobs. One of them—a mocker and a strutter with too much coconut oil in his hair—once told me the reason why.

"Don't worry," he'd said when I mentioned my fear of taking the road to the *kampong* in the dark. "No one would dare touch you."

"I'm not that great," I said, thinking he was flattering me.

"Not that great, no," he laughed. "I mean no one would touch you because you're cursed."

I sat on the front steps looking down at the swarm of flickering lights in the *kampong,* waiting for my aunt long after I knew it was too late to expect her that night. When the lights were snuffed out one by one, I went inside to Auntie's room where I had slept on a bedroll on the floor since the day of the crash, when I'd given up my bed to the man in it now. With Auntie gone I lay on her bed, not bothering with the bedroll. The *kampong* noises had died down for the night; the palm trees rattled, but gently, in the breeze that had picked up finally after the breathless heat of the day. Still, it was not a night for sleep. I got up and went into my room, where the large, motionless figure filled my bed. Moonlight flooded through the open window and turned the hair on his head and chest to phosphorescence, like the surf on certain nights.

I sat at the foot of the bed, weary but bolt awake. The moon made me think of my mother. It was on a night like this that she had walked into the sea. Auntie had told me a story that came back to me now.

When my mother was pregnant, there was a drought in the dry zone, where the oil fields were concentrated, and where she kept house for my father at the time. It was the worst water shortage in years, and even the Europeans were under ration. That's when the first of the strikes began in the refineries, followed by the riots. In the turmoil of the next days the faucets in the European quarter were stone dry, and even the odd waterseller was nowhere in sight.

My mother had saved just enough drinking water to last a few days.

"For three days she took just enough from the canteen to moisten her lips," said Auntie. "While your father guzzled, thoughtless. And there she was, a child in her belly, herself not much more than a child. Later, when he went off and left her, she told me about the drought. I yelled at her. 'Stupid thing! Suppose the drought had gone on? What then?'

"Then, she said, she would have cut open a piece of her flesh to give him her blood to drink."

My mother—dead at sixteen—must have been exactly my age at the time of the drought. And my father? How old was he then? The same age, could it be, as this wounded man lying in front of me? "How old are you?" I whispered, although there was no need to. Suddenly, the moonlight felt cold on my skin, and my head swam from fatigue. I lay alongside him, pressing myself very close. After a while I loosened the sarong around his waist and crawled in until we lay side by side, cocooned.

I woke with the sun in my eyes and a bitter taste in my parched mouth. I had been dreaming of drought. The rebels, in the dream, had cut the water lines, and I was stranded on a beach, gagging on mouthfuls of saltwater.

My head was still on his chest. My neck was stiff, and when I started to rub it I found my fingers were wet. But what from? I swept my hand down across his belly—and there near his crotch was the wet patch. The moisture trailed out of the tip of his sex which lay horizontally—fuller than I remembered— across his thigh. I touched the moisture, which was clear and a little slippery. There was no odor to it. But it tasted slightly salty.

Someone from the *kampong*, one of the headman's sons, brought me the news about Auntie later that day. On the mainland, where she had been shopping, the police had made a sweep, arresting people by the lorry load. She was among those detained.

Detained. What did that mean, exactly? How long would they keep her? The headman's son couldn't tell me. "Not too long," he said, vague like the doctor. But the next bit of news hit me even harder.

"How's the Tuan?" he asked, cocking his head in the direction of my bedroom. I had forgotten that he was one of the men present on the day of the crash—was it just two weeks ago?

"Better," I lied, "much better." That wasn't a lie exactly. At least he had come to; at least we could feed him; at least he was alive.

"Not to worry!" said the headman's son; "day-after-tomorrow they're coming to take him to hospital."

The news made me dizzy, and for a moment I couldn't see straight. Looking over the shoulder of the man facing me, I fancied that the thin palm trees beyond were growing at even crazier angles than the ones along the beach, where they were almost horizontal.

"He's not ready!" I almost cried out, but knew better. The man would have wondered.

I wasn't ready. I wanted to keep him with me, as he was, without improvement if necessary. Once he was gone, nothing would stand between me and the void just waiting to swallow me whole. War would come to our island, I had no doubt of that now. The streams would run red, just like that reservoir up north. My aunt—like my mother, like my father—would never come back for me. And there would be a drought.

Just two more days! I couldn't leave his side. I couldn't

bear it. Nothing seemed pressing anymore save the need, the urgent need, to hold him hostage. I didn't neglect to feed him the boiled rice—or to sustain myself on the remains. I didn't neglect the spongings, either. Nothing else mattered to me. Nothing.

When night came I got into bed with him, crawling into his sarong once more. I wanted rest but not sleep. Yet it was hard to fight the drowsiness brought on by the steady shushing of the sea. Trying to stay awake, I rummaged between his legs. Almost immediately, my fingers were wet.

By daylight, when I could see, all I wanted was to keep the liquid flowing—the little bit of liquid that emerged bead by bead at the nick of the crown on his mushroom-shaped sex. The first time I bent over to taste it at the source, I did it with utmost care, as though licking nectar off a thorn. But soon I grew reckless from a kind of greed, kneeling to face him as I continued the milking. I'd never known such power over another being—there he was, at my feet, exposed, unknowing, wholly at my mercy. So what if his eyes flared open without warning, and he watched me with that roaming gaze, a gaze less than pleasurable, less than human really? So what if he made those gargling noises? It would have taken a lot more to wrest me from my task, my dogged extraction of the juice that kept coming—only by the eyedropperful, it's true; but the miracle was that it kept coming.

No sooner had I licked up a droplet than another would seep through the nick in that tender flesh like a runnel of sap. A little kneading, a little rubbing, and out it oozed. Was it the slight saltiness that set off the thirst in me—a thirst that drink alone couldn't slake? Again and again I got up from bed for air. And for endless sips of water. I gave him to drink too—the thirst had seized him as well for all I knew: his lips were dry and white at the corners. No, I didn't deprive him. I even remembered to feed him his rice, a mouthful or two at a time. But being on my feet was a strain. Lightheaded, heavy-footed, I moved as in a delirium, craving only to return to bed, and to that little spot of moisture seeping through his sex. That was what gave me satisfaction. That. Not the tepid, tasteless water I drank and drank.

Is it surprising that by now I was rubbing between my own legs as well, in rhythm with the steady tapping of his sap? Pleasuring myself was hardly new to me. Maybe if things had been different, if someone—anyone—in the *kampong* had dared touch me, I might not yet have learned to touch myself so capably. But no one did; and so I did. How many times had I stood squarely in front of the window of my room, fingering myself with my sarong hitched up in front, while an unsuspecting male, the object of my heated fancy, went about his business in the *kampong* below! Even when they—for there were many such males—happened to look up and catch me framed at the window, whatever they saw of me from the chest up revealed nothing of how I busied myself below the window line. Skinny boys in their teens, paunchy men—I wasn't choosy about these targets. Once, it was an old Hindu in a ragged loincloth, bending over to stack cordwood. That time I was somewhat more ashamed than usual afterward. But shame is not unlike a lump of ice: painful to swallow, but only for a stinging instant. Then it melts, it goes away.

Given what I knew already, it wasn't so hard to finger myself with one hand, coaxing the drip out of him with the other—while also managing to lick. All the while I marveled at the slick rosy tip of his strange, strange growth, rubber-soft one minute and hard enough the next so that the veins beat against my fingertips. At last my licking gave way to outright sucking, in time to the sucking that pulsed between my legs just before the long tremor kicked in.

By night I was wild with abandon. I shed all my clothes—a thing I'd never done in his presence—dropping my sarong on top of his, which lay on the floor, in a coil, where I'd flung it. I bent down to look into his face and saw that his eyes were open, fixed just past me with the shock of a man gazing at a ghost. Was it my hair, I wondered—my neglected mass of frizz? He closed his eyes then, as though to shut out the disturbing vision, whatever it was.

I got up onto the bed and knelt beside him, facing his feet. The air in the room was so warm and close that I could smell my own sweat—a sour, sickly smell—along with the familiar fumes given off by his body. It felt no different from a fever— the sweating, the shortness of breath, the thirst. Naturally, I went for the liquid. Like the water I squandered while fearing drought, I kept returning to this salty, thirst-making moisture to quench my thirst.

As I squatted over him on the bed, facing his feet and bending over to drink at the source, I happened to lower my crotch onto his hand, which lay with its fingers curled, palm up, by his side. That touch, so slight, grazed me to the quick, and all I had to do—without interrupting the sucking—was to rock back and forth, back and forth, over his open hand while I climbed to that edge from which the body aches to plummet. I plummeted. I shot forward until my head came to rest at his feet. After a while I turned around and nuzzled his hand, only to discover a slickness on his fingers, so like the slickness on mine. Did our liquids also taste alike?

They did. I wanted him to taste them both. I wiped his wet hand on one of my breasts and brought that nipple up to his mouth, where I pressed it against his lips. Then I lowered my other breast down to the moisture at the tip of his sex, rubbing it around before doing what I'd done with the other breast.

The thirst was so acute now I could barely swallow. I placed my mouth over his, probing deep with my tongue—over and under his, all along his teeth, between his gums and lips. His breath was musty, his taste sour-sweet. The combination made my mouth water. I went for his ears now, first one and then the other, licking along the curves and dents and into the hole, to fetch up the bitterish taste of wax. I moved down to the armpits, burying my nose in the pungent thicket of hair; down over his chest and belly to lick his navel; and down into the depths of his genitals.

I'd never stopped to lick the sac before. I trailed my tongue over it now, over the ridged hairy skin, before lifting it to lick under as well, down the line running into his crack. I stopped at its rim, to catch my breath; then, lifting his legs at the knees, parting the cheeks, I plunged my tongue right down into the recess, as deep as it would go.

A dark bitter taste exploded through my palette; the taste of a poisonous plant, perhaps—some wild, inedible onion. The discovery was dizzying. I wanted to subject him to something comparable. That's when I moved up to straddle his face. I faced him on my knees, shifting them farther and farther apart until the very core, the very heart of that hidden cleavage between my legs was split wide open and planted squarely on his mouth. Now we were engaged in a long wet kiss; it was my lips, I should say—those other lips—that were doing the kissing as they smeared their saliva onto his. *Taste!* I said, pressing down harder on my haunches, circling faster, kissing deeper. I was dying of thirst. I was dying, dying ... and in the throes of the shudders that sent me sprawling across his face, I glimpsed what it was like, that letting go and slipping away from the surge of inseparable pleasure and pain.

After a while my skin prickled and I sensed, before I saw, the light I was lying in, a light that chilled rather than warmed me. I opened my eyes onto the full face of the moon, filling my window, staring me down.

I picked up my sarong and tied it around my chest. Outside, I stood on the veranda briefly to absorb the night: the indigo shadows and shapes of the *kampong* roofs, the crooked palms and fuzzy shoreline of the sea. How still it was—not a breeze, not a drizzle to break the spell and let the monsoon in. Those yellow flowers had bloomed and withered in a burst of false promise.

The moon was not so close now; it had retreated to a distance from which it shed its path of light. The path led directly from the stairs of the veranda, down the incline, in a straight line to the sea. I set out without the slightest hesitation; nothing seemed more natural or more inevitable than walking its beam. I followed it until the sand turned wet underfoot. From there the path glittered like a welcoming carpet rolled out, in my honor, across the surface of the sea. I took my first step into the waves. It was easy, it was nothing, I could feel the slightest undertow pulling me in.

But on the threshold of that walk into the waves I turned —
I don't know why — to take a few steps along the beach ... and
found the beam trailing me. I stopped and turned in the other
direction — and there was the moonbeam, still at my side. Back
I wheeled once more, breaking into a run; and back it tagged
alongside me.

Whichever way I went, up and down the beach, the path of
light was doggedly at my heels.

It wasn't the moon that was doing the bidding; it was taking the lead from me — it was I who was guiding the beam! I
darted this way and that, stopping and starting, giddy from
running circles round the moon.

When I could run no more I headed home, the sea behind
me, the moon in tow.

There was time to give him a sponging. I hadn't planned on
it; I hadn't thought I'd be returning. Yet here I was back home,
in time for one last wash.

I hadn't thought I could do the other thing either. But that
too I did.

I let him go.

AUTHOR'S NOTE

When I began this, it was the setting I had to think about;
the action in an erotic story, after all, is a given. I grew up in the
tropics, but that's not entirely why I came to select them as the
background here. Rather, it was also because of a powerful
construct of the tropics shaped by the likes of Conrad, Orwell,
Melville, Malraux, et al. All of them captured — and sometimes
brilliantly misrepresented — this region as a zone of mythic heat
and torpor that destroys decorum, breaks down morality, and
erodes the will. It is to them that I owe my having settled on a
tropical island as the backdrop for my story. Where else but in
a steamy jungle could such a switch in rules take place? Where
else could exploitation occur so illicitly?

The old tropical stereotypes, yes. But why fight them, if
instead you can stand them on their head? "Drought" is my
version of what happens when a restless native tends a
wounded knight.

OH, BROTHER

❧❧❧❧❧❧❧

By Bea Wilder

*The lively comic charm of this monologue beautifully comple-
ments its vision of the tenderness that can spring up even
between two new lovers whose erotic impulses are helped along
by propinquity. Bea Wilder, like Susan Dooley, gives us a por-
trait of a woman at home in her body, who knows and cherishes
her own ability to give and receive pleasure ... and her relish is,
I think, infectious.*

I was deflowered in the City of Brotherly Love twenty-five
years ago. Perhaps this explains my penchant for friends'
brothers, or maybe it's because I never had one, growing up as
I did in a one-gender family of three younger sisters, a domi-
neering mother, and a large cranky female cat. I've simply
always been completely fascinated with the idea of having boys
around the house—boys you could touch, hug, and kiss, but
never screw, of course. So when Carolyn invited me out of the
city in the middle of August, my first inclination was to say no.
(I already had plans to go to a Red Sox game on Sunday with
an old lover and friend, and who needed extra traffic hassles?)

But then she let drop that at this birthday party for her, at her family's summer house, her New York-dwelling brother Jonathan would be in attendance; not surprisingly, although she didn't know it, this turned out to be the very incentive I needed to tank up my car and hit the road early that Saturday morning.

In Cambridge, recycling old boyfriends and husbands and coming across with brothers and other relatives is de rigueur, but Carolyn had only been forthcoming to the extent that I knew Jonathan was in his midforties and unattached. That was enough though, and the promise of a "live one" fresh off the train from the Big Apple remained a tantalizing prospect all the way up the highway north to New Hampshire. Anyway, her directions were good, and in exactly the time she said it would take, I was turning off Route 69 onto the bumpy dirt road that led up a hill to her mother's driveway. No other cars were in evidence, and I remembered hearing something about how they'd be grocery shopping if they weren't there when I arrived. Hordes of daunting relatives were promised for the birthday soiree, so these peaceful moments were fleeting and precious. I unloaded my tote bag, birthday present, and tennis racquet and pushed open the front screen door to the kitchen. I put my stuff down and looked through the living room to a nice deck with a spectacular mountain view, and then I realized I was not alone. Card-shuffling noises emanated from the breakfast nook, and there was a large bearlike creature intently playing solitaire. I coughed nervously, and it got up and smiled. He had opaque brown eyes and a tender smile. "Oh, you must be Carrie's friend. I'm Jonathan."

He seemed tentative and shy, and I was a bit taken aback, but I managed a "Yes, I'm Jean. What shall I do with my stuff?" Now he looked confused, and he sort of pointed at the living room and said to stick it there for the time being. Then he went back to his card game, and I stammered about the nice view and he agreed, and then I said I was going out on the deck to look. He showed up a few minutes later, and we made desultory conversation about Carrie and mother gone shopping and would be back soon and about what an easy trip up it was and about how I hoped we would play tennis and about his documentary on a famous deceased Democrat and my Suburban Hunger study. He seemed kind and sensitive and self-effacing, different from his sister, and just as I sensed the beginnings of sweet sexual tension a noisy car jarred my mood. Carolyn and their mother had arrived.

We all converged in the kitchen, and Carolyn gushed over my early arrival and Mrs. Steele said she hoped I was ready for some tennis before it got too hot as we all put the bottles and cans and jars away. No one introduced me to Jonathan. Mugs of coffee were filled, and we sat on the deck with various newspapers commenting on interesting items here and there. I felt a bit strange and distinct from this family unit. Jonathan was very quiet but pleasant in a sort of detached way that made me curious about and interested in him. We made eye contact a few times and laughed together about a pun Carolyn didn't get. After a while, Carolyn announced that I should bring my tote upstairs to a room down the hall from Jonathan because she preferred a sort of finished basement room with only one bed. She took me on a brief tour and showed me where to drop off my bag, and then we all changed for the tennis game and met at the court nearby. Jonathan and his mother teamed up against Carolyn and me.

The woman is almost eighty, after all, and Jonathan said he rarely played, but they beat us handily. I played poorly, which is unusual, but I was thinking much more about how I hoped Jonathan liked my long tan legs in my short tennis dress than about watching the ball. Luckily it was too hot to play for too long, and we went back to the house for bathing suits because Carolyn wanted to show me the swimming hole. Her mom opted to stay and mix up chicken salad, and Jonathan came with us to swim. Despite the heat, the water temperature was subfreezing so Carolyn and I only jumped in and out and then sat on a rock in the sun and talked. Jonathan stood in the water stomach-deep and cooled off his oversized physique, and I pretended to be engrossed in Carolyn's boring tales of their childhood summers.

The hot day wore on till it was time for an agreed-upon

nap. It was about 2:00 P.M., and the guests were due at 5:30. Carolyn went downstairs to her bedroom, and I went upstairs and fell on my bed naked. I couldn't really sleep wondering where Jonathan was and listening for signs of him on the stairs. It crossed my mind that masturbating would relieve some of the tension I felt, but I didn't know if I really wanted to let go of it and besides the bedsprings were so creaky. Instead I fantasized about what it would be like if he walked in and took me in his arms and licked me all over. I became so aroused, I had to have some relief, so I licked my fingers and tweaked my straining, diamond-hard nipples, then ran them down my front to the moist fuzzy outskirts of my clit. I pressed it hard then in gentle circles. Within seconds I felt the wonderful spasms of relief all through my body to my toes. I hoped I hadn't gasped too loudly. I rolled over pressing my breasts to the cool cotton sheets, happy that I could make myself feel so good, and fell asleep.

When I awoke I was sweating and disoriented. I was worried I had slept through the party. I pulled on my bathing suit and went downstairs to look for a clock. The one on the mantle said 4:30. Jonathan was in the far corner of the living room reading, and he looked up. "Aren't you ever going to get dressed?" he said smiling. "Oh, yes, I mean I just came down to see what time it was. I fell asleep, and I thought it might be later," I managed. "Why SHOULD she get dressed?" his mother, unexpectedly charging around the corner, boomed. "If I looked that good in a bathing suit, I'd never take it off. She isn't chubby like you and me, Jon," she added. Jonathan blushed visibly and mumbled something about taking a shower. He brushed by me, and I wanted to hug him and show him that we were allied against rude mothers and tell him I would never embarrass him like that, but, of course, I just stepped out of the way. Then Mrs. Steele started again, "Come help me put out the hors d'oeuvres, my dear. Carolyn's out looking for my cat who has been missing all day. She'll be back when she's found her."

I grabbed a vegetable platter and some Boursin and crackers and put them on coffee tables, and then I fraternized with the enemy a bit, she was after all my hostess, and went upstairs to dress.

I came down in my black and white polka-dotted jumpsuit (once, someone at another summer place had called it a "clown suit," but I thought it very chic) and gold sandals. Carolyn's uncle, who's a preeminent Chinese scholar and his wife had arrived. Carolyn was with them on the deck in a wonderful rust-colored handkerchief dress (she did have style), and she introduced us and told us to help ourselves to drinks. I was getting ice cubes out of the bucket when a large group of cousins came in the door shrieking and kissing. I reached for the vodka and tonic and went out to the Chinese scholar who recently had a building at Harvard named for him. He was very old, and his wife was ensconced with the cousins, so I sat near him and asked him questions about our surroundings. We talked at great length, and Mrs. Steele came by on several occasions and whispered offers of replacing me so I could "mingle," but I was very content.

I could see Jonathan across the crowded deck, and he looked uncomfortable even though it was his chance to shine about his documentary, with its initial broadcast on public television due in a month. Carolyn herself was madly mingling and soon started opening cards and gifts. The aged Chinese scholar talked about how he missed Carolyn's father because he had had such a good mind, which would be refreshing at occasions like this. Then he started to nod off, and I decided to find a bathroom. When I emerged the party was delightfully dispersing except for one maiden aunt who was invited to eat duck and play bridge with us later, "because Carrie never likes to play." I guess it was assumed that Jonathan and I would. Carolyn seemed locked in conversation with a Connecticut cousin, so I scurried around the kitchen and helped get the meal set out on the dining room table.

The duck was superb, which was surprising. Mrs. Steele was a good artist, but her kitchen here, and in Cambridge, had none of the inviting signs of an accomplished cook. The bridge was fun, too, and we all fell into an amusing round of harmless gossip while Carolyn cleaned up. Then, just when I was starting to feel at ease with Carolyn and her family, she announced she was retiring. It was only about ten, but she said she hadn't slept well the night before, thanked us again for our birthday efforts, and descended to her bedroom. When the rubber ended, Mrs. Steele also retired, and Jonathan was asked to walk the aunt home. I wasn't at all tired, but I did feel a chill of isolation and abandonment. I walked out on the deck and made a silent prayer that Jonathan would come home and keep me company. After a few very long minutes, the front door opened and shut, and I could hear him in the kitchen rustling around. The sliding door to the deck opened, he came out, sat down behind me, and lit a joint. I turned my chair around, and we stared at each other.

"Want some of this?" he offered as he held out the rolled cigarette. I hadn't smoked dope in ages and I didn't usually like it, but I didn't want to offend him in any way so I reached for it and inhaled. "How did you like the Jesus freaks?" he asked. I looked confused, so he regaled me with a tale of cousins I had met earlier who had discovered the ways of Satan and had joined the First Assembly of God. I laughed and said I hadn't noticed, but that I had that in my family too, and he laughed and we toked some more. He pointed out their house across the meadow, and we pretended to hear Satanic rituals being performed and laughed some more. He told me we should try to talk softly because his mother's room had a window on the deck. I felt like we were naughty children sneaking around after the adults had gone to sleep, and it was forbidden and fun and the way I imagined it would be with a brother in the house. I had a sudden urge to lie down on the bench near his chair and put my head in his lap, but instead I asked if I could sip his ice water.

I drank it all, then offered to get some more from the kitchen. I was a bit tipsy, but I managed to get to the kitchen and had just opened the refrigerator door when I felt him behind me. He put his hand over mine and closed the fridge door. I turned around, and he sort of pinned me with his arms against it and kissed me in the most unforgettable way. First it was tentative and probing, then as we relaxed into it and found our rhythm we simultaneously hugged and rubbed each other with our arms, still sucking on each other's tongues and exploring for what seemed like a very long time. I guess some of it was the dope, but I honestly can say I had never kissed like that before. Jonathan took my face in his hands then my hand and led me over to a large comfortable chair in the living room. We collapsed into it and kissed more and more, and I could feel my whole body responding and aching for more. I took his hand and placed it on a breast, and he stopped kissing and looked to see where to put it. Then he gently pinched my nipple and stuck his tongue in my ear.

"You're beautiful," he groaned. I was panting, and I grabbed for his shirt and felt his smooth soft skin, and he moaned softly. Then he whispered in my ear: "You go upstairs first and open your door and close it and listen for me to come up and then sneak into my room." I tried to sit up straight and unconvincingly said, "But, Jonathan, I don't think we should do obscene things in your mother's house."

"We don't have to," he whispered, "but don't you want to kiss some more?"

"Oh, yes," I agreed. "Let's."

I followed his instructions about entering my room and listening for him, and then I quietly opened my door and crept down the hall to his room. He was lying on his bed with his shirt off, and I longed to rest my breasts on his chest. As if mind reading, he fumbled at the large buttons on the front of my jumpsuit until they opened. I was bra-less, and he rubbed my breasts, and we lay chest to chest for several minutes. Then he said rather naively, "Did you ever expect that today would end up like this?" "I was hoping it would, weren't you?" I asked. "Yeah, it's just that Carrie and I don't usually like the same people," he explained. "It's not as if she's been particularly friendly today, so it's nice that you are," I murmured, as I reached down to rub his cock. "Mmmm," he grunted as he helped me unzip his fly and put my hand on his throbbing erection. Then he took my hand off and said, "I might finish too soon, so let's concentrate on you for a bit."

He encircled my breasts and very slowly and softly stroked

my stomach and thighs. I felt very wet and juicy and almost cried out when he found my clit with one finger and put another up my vagina. He took that finger away and put it up to my lips to remind me to be quiet, and I could smell my female juices on his finger, which turned me on even more. He stuck his tongue in my mouth and we kissed some more, then his tongue followed the path his finger had made around my breasts and down my stomach to my overflowing cunt. He gently sucked on my clit and reinserted his finger, and I held onto his head while I lurched in an orgasm unknown to me. Waves of chills all the way to my toes seized my flailing body over and over again. When I was spent, I felt relaxed and happy and warm all over. He grazed gently on my front some more and rested his hand on my moist bush, and I reached over to his semihard penis. He took my hand and licked it and then put it back on his cock and I rubbed it slowly. "Touch my balls," he requested softly, and he moaned when I grabbed them.

His cock was glistening with a few drops of sperm, and I could feel my excitement rising up again. I licked him the way he had me all down his front, and then I teased his tip until he begged me to take him. Still I ran my hand up and down his shaft and licked only the tip of his cock while he thrust himself into my mouth. I removed the penis and coddled it in the cleavage of my breasts. "Please, please," he groaned, as I held him and rubbed him across my hard nipples, then put him back in my mouth, sucking up and down and carefully keeping my teeth out of the way. He found my clit again with a spare hand, and we writhed around together until I could taste his sperm. He was delicious, and I loved the Chinese food taste of him. We lay all wrapped up in each other for a very long time until I felt him reach for a clock. We looked at the glow-in-the-dark hands together. It was 3:30. I would be an utter wreck at the baseball game if I didn't try for a few hours of sleep, but I couldn't let go of him. He kissed me again, and we entwined tongues. Then he gently lifted me up in his arms and crept down the hall to my room. He lay me down on the bed and kissed my bush. "You have a beautiful pussy," he said. I wanted him again, but I knew we should stop. "So much for not doing obscene things in your mother's house," I whispered. "No penetration," he said smiling. Then he was gone. I fell into deep satisfied sleep.

The next morning was a rush of showering, dressing, packing, morning salutations, thank-yous, and English muffins, with everyone at the breakfast table when I got there. Jonathan and I had our furtive exchanges, and when it was time to go, he walked me out to the car with my bag. He put the bag in the trunk and stood staring at me as I started the car. I rolled down the window and winked at him. "I sure hope you're in the book," he said. "Have a safe trip."

"I am," I replied. "Oh, brother," I thought as I drove down the road.

AUTHOR'S NOTE

I wrote this story one year after the weekend on which it is loosely based. It is an anniversary reflection on the beginnings of a memorable affair of the heart, with a few adjustments for fantasy, though it was a genuinely good time. I have enjoyed several of my friends' brothers over the years and remain fascinated with the brother-sister relationship, which I am only starting to understand.

NINETY-THREE MILLION MILES AWAY

By Barbara Gowdy

There are relationships with strangers, and then there are strange relationships. In "Ninety-Three Million Miles Away" Barbara Gowdy mixes the two, adding, as well, a paradox: the intense intimacy of distance. It is across this space, she suggests, that we might find a singular opportunity to be most ourselves. While certainly an intriguing notion of itself, it is accompanied by another, equally provocative one—that most women have in them an instinctive streak of exhibitionism, which is, Gowdy posits, "a side effect of being the receptor in the sex act." However, her concluding message, reminding us as it does that the sensation of feeling desire always carries with it the potential for surprise, is unassailable.

At least part of the reason Ali married Claude, a cosmetic surgeon with a growing practice, was so that she could quit her boring government job. Claude was all for it. "You only have one life to live," he said. "You only have one kick at the can." He gave her a generous allowance and told her to do what she wanted.

She wasn't sure what that was, aside from trying on clothes in expensive stores. Claude suggested something musical—she loved music—so she took dance classes and piano lessons and discovered that she had a tin ear and no sense of rhythm. She fell into a mild depression during which she peevishly questioned Claude about the ethics of cosmetic surgery.

"It all depends on what light you're looking at it in," Claude said. He was not easily riled. What Ali needed to do, he said, was take the wider view.

She agreed. She decided to devote herself to learning, and she began a regime of reading and studying, five days a week, five to six hours a day. She read novels, plays, biographies, essays, magazine articles, almanacs, the New Testament, *The Concise Oxford Dictionary, The Harper Anthology of Poetry.*

But after a year of this, although she became known as the person at dinner parties who could supply the name or date that somebody was snapping around for, she wasn't particularly happy, and she didn't even feel smart. Far from it, she felt stupid, a machine, an idiot savant whose one talent was memorization. If she had any *creative* talent, which was the only kind she really admired, she wasn't going to find it by armoring herself with facts. She grew slightly paranoid that Claude wanted her to settle down and have a baby.

A few days before their second wedding anniversary she and Claude bought a condominium apartment with floor-to-ceiling windows, and Ali decided to abandon her reading regime and to take up painting. Since she didn't know the first thing about painting or even drawing, she studied pictures from art books. She did know what her first subject was going to be—herself in the nude. Several months earlier she'd had a dream about spotting her signature in the corner of a painting, and realizing from the conversation of the men who were admiring it (and blocking her view) that it was an extraordinary rendition of her naked self. She took the dream to be a sign. For several weeks she studied the proportions, skin tones, and muscle definitions of the nudes in her books, then she went out and bought art supplies and a self-standing, full-length mirror.

She set up her work area in the middle of the living room. Here she had light without being directly in front of the window. When she was all ready to begin, she stood before the mirror and slipped off her white terry-cloth housecoat and her pink flannelette pajamas, letting them fall to the floor. It aroused her a little to witness her careless shedding of clothes. She tried a pose: hands folded and resting loosely under her stomach, feet buried in the drift of her housecoat.

For some reason, however, she couldn't get a fix on what she looked like. Her face and body seemed indistinct, secretive in a way, as if they were actually well-defined, but not to her, or not from where she was looking.

She decided that she should simply start, and see what happened. She did a pencil drawing of herself sitting in a chair and stretching. It struck her as being very good, not that she could really judge, but the out-of-kilter proportions seemed slyly deliberate, and there was a pleasing simplicity to the reaching arms and the elongated curve of the neck. Because flattery hadn't been her intention, Ali felt that at last she may have wrenched a vision out of her soul.

The next morning she got out of bed unusually early, not long after Claude had left the apartment, and discovered sunlight streaming obliquely into the living room through a gap between their building and the apartment house next door. As far as she knew, and in spite of the plate-glass windows, this was the only direct light they got. Deciding to make use of it while it lasted, she moved her easel, chair, and mirror closer to the window. Then she took off her housecoat and pajamas.

For a few moments she stood there looking at herself, wondering what it was that had inspired the sketch. Today she was disposed to seeing herself as not bad, overall. As far as certain specifics went, though, as to whether her breasts were small, for instance, or her eyes close together, she remained in the dark.

Did other people find her looks ambiguous? Claude was always calling her beautiful, except that the way he put it—

"You're beautiful to me," or "I think you're beautiful"—made it sound as if she should understand that his taste in women was unconventional. Her only boyfriend before Claude, a guy called Roger, told her she was great but never said how exactly. When they had sex, Roger liked to hold the base of his penis and watch it going in and out of her. Once, he said that there were days he got so horny at the office, his pencil turned him on. She thought it should have been his pencil sharpener.

She covered her breasts with her hands. Down her cleavage a drop of sweat slid haltingly, a sensation like the tip of a tongue. She circled her palms until her nipples hardened, and imagined a man's hands ... not Claude's—a man's hands not attached to any particular man. She looked out the window.

In the apartment across from her she saw a man.

She leapt to one side, behind the drapes. Her heart pounded violently, but only for a moment, as if something had thundered by, dangerously close. She wiped her wet forehead on the drapes, then, without looking at the window, walked back to her easel, picked up her palette and brush, and began to mix paint. She gave herself a glance in the mirror, but she had no intention of trying to duplicate her own skin tone. She wanted something purer. White with just a hint of rose, like the glance of color in a soap bubble.

Her strokes were short and light to control dripping. She liked the effect, though ... how it made the woman appear as if she were covered in feathers. Paint splashed on her own skin, but she resisted putting her smock on. The room seemed preternaturally white and airy; the windows beyond the mirror gleamed. Being so close to the windows gave her the tranced sensation of standing at the edge of a cliff.

A few minutes before she lost the direct sun, she finished the woman's skin. She set down her palette and put her brush in turpentine, then wet a rag in the turpentine and wiped paint off her hands and where it had dripped on her thighs and feet. She thought about the sun. She thought that it is ninety-three million miles away and that its fuel supply will last another five billion years. Instead of thinking about the man who was

watching her, she tried to recall a solar chart she had memo-
rized a couple of years ago.

The surface temperature is six thousand degrees Fahren-
heit, she told herself. Double that number, and you have how
many times bigger the surface of the sun is compared to the
surface of the earth. Except that because the sun is a ball of hot
gas, it actually has no surface.

When she had rubbed the paint off herself, she went into
the kitchen to wash away the turpentine with soap and water.
The man's eyes tracked her. She didn't have to glance at the
window for confirmation. She switched on the light above the
sink, soaped the dishcloth, and began to wipe her skin. There
was no reason to clean her arms, but she lifted each one and
wiped the cloth over it. She wiped her breasts. She seemed to
share in his scrutiny, as if she were looking at herself through
his eyes. From his perspective she was able to see her physical
self very clearly—her shiny, red-highlighted hair, her small
waist and heart-shaped bottom, the dreamy tilt to her head.

She began to shiver. She wrung out the cloth and folded it
over the faucet, then patted herself dry with a dish towel. Then,
pretending to be examining her fingernails, she turned and
walked over to the window. She looked up.

There he was. Her glance of a quarter of an hour ago had
registered dark hair and a white shirt. Now she saw a long,
older face ... a man in his fifties maybe. A green tie. She had
seen him before this morning—quick, disinterested (or so she
had thought) sightings of a man in his kitchen, watching television, going from room to room. A bachelor living next door.
She pressed the palms of her hands on the window, and he
stepped back into shadow.

The pane clouded from her breath. She leaned her body
into it, flattening her breasts against the cool glass. Right at the
window she was visible to his apartment and the one below,
which had closed vertical blinds. "Each window like a pill'ry
appears," she thought. Vaguely appropriate lines from the
poems she had read last year were always occurring to her. She
felt that he was still watching, but she yearned for proof.

When it became evident that he wasn't going to show himself, she went into the bedroom. The bedroom windows didn't face the apartment house, but she closed them anyway, then got into bed under the covers. Between her legs there was such a tender throbbing that she had to push a pillow into her crotch. Sex addicts must feel like this, she thought. Rapists, child molesters.

She said to herself, "You are a certifiable exhibitionist." She let out an amazed, almost exultant laugh, but instantly fell into a darker amazement as it dawned on her that she really was ... she really *was* an exhibitionist. And what's more, she had been one for years, or at least she had been working up to being one for years.

Why, for instance, did she and Claude live here, in this vulgar low-rise? Wasn't it because of the floor-to-ceiling windows that faced the windows of the house next door?

And what about when she was twelve and became so obsessed with the idea of urinating on people's lawns that one night she crept out of the house after everyone was asleep and did it, peed on the lawn of the townhouses next door ... right under a streetlight, in fact.

What about two years ago, when she didn't wear underpants the entire summer? She'd had a minor yeast infection and had read that it was a good idea not to wear underpants at home, if you could help it, but she had stopped wearing them in public as well, beneath skirts and dresses, at parties, on buses, and she must have known that this was taking it a bit far, because she had kept it from Claude.

"Oh, my God," she said wretchedly.

She went still, alerted by how theatrical that had sounded. Her heart was beating in her throat. She touched a finger to it. So fragile, a throat. She imagined the man being excited by her hands on her throat.

What was going on? What was the matter with her? Maybe she was too aroused to be shocked at herself. She moved her hips, rubbing her crotch against the pillow. No, she didn't want to masturbate. That would ruin it.

Ruin what?

She closed her eyes, and the man appeared to her. She experienced a rush of wild longing. It was as if, all her life, she had been waiting for a long-faced, middle-aged man in a white shirt and green tie. He was probably still standing in his living room, watching her window.

She sat up, threw off the covers.

Dropped back down on the bed.

This was crazy. This really was crazy. What if he was a rapist? What if, right this minute, he was downstairs, finding out her name from the mailbox? Or what if he was just some lonely, normal man who took her display as an invitation to phone her up and ask her for a date? It's not as if she wanted to go out with him. She wasn't looking for an affair.

For an hour or so she fretted, and then she drifted off to sleep. When she woke up, shortly after noon, she was quite calm. The state she had worked herself into earlier struck her as overwrought. So, she gave some guy a thrill, so what? She was a bit of an exhibitionist ... most women were, she bet. It was instinctive, a side effect of being the receptor in the sex act.

She decided to have lunch and go for a walk. While she was making herself a sandwich she avoided glancing at the window, but as soon as she sat at the table, she couldn't resist looking over.

He wasn't there, and yet she felt that he was watching her, standing out of the light. She ran a hand through her hair. "For Christ's sake," she reproached herself, but she was already with him. Again it was as if her eyes were in his head, although not replacing his eyes. She knew that he wanted her to slip her hand down her sweatpants. She did this. Watching his window, she removed her hand and licked her wet fingers. At that instant she would have paid money for some sign that he was watching.

After a few minutes she began to chew on her fingernails. She was suddenly depressed. She reached over and pulled the curtain across the window and ate her sandwich. Her mouth, biting into the bread, trembled like an old lady's. "Trembled like a guilty thing surprised," she quoted to herself. It wasn't guilt, though, it wasn't frustration, either, not sexual frustration. She was acquainted with this bleached sadness—it came upon her at the height of sensation ... after orgasms, after a day of trying on clothes in stores.

She finished her sandwich and went for a long walk in her new toreador pants and her tight, black, turtleneck sweater. By the time she returned, Claude was home. He asked her if she had worked in the nude again.

"Of course," she said absently. "I have to." She was looking past him at the man's closed drapes. "Claude," she said suddenly, "am I beautiful? I mean not just to you. Am I empirically beautiful?"

Claude looked surprised. "Well, yeah," he said. "Sure you are. Hell, I married you, didn't I? Hey!" He stepped back. "Whoa!"

She was removing her clothes. When she was naked, she said, "Don't think of me as your wife. Just as a woman. One of your patients. Am I beautiful or not?"

He made a show of eyeing her up and down. "Not bad," he said. "Of course, it depends on what you mean by 'beautiful.'" He laughed. "What's going on?"

"I'm serious. You don't think I'm kind of ... normal? You know, plain?"

"Of course not," he said lovingly. He reached for her and drew her into his arms. "You want hard evidence?" he said.

They went into the bedroom. It was dark because the curtains were still drawn. She switched on the bedside lamp, but once he was undressed, he switched it off again.

"No," she said from the bed, "leave it on."

"What? You want it on?"

"For a change."

The next morning she got up before he did. She had hardly slept. During breakfast she kept looking over at the apartment house, but there was no sign of the man. Which didn't necessarily mean that he wasn't there. She couldn't wait for Claude to leave so that she could stop pretending she wasn't keyed up. It was gnawing at her that she had overestimated or somehow misread the man's interest. How did she know? He might be gay. He might be so devoted to a certain woman that all other women repelled him. He might be puritanical ... a priest, a born-again Christian. He might be out of his mind.

The minute Claude was out the door, she undressed and began work on the painting. She stood in the sunlight mixing colors, then sat on the chair in her stretching pose, looking at herself in the mirror, then stood up and—without paying much attention, glancing every few seconds at his window—painted ribs and uplifted breasts.

An hour went by before she thought, he's not going to show up. She dropped into the chair, weak with disappointment, even though she knew that, very likely, he had simply been obliged to go to work, that his being home yesterday was a fluke. Forlornly she gazed at her painting. To her surprise she had accomplished something rather interesting: breasts like Picasso eyes. It is possible, she thought dully, that I am a natural talent.

She put her brush in the turpentine, and her face in her hands. She felt the sun on her hair. In a few minutes the sun would disappear behind his house, and after that, if she wanted him to get a good look at her, she would have to stand right at the window. She envisioned herself stationed there all day. You are ridiculous, she told herself. You are unhinged.

She glanced up at the window again.

He was there.

She sat up straight. Slowly she came to her feet. Stay, she prayed. He did. She walked over to the window, her fingertips brushing her thighs. She held her breath. When she was at the window, she stood perfectly still. He stood perfectly still. He had on a white shirt again, but no tie. He was close enough that she could make out the darkness around his eyes, although she couldn't tell exactly where he was looking. But his eyes seemed to enter her head like a drug, and she felt herself aligned with his perspective. She saw herself—surprisingly slender, composed but apprehensive—through the glass and against the backdrop of the room's white walls.

After a minute or two she walked over to the chair, picked it up, and carried it to the window. She sat facing him, her knees apart. He was as still as a picture. So was she, because she had suddenly remembered that he might be gay or crazy. She tried to give him a hard look. She observed his age and his sad, respectable appearance ... and the fact that he remained at the window, revealing his interest.

No, he was the man she had imagined. I am a gift to him, she thought, opening her legs wider. I am his dream come true. She began to rotate her hips. With the fingers of both hands she spread her labia.

One small part of her mind, clinging to the person she had been until yesterday morning, tried to pull her back. She felt it as a presence behind the chair, a tableau of sensational, irrelevant warnings that she was obviously not about to turn around for. She kept her eyes on the man. Moving her left hand up to her breasts, she began to rub and squeeze and to circle her fingers on the nipples. The middle finger of her right hand slipped into her vagina, as the palm massaged her clitoris.

He was motionless.

You are kissing me, she thought. She seemed to feel his lips, cool, soft, sliding, and sucking down her stomach. You are kissing me. She imagined his hands under her, lifting her like a bowl to his lips.

She was coming.

Her body jolted. Her legs shook. She had never experienced anything like it. Seeing what he saw, she witnessed an act of shocking vulnerability. It went on and on. She saw the charity of her display, her lavish recklessness and submission. It inspired her to the tenderest self-love. The man did not move, not until she had finally stopped moving, and then he reached up one hand—to signal, she thought, but it was to close the drapes.

She stayed sprawled in the chair. She was astonished. She couldn't believe herself. She couldn't believe him. How did he know to stay so still, to simply watch her? She avoided the thought that right at this moment he was probably masturbating. She absorbed herself only with what she had seen, which was a dead-still man whose eyes she had sensed roving over her body the way that eyes in certain portraits seem to follow you around a room.

The next three mornings everything was the same. He had on his white shirt, she masturbated in the chair, he watched without moving, she came spectacularly, he closed the drapes.

Afterward she went out clothes shopping or visiting people. Everyone told her how great she looked. At night she was passionate in bed, prompting Claude to ask several times, "What the hell's come over you?" but he asked it happily, he didn't look a gift horse in the mouth. She felt very loving toward Claude, not out of guilt but out of high spirits. She knew better than to confess, of course, and yet she didn't believe that she was betraying him with the man next door. A man who hadn't touched her or spoken to her, who, as far as she was concerned, only existed from the waist up and who never moved except to pull his drapes, how could that man be counted as a lover?

The fourth day, Friday, the man didn't appear. For two hours she waited in the chair. Finally she moved to the couch and watched television, keeping one eye on his window. She told herself that he must have had an urgent appointment, or that he had to go to work early. She was worried, though. At some point, late in the afternoon when she wasn't looking, he closed his drapes.

Saturday and Sunday he didn't seem to be home—the drapes were drawn and the lights off ... not that she could have done anything anyway, not with Claude there. On Monday morning she was in her chair, naked, as soon as Claude left the house. She waited until 10:30, then put on her toreador pants and white, push-up halter top and went for a walk. A consoling line from *Romeo and Juliet* played in her head: "He that is stricken blind cannot forget the precious treasure of his eyesight lost." She was angry with the man for not being as keen as she was. If he was at his window tomorrow, she vowed she would shut her drapes on him.

But how would she replace him, what would she do? Become a table dancer? She had to laugh. Aside from the fact that she was a respectably married woman and could not dance to save her life and was probably ten years too old, the last thing she wanted was a bunch of slack-jawed, flat-eyed drunks grabbing at her breasts. She wanted one man, and she wanted him to have a sad, intelligent demeanor and the control to watch her without moving a muscle. She wanted him to wear a white shirt.

On the way home, passing his place, she stopped. The building was a mansion turned into luxury apartments. He must have money, she realized ... an obvious conclusion, but until now she'd had no interest whatsoever in who he was.

She climbed the stairs and tried the door. Found it open. Walked in.

The mailboxes were numbered one to four. His would be four. She read the name in the little window: "Dr. Andrew Halsey."

Back at her apartment she looked him up under "Physicians" in the phone book and found that, like Claude, he was a surgeon. A general surgeon, though, a remover of tumors and diseased organs. Presumably on call. Presumably dedicated, as a general surgeon had to be.

She guessed she would forgive his absences.

The next morning and the next, Andrew (as she now thought of him) was at the window. Thursday he wasn't. She tried not to be disappointed. She imagined him saving people's lives, drawing his scalpel along skin in beautifully precise cuts. For something to do she worked on her painting. She painted fishlike eyes, a hooked nose, a mouth full of teeth. She worked fast.

Andrew was there Friday morning. When Ali saw him she rose to her feet and pressed her body against the window, as she had done the first morning. Then she walked to the chair, turned it around and leaned over it, her back to him. She masturbated stroking herself from behind.

That afternoon she bought him a pair of binoculars, an expensive, powerful pair, which she wrapped in brown paper, addressed, and left on the floor in front of his mailbox. All weekend she was preoccupied with wondering whether he would understand that she had given them to him and whether he would use them. She had considered including a message: "For our mornings" or something like that, but such direct communication seemed like a violation of a pact between them. The binoculars alone were a risk.

Monday, before she even had her housecoat off, he walked from the rear of the room to the window, the binoculars at his eyes. Because most of his face was covered by the binoculars and his hands, she had the impression that he was masked. Her legs shook. When she opened her legs and spread her labia, his eyes crawled up her. She masturbated but didn't come and didn't try to, although she put on a show of coming. She was so devoted to his appreciation that her pleasure seemed like a siphoning of his, an early, childish indulgence that she would never return to.

It was later, with Claude, that she came. After supper she pulled him onto the bed. She pretended that he was Andrew, or rather she imagined a dark, long-faced, silent man who made love with his eyes open but who smelled and felt like Claude and whom she loved and trusted as she did Claude. With this hybrid partner she was able to relax enough to encourage the kind of kissing and movement she needed but had never had the confidence to insist upon. The next morning, masturbating for Andrew, she reached the height of ecstasy, as if her orgasms with him had been the fantasy, and her pretenses of orgasm were the real thing. Not coming released her completely into his dream of her. The whole show was for him—cunt, ass, mouth, throat offered to his magnified vision.

For several weeks Andrew turned up regularly, five mornings a week, and she lived in a state of elation. In the afternoons she worked on her painting, without much concentration though, since finishing it didn't seem to matter anymore in spite of how well it was turning out. Claude insisted that it was still very much a self-portrait, a statement Ali was insulted by, given the woman's obvious primitivism and her flat, distant eyes.

There was no reason for her to continue working in the nude, but she did, out of habit and comfort, and on the outside chance that Andrew might be peeking through his drapes. While she painted she wondered about her exhibitionism, what it was about her that craved to have a strange man look at her. Of course, everyone and everything liked to be looked at to a certain degree, she thought. Flowers, cats, anything that preened or shone, children crying, "Look at me!" Some mornings her episodes with Andrew seemed to have nothing at all to do with lust; they were completely display, wholehearted surrender to what felt like the most inaugural and genuine of all desires, which was not sex but which happened to be expressed through a sexual act.

One night she dreamed that Andrew was operating on her. Above the surgical mask his eyes were expressionless. He had very long arms. She was also able to see, as if through his eyes, the vertical incision that went from between her breasts to her navel, and the skin on either side of the incision folded back like a scroll. Her heart was brilliant red and perfectly heart-shaped. All of her other organs were glistening yellows and oranges. Somebody should take a picture of this, she thought. Andrew's gloved hands barely appeared to move as they wielded long, silver instruments. There was no blood on his hands. Very carefully, so that she hardly felt it, he prodded her organs and plucked at her veins and tendons, occasionally drawing a tendon out and dropping it into a petri dish. It was as if he were weeding a garden. Her heart throbbed. A tendon encircled her heart, and when he pulled on it she could feel that its other end encircled her vagina, and the uncoiling there was the most exquisite sensation she had ever experienced. She worried that she would come and that her trembling and spasms would cause him to accidently stab her. She woke up coming.

All day the dream obsessed her. It *could* happen, she reasoned. She could have a gall bladder or an appendicitis attack and be rushed to the hospital and, just as she was going under, see that the surgeon was Andrew. It could happen.

When she woke up the next morning, the dream was her first thought. She looked down at the gentle swell of her stomach and felt sentimental and excited. She found it impossible to shake the dream, even while she was masturbating for Andrew, so that instead of entering *his* dream of her, instead of seeing a naked woman sitting in a pool of morning sun, she saw her sliced-open chest in the shaft of his surgeon's light. Her heart was what she focused on, its fragile pulsing, but she also saw the slower rise and fall of her lungs, and the quivering of her other organs. Between her organs were tantalizing crevices and entwined swirls of blue and red—her veins and arteries. Her tendons were seashell pink, threaded tight as guitar strings.

Of course she realized that she had the physiology all wrong and that in a real operation there would be blood and pain and she would be anesthetized. It was an impossible, mad fantasy; she didn't expect it to last. But every day it became more enticing as she authenticated it with hard data, such as the name of the hospital he operated out of (she called his number in the phone book and asked his nurse) and the name of the surgical instruments he would use (she consulted one of Claude's medical texts), and as she smoothed out the rough edges by imagining, for instance, minuscule suction tubes planted here and there in the incision to remove every last drop of blood.

In the mornings, during her real encounters with Andrew, she became increasingly frustrated until it was all she could do not to quit in the middle, close the drapes, or walk out of the room. And yet if he failed to show up, she was desperate. She started to drink gin and tonics before lunch and to sunbathe at the edge of the driveway between her building and his, knowing he wasn't home from ten o'clock on, but laying there for hours, just in case.

One afternoon, lightheaded from gin and sun, restless with worry because he hadn't turned up the last three mornings, she changed out of her bikini and into a strapless, cotton dress and went for a walk. She walked past the park she had been heading for, past the stores she had thought she might browse in. The sun bore down. Strutting by men who eyed her bare shoulders, she felt voluptuous, sweetly rounded. But at the pit of her stomach was a filament of anxiety, evidence that despite telling herself otherwise, she knew where she was going.

She entered the hospital by the Emergency doors and wandered the corridors for what seemed like half an hour before discovering Andrew's office. By this time she was holding her stomach and half believing that the feeling of anxiety might actually be a symptom of something very serious.

"Dr. Halsey isn't seeing patients," his nurse said. She slit open a manila envelope with a lion's head letter opener. "They'll take care of you at Emergency."

"I have to see Dr. Halsey," Ali said, her voice cracking. "I'm a friend."

The nurse sighed. "Just a minute." She stood and went down a hall, opening a door at the end after a quick knock.

Ali pressed her fists into her stomach. For some reason she no longer felt a thing. She pressed harder. What a miracle if she burst her appendix! She should stab herself with the letter opener. She should at least break her fingers, slam them in a drawer like a draft dodger.

"Would you like to come in?" a high, nasal voice said. Ali spun around. It was Andrew, standing at the door.

"The doctor will see you," the nurse said impatiently, sitting back behind her desk.

Ali's heart began to pound. She felt as if a pair of hands were cupping and uncupping her ears. His shirt was blue. She went down the hall, squeezing past him without looking up, and sat in the green plastic chair beside his desk. He shut the door and walked over to the window. It was a big room; there was a long expanse of old green and yellow floor tiles between them. Leaning his hip against a filing cabinet, he just stood there, hands in his trouser pockets, regarding her with such a polite, impersonal expression that she asked him if he recognized her.

"Of course I do," he said quietly.

"Well—" Suddenly she was mortified. She felt like a woman about to sob that she couldn't afford the abortion. She touched her fingers to her hot face.

"I don't know your name," he said.

"Oh. Ali. Ali Perrin."

"What do you want, Ali?"

Her eyes fluttered down to his shoes—black, shabby loafers. She hated his adenoidal voice. What did she want?

What she wanted was to bolt from the room like the mad woman she suspected she was. She glanced up at him again. Because he was standing with his back to the window, he was outlined in light. It made him seem unreal, like a film image superimposed against a screen. She tried to look away, but his eyes held her. Out in the waiting room the telephone was ringing. What do *you* want, she thought, capitulating to the pull of her perspective over to his, seeing now, from across the room, a charming woman with tanned, bare shoulders and blushing cheeks.

The light blinked on his phone. Both of them glanced over at it, but he stayed standing where he was. After a moment she murmured, "I have no idea what I'm doing here."

He was silent. She kept her eyes on the phone, waiting for him to speak. When he didn't, she said, "I had a dream ..." She let out a disbelieving laugh. "God." She shook her head.

"You are very lovely," he said in a speculative tone. She glanced up at him, and he turned away. Pressing his hands together, he took a few steps along the window. "I have very much enjoyed our ... our encounters," he said.

"Oh, don't worry," she said. "I'm not here to —"

"However," he cut in, "I should tell you that I am moving into another building."

She looked straight at him.

"This weekend, as a matter of fact." He frowned at his wall of framed diplomas.

"This weekend?" she said.

"Yes."

"So," she murmured. "It's over then."

"Regrettably."

She stared at his profile. In profile he was a stranger — beak-nosed, round-shouldered. She hated his shoes, his floor, his formal way of speaking, his voice, his profile, and yet her eyes filled and she longed for him to look at her again.

Abruptly he turned his back to her and said that his apartment was in the east end, near the beach. He gestured out the window. Did she know where the yacht club was?

"No," she whispered.

"Not that I am a member," he said with a mild laugh.

"Listen," she said, wiping her eyes. "I'm sorry." She came to her feet. "I guess I just wanted to see you."

He strode like an obliging host over to the door.

"Well, good-bye," she said, looking up into his face.

He had garlic breath and five o'clock shadow. His eyes grazed hers. "I wouldn't feel too badly about anything," he said affably.

When she got back to the apartment the first thing she did was take her clothes off and go over to the full-length mirror, which was still standing next to the easel. Her eyes filled again because without Andrew's appreciation or the hope of it (and despite how repellent she had found him) what she saw was a pathetic little woman with pasty skin and short legs.

She looked at the painting. If *that* was her, as Claude claimed, then she also had flat eyes and crude, wild proportions.

What on earth did Claude see in her?

What had Andrew seen? "You are very lovely," Andrew had said, but maybe he'd been reminding himself. Maybe he'd meant, "lovely when I'm in the next building."

After supper that evening she asked Claude to lie with her on the couch, and the two of them watched TV. She held his hand against her breast. "Let this be enough," she prayed.

But she didn't believe it ever would be. The world was too full of surprises, it frightened her. As Claude was always saying, things looked different from different angles, and in different lights. What this meant to her was that everything hinged on where you happened to be standing at a given moment, or even on who you imagined you were. It meant that in certain lights, desire sprang up out of nowhere.

AUTHOR'S NOTE

"Ninety-Three Million Miles Away" was conceived as a response to Alberto Moravia's novel, *The Voyeur*. I wanted to turn the perspective around and write from the viewpoint of the object rather than the subject, although in so doing I made the (perhaps obvious) discovery that the object of desire is simultaneously the subject.

I also wanted to write a story about teetering on the edge, so I let my exhibitionist take her fantasy right to its logical extreme.

THE SHAME GIRL

❧❧❧❧❧❧❧

By Carolyn Banks

*When one speaks of erotic fantasy, it is not normally the super-
natural to which one is alluding. However, as we all know, there
are certain potential drawbacks to any earthbound human
lover—dandruff, say, and the ability to forget important
anniversaries being only the least of them. And so Carolyn
Banks imagines a young girl's sexual awakening not as just
the prosaic or ultimately disappointing occurrence it so easily
can be but rather as a moment that magic moves out of time.
What we sense is the contentment felt by Banks' narrator, the
awareness of her sexual self ignited so long before and still
brightly alive within her.*

D addy says our creek is where the mer-maids come to rest."
My grandchild Miranda's voice, bright and shrill.

Then that of her father, Ed, my son-in-law. "To hear your
mother talk," he says, "mer-men as well."

I watch my daughter blush. "Edmund," she says, stepping
in toward him, bumping his hip with her own.

My heart leaps at this, at their intimacy, and at the possibility ... "Anything can happen," I say.

Miranda reaches both arms up, and I bend into her embrace. She smells like popcorn and wool. How old is she now? I think five. "Hello, Grandma," she says, her lips fall wet against my cheek.

"Isn't it kind of cold for you to be out here like that?" Ed gestures at my sweater. He and Jill wear matching sheepskin jackets. Their cheeks are red, their breath is visible.

"I suppose." I take Miranda's mittened hand, but she pulls away, runs down the path and past the house, out onto the edge of the lawn where the creek can be seen.

"What about the mer-maids?" she turns and asks.

We have all three stumbled behind her. I look over at Jill. She is flushed again. Ed's eyebrows arch, as if to ask what he should answer now. "Well," I remind the little girl, "this is a bywater, a salt creek that lifts and falls with the tide. It might harbor mer-folk."

"Mer-folk," she repeats, laughing. Then she shifts her focus abruptly, as children often do. "Is it true that all your friends wear pantyhose under their bathing suits?"

Her parents rush at her, shooshing. They tell me not to mind. "I don't know where she gets these things," Jill says. She glares at her child, takes her shoulders, and nudges her toward the house. "Enough of this," she says. "Inside."

But Miranda doesn't take this seriously. She laughs with every stride. And the minute that she's indoors, while, in fact, she's yanking off her cap and mittens, she asks about the pantyhose again.

I wave her mother off. "The truth is," I tell her, "one or two of my friends do. Wear pantyhose, I mean. Nude pantyhose. They think it makes their legs look better, and actually, from far away, it does. But the wonder is that they wear bathing suits at all."

Ed laughs uncomfortably and looks at Jill.

I realize what he thinks I mean. I correct myself. "I mean most women their age don't swim," I say.

"Oh!" Ed is relieved.

Miranda is bored with my answer. She is scouting what my husband called Our Great Room. Here the ceiling is two stories high and huge fish—tarpon, blue, and sail—arc in taxidermic splendor on the walls. Here, too, tarnished silver cups hold things they shouldn't: pencils, a ruler, some receipts, and maybe even bills. There are paintings, also—shipyards, yachts, the sea. And there is "The Shame Girl," an almost photographic painting that our cook—long ago, back when I was small—once named.

The Shame Girl sits naked on a rock, her privates hidden discreetly by the way she wraps herself with her arms. The water that surrounds the rock, still as a mirror, offers the same demure reflection. There is something very formal about that water. Not just its stillness but the sculpted vegetation on its shore. Not like the vegetation here at waterside: thick, impenetrable, unruly.

"Mer-maids," I say, "Indeed. And mer-men! What an astounding thing." I look at my daughter with new eyes. If I asked her, would she tell me? I rather doubt it, for what would she say?

I told someone once—my roommate at school—and I wasn't believed. Our theme for the day was First Sexual Encounter, and I'd already heard hers, a tawdry scuffle in the backseat of her boyfriend's parents' car.

"I remember it so clearly," I began. For my turn, I had made my roommate sit within a nest of throw pillows I'd collected from the dayroom. I had wanted the mood to be right and had chosen something in the pasha mode.

"Wait, wait!" she'd said, arranging the pillows another way, some beneath her knees, others behind her head.

I was, by now, eager to go on. "Ready?" I asked.

I set the scene quite carefully, as I will now:

My parents were having their annual summer party. As usual, there would be no young people there. For me the excitement was in the preparation, the hanging of the lanterns, especially.

My father would stand on a ladder beneath a line of bare

bulbs he'd earlier strung. Cook would be on the ground, at the ladder's side. I would punch each lantern open—they were boxed and folded flat, but when you pressed them, they'd expand into bright ribbed bells made of the thinnest paper. I would hand the open lantern to Cook, who would then give it to my dad. And my mother, she would stand off to the side saying, "No, it leans a bit to the left," or "Ah! Just so."

And every year it would be the same. My father would come down after hanging the last lantern, hug my mother, and say something quietly in her ear. Then he'd boom again, "What an assembly line we make, eh?" And he'd thank me and thank Cook, and he'd take my mother away.

Cook would fuss over me lest I feel excluded, but the fact was, I never minded any of this. One year I even repeated to Cook what I had been told—that Daddy had only heard the mer-maids sing. I knew already that this was the euphemistic— or so I thought—phrase that he often used to signal his desire.

But this time I was sixteen, old enough to move among the party guests as an equal, I thought. When I said so, however, my father had smiled his indulgence and my mother had feathered her fingers through my hair. I still burned beneath my sense of insult.

So, when the party was well under way and darkness had taken hold, I donned a hooded jersey and a pair of blue jeans and decided to swim out to a large flat rock and sprawl there, looking back at the colored lights and spying on the guests.

I had never gone into the water at night. Nor had I swum in other than a one-piece suit. Three strokes in, the clothing I'd selected grew so cumbersome and heavy that I found myself near panic.

I gained the rock and pulled myself up on it. Then I began, with difficulty, shedding what I'd worn. When I was naked, however, I was also quite cold. Without thinking, I assumed "The Shame Girl" pose.

On shore, the colored lights were turning the people beneath them tints of fuchsia and green. I somehow grew cynical and thought the partygoers clumsy and silly and not worth observing after all.

I was sorry that I hadn't stayed in my room. I had things to do, books to read. It seemed to me then that grown-up parties relied more on laughter than words, but I thought the latter were far superior and so was scornful.

I slipped into the water; it was time, I knew, to leave this childish business of spying behind. The water was warmer, more welcoming than air. I dawdled near the rock, my legs waving as I reached to touch the soft beard of moss on the granite underside.

It was then that someone's fingers flashed against my own.

I gasped and attempted to lift myself onto the rock again, but the strength in my arms failed me. I tried again with the same result. I clung to the rock, panting, and attempted to coax myself back to a state of calm.

I did this by concentrating on the onshore colors and sounds, the jazzy lyric that floated out over the water from my parents' wind-up phonograph: "Oh, honey wait for me, oh, honey wait ..."

Was *I* waiting? And for what?

While I wondered, a warmer swirl of water began to play at my hips and thighs. I felt that everywhere it touched me I was glowing.

Glowing! I would be seen from shore! I let go my hold on the rock, curled, and let my body plummet down.

It was black down there. I hadn't been glowing at all, at least not in any visible way. But when I felt a hand snake between my legs and across my buttocks, the radiance, the glow, the *heat* increased.

I gave myself to the water and its' sensations, gave myself to what was now a cool and steady pull of current against my knees and calves and toes.

Soon something very like hair brushed against my belly and then moved away. Seconds later, it brushed yet again, my belly, hips, thighs. I reached down, my fingers floating, and I touched, though fleetingly, what seemed a human face: forehead, nose, lids and lashes, lips.

I surfaced like a shot and looked for the rock, the shore, the things that kept me earthbound. Just then, they seemed so far away. In the same breath-stopping instant, legs pressed and even wrapped around my own.

It was at this point that my roommate interrupted me. She sat straight up and hollered "Foul," as if this were a game. I was irritated and demanded to know why I had been stopped. "Because you said his *legs*. If this is about a mer-man, he *can't* have legs."

"But he did have legs. He did. He just didn't have feet."

"All right," she said, "Suspension of disbelief." She assumed her former pose. "Go ahead."

"Thank you."

The legs again.

"No, no! Don't!" someone, a woman, said from shore. Did she mean me? I looked back toward the house, the lawn. At this distance, the lanterns made the water wink and gleam. The same woman was laughing now. "Well, all right," she said.

With that, a tendril of fear began to coil within me. I thought of my parents' friends, of the fuchsia and green people, of the men. Was this one of them? The thought of it, of someone so old, made me thrash and pull away.

I made for shore as purposefully as I could, though all the while I swam, a sinewy body kept sweeping past me—back and forth and around—in the water.

This was no one that I or my parents knew.

"Were you still glowing?" my roommate asked sarcastically.

"Yes," I answered, beyond impatience.

As I stroked, the body in the water began to touch and play against my own, against my shoulders and my breasts and along my neck, my spine, against my buttocks, between my legs. My will to reach the shore began to fade. I let the water buoy me.

"You wouldn't dare," a woman shrieked from shore.

"Don't bet on it," a man's voice replied. Then there was the sound of glass breaking.

"Well, last year …," I heard my father begin. He pronounced "last" as if it were "lust."

Meanwhile, I had the distinct feeling that I was being held and carried. I began to move through the water with a force that was not my own. I plunged and rolled and bobbed as if I were a dolphin in an open sea. And whenever I felt my lungs would explode, I would be lifted through the air for an instant or two. I was still very near my parents' home, I noted, for I saw ribbonlike streaks of green and of fuchsia every now and again.

And then whatever gripped me arced and took me deep and deep and deep. Shells crushed against my shoulders and my back, and bits of furry weed caught in my nostrils and my hair. I caught hold of whatever it was that held me—in that moment, I did so need to—and, in answer, a sharp fin lashed out, slicing into the flesh of my hand.

And then there was nothing, no one, only the roar of my heart.

I surfaced and paddled toward an eroded part of shore. Once there I pressed my face against the earth. I was alone and hurt, the blood from my hand mingling black with the water of the creek.

Then someone softly reached from below, took my hand, licked and sucked at the edges of my cut until the bleeding stopped. I closed my eyes and tried to conjure him: his face, his jaw, his seaweed-tangled hair.

"The Mysterious Stranger motif," my roommate offered. I was silent, angry. Then she relented. "Come *on*," she said, "get back to the good part." (She later went to New York and became an important editor.)

Afterward, the water lapped at me. I swayed to its lilt. The whole of my body felt its kiss, as though all of me had been wrapped in inky, liquid silk.

"Oooh, inky silk!" my roommate cooed. "That's good."

✿　✿　✿

On shore the lanterns had been doused. I knew that it was time. I slipped beneath the water, floated with the presence somewhere near me in the night. There was no urgency now, no fervor. When we neared the pilings of our dock I let my head and shoulders break the surface.

Beyond the steep roof of my parents' house, a car door slammed and then another. An engine fired into life.

"Is someone out here?" My mother's voice was so close, too close.

"And then?"

"And then he swam away. He was a mer-man. I'm sure of it."

My roommate sighed. "Good story," she said, in a languor. "Even if it's stupid," she went on, "it's good."

"But it could be," I told her, remembering what my father had once told me. I even used his words: "For ours is a bywater, subject to tides. It's connected to the bay and then the sea."

She raised her arm, laid her hand across her forehead, raised her head with great drama, "For ours is a bywater," she intoned.

I lifted a pillow and clapped it down upon her head.

I still had the scar on my hand where the fin had cut me. I mentioned this, so wanting my roommate to believe. I reminded her of my father's seemingly euphemistic phrase. About the mer-maids.

"Quoting Eliot," she gibed.

But was it only that? My father, after all, had grown up on this tidal creek.

Eventually, I inherited it all: house, creek, paintings, trophies, stuffed fish. And "The Shame Girl," which I took to staring at, long and hard.

In a certain light, after a glass or two of port, admittedly, I could see a mer-something deep within the water. Mer-man. Of course that didn't explain why the Shame Girl clutched at herself, but maybe she was taunting him, daring him out of the water. (Now I think that maybe our cook saw him, the merman, after all. Saw him in the painting long before I ever thought to look. There is no way to know. Cook is long years dead, buried when Jill was younger than Miranda is now. At Cook's funeral, Father—he walked with two canes by then— summed her up, telling me, "She was fat as a goose. Her passion, all of it, went into those meals. Lord, those wonderful meals.")

At any rate, by then there was another proof, the words of my husband, whom I had never dared to tell. "You smell just like the sea," he would say admiringly. (Oh, but how I remember him, square face, soft lips, fierce daily stubble! Even now I know exactly how his breath felt in my ear, against my cheek, along my neck. Or at my navel or pubis or thigh.) Why the sea?

But now, today, there is the blush that crossed my daughter's face.

"Do you like this painting?" I ask her. I am indicating "The Shame Girl," of course.

"Frankly, mother ... ," Jill begins, in a way that tells me, no, she does not see him there, not yet at any rate.

"She thinks it's dumb," my granddaughter says.

"I find 'The Shame Girl' rather interesting," Ed puts in. We all call it by the name Cook gave it, have for decades now, and no one bats an eye.

I stand, walk to the window, look down at the creek. With the fingers of my left hand, I trace the silvery scar on my right. "In summertime, I still swim," I announce.

I turn. Then I remember what Miranda asked me earlier about those friends of mine. "And I don't wear pantyhose under my suit when I go out there, either." I wag my finger and speak sternly to the little girl, making this a joke.

"Shame Girl, Shame Girl, Shame Girl!" Miranda accuses, giggling and stomping and wagging back.

We all laugh. We're all happy. I, here at waterside, perhaps a little more than they.

AUTHOR'S NOTE

I don't think there's anything sexier than touching underwater: it's slower and silkier. This, then, was where I wanted to set my story. But I also liked the taboo aspect of portraying the narrator's sexual coming of age within sight of her parents' party on shore. And, of course, the generational aspect appealed to me, the notion that others in the family had been or would be visited by the mer-folk.

THE FOOTPATH OF PINK ROSES

❧❧❧❧❧❧❧

By Carol Lazare

Sometimes, especially when regarding the complex issues of sexual power/sexual pleasure, it is easy to know what to think and hard to know what to do. Or would you prefer the opposite? The fact that Carol Lazare openly and honestly confronts the rape-versus-ravishment problem ("rape is ravishment defiled") does not mean that her answers are everyone's. On "The Footpath of Pink Roses" she leads us down, however, one thing is certain: erotic sensation—soft, sharp, sweet, enveloping—mimics those flowers whose petals fall all around.

Sex was always on my mind. I was fifteen and fantasized about being overcome with desire, being taken wantonly, with no holds barred, to the point of utter, complete, absolute abandon, bliss, ecstasy, and exhaustion. In a word, ravished.

A rape had been reported down by the river near a footpath where pink roses grew. Myself, I worried over the difference between ravishment and rape, and I wrote a poem about it.

If a stranger confronts me and I am attracted to him,
If he is after rape and I am after ravishment,
If the act occurs, what will it be called?
At what point does my desire to be ravished by an attractive
    stranger
Become rape by a horrific criminal?

I analyzed the difference. "'She was asking for it.' 'She wanted it.'" If she was like me, ravishment was what she wanted. Perhaps the rapist thought that he was ravishing her, giving her what she wanted. Perhaps our natural instincts have become so perverted that ravishment is no longer possible. Perhaps, I will never be ravished. Perhaps my definition of ravishment is really this society's definition of rape. And rape is ravishment defiled.

A year later the rape/ravishment dilemma continued, and I was on my way home from the Deluxe Theatre. There had been a Saturday double bill, and I was feeling warm and contented after having just seen two Hollywood movies full of Paul Newman. I had to walk down Carruthers Street which is like a back lane. There are no front doors facing the street. On one side are backyards, clotheslines, gardens, and garages and on the other side of the street, the bus barn. The huge, vertical, sliding door of the barn was half open, and I could see the bottoms of the orange buses and pairs of legs engaged in chores and wordless conversation. A world of thigh-to-toe legs, half-ladders, and half-mops. What response would a cry of distress from Carruthers bring? Would whole bodies come running? Or would Dalilike legs, in worker overalls, brush under the half-open barn door and dodge around and about the empty buses on the lot? One never knew what might be crouched behind an empty orange bus. I doubled my stride as I passed them and hoped that fate would once again deal me safe passage.

It was twilight too, that time of day just before dusk when you can practically see the air, when the molecules seem big enough to push aside like a veil, when time is in limbo and unusual things can happen. I moved with anticipation and S.F.s (sinking feelings) through the molecules. In ten minutes it would be dusk, the air would be normal again, and I would be home and safe.

As I neared the intersection at the end of the block, a huge boatlike car entered Carruthers and came toward me with the driver's window down. Through it I could hear the sweet voice of Todd Rundgren singing a familiar song. I was humming along when the driver stuck his head out at me and crowed, "Hey honey, I'm lookin' for some tight, young slit." I looked at him, and the molecules of his face mixed with the molecules of car that mixed with the molecules of air, like an illusory dream mixing and moving in the twilight. For an instant I tried to answer him until adrenaline kicked me into action, and I ran toward safety and the dusk.

"I'm lookin' for some tight, young slit." How could anyone who listens to Todd Rundgren be saying that? This was new vocabulary and it filled me with fear: fear of forced surrender, to power, rape. There was no fear in ravishment, only willful surrender to ecstasy.

My sexual adventures in the past twelve years have been uneventful. There has been, thankfully, no rape, but, unfortunately, no ravishment either. I've become a woman with a potentially insatiable sexual appetite. My nipples are usually visibly erect, a strong indication, so I've read, of an aroused woman. They can be seen pushing out a T-shirt or a dress while picking out a pound of beans or scrubbing off baked-on grease or rolling twenty dollars worth of pennies. And it's not the cold weather. My nipples are erect in any season, day or night. Because I can't walk around at all times flashing my aroused-woman insignia, I have often chosen to wear the "layered look." Two or three layers over erect nipples lessens the impression that I'm a slave to carnal knowledge.

When I was nineteen or twenty, I experienced one of my more memorable uneventful sexual adventures with a young man named Marshall. He was self-assured and absolutely confident about his attractiveness to women. My mother, like many Jewish mothers, has been loving and devoted to me. I've found that with the sons of Jewish mothers the care can be more extreme. Because they are so worshiped and pampered at home, they transfer this expectation to the women they meet in their private lives. Marshall, not for one millionth of a millisecond doubted his power to excite me. He knew, like no other, that the key to my arousal was my nipples. He would lightly brush them, tug them, flick them, turn them, swirl them, kiss them, lick them. I learned many things from Marshall, but my sexual education was still limited. He may have taken my breasts to university, but the rest of me remained in grade school.

One uninspired encounter after another led me to the belief that the best sex is in the mind. Free of self-consciousness, free of guilt, free to experiment, my mind had brought me to the brink of ravishment with "him," my perfect lover. He filled all my requirements, handsome, well-built, tender, attentive, and slow, very slow. I chose my perfect lover from the Cree Nation—for his piercing black almond eyes, his long, thick, black hair, his cheekbones that could fill my palms. My engagement as a field worker for social services had brought me in contact with many native people, and I began to appreciate the traditional North American native way of life. I had many questions about the troubled state of the earth. It offered me an answer—respectful coexistence in all things including the relationship between man and woman.

It is a midsummer day just before dusk. Twilight. I am twenty-eight and walking with anticipation and S.F.s along the river near the footpath of pink roses. I think about my state of readiness and my yellow karate belt. I imagine it wound neatly around my karate *gi* and am visualizing a block to my chest, when, in that instant, I feel an actual blow to my upper back. It forces me to lose my balance and my wind. Gasping for air I try to regain my balance and am helped by being grasped at the shoulder, straightened, and held with a man's hand over my mouth and my neck squeezed into the V formed by the bicep and forearm of a man's arm. In an instant we are sharing an intimacy that can often take weeks to achieve under normal circumstances. My upper back is held tightly against his chest. I can feel the contours of his body and know that he worked at it. As he pulls me backward I can feel the muscles of his upper thighs brush against my buttocks. The elbow of the arm wrapped around my neck rests on my breast and with each movement grazes my nipple until it stiffens. Can he feel it? Will he think it is arousal? Is it?

As he drags me toward the footpath of pink roses I try for a moment to convince myself that I am having a trancelike experience. As my mother would describe, "Going to one of those windy places" I am prone to go. I attempt to follow her advice, breathing deeply from the diaphragm, chastising myself for not eating that day. As I breathe in I can smell the skin surrounding my face. He smells of the outdoors and smoke, not of cigarettes but burning cedar. One of his fingers is cushioned between my lips, and I can taste the salt from his skin and sour cream and onion potato chips. My senses are acute and trustworthy. I am not on the edge or going over it into madness. I am being dragged, by a man, into the rosebushes.

As I strain my eyes, forcing their muscles into an unnatural elongation, a discomforting downward look, I see the skin of his forearm, chestnut brown and hairless. An Indian. Despite my reason that has urged me to prepare for my defense, my instinct fixates on his brown-skinned forearm and the possibility of fulfilling my fantasy. Perhaps, in this moment, with my innate will to survive, I can convince myself that what will happen next is within my power and control. My choice. The illusion of choice is vital to me. Ravishment or rape. I choose to surrender to ecstasy.

He stopped and dropped to the ground, his hand still over my mouth and his arm in a V around my neck. His legs formed another V and my lower back was pressed against his penis, my back and head at his heart. His chest was heaving, and like a rider out of sync with her horse, my body bounced off of his. He pressed me closer to correct the bounce. Force or willful surrender. The scent of roses enveloped me. I corrected my rhythm and we rode as one.

As his breathing normalized, his penis grew erect in the small of my back. "Gimme your money," he said. I was thrown by this. I had been readying myself for one of the most profoundly rationalized experiences of my life, only to find out that I was to be neither raped nor ravished, but robbed! Mugged for money! "Gimme your money," he said again. The V of his arm tightened around my throat. I cupped my hands around the hard muscle of his forearm. His voice deceived me too. It was a whisper, a warm breeze over my forehead with a hint of fake parsley. I moved my fists into the proper karate pose, positioned them, one on each side of his rib cage, then I punched. "AAAAA-Ah!!" I growled. He fell back into a rosebush, his arms circling his chest. I scrambled away on all fours and turned to face him. Here was my perfect Cree lover, and I was looking him straight in the eye. His face was framed by tiny pink roses like the cherubic angels of seventeenth-century religious paintings. An ingenuous mugger.

"That hurt. Y' fuckin' yahoo," he said.

"*Gulliver's Travels*," I said.

"Whose?" he asked.

"The yahoo in *Gulliver's Travels*. Have you read it?" I asked.

"Ya sure. Two or three times," he said.

"Not my favorite," I said.

"Me neither," he said.

"What's yours?" I asked.

"*The Ocean Almanac*," he answered.

"I don't know it."

"It fuckin' hurts. What did you do?"

"Karate," I said.

"Like black belt."

"No, just yellow," I said.

"Probably busted my floating rib again. Fuck."

"You really frightened me," I said.

"Don't go wanderin' around here. Full moon t'night," he said.

The moon was low on the horizon. As I often would, I gave myself the challenge of a fake deadline and wondered where I would be when it was high in the sky. I could have walked away. I kept talking.

"Are you a drug addict?" I asked.

His mouth broadened into a wide, white-toothed smile, a practiced smile, one that was proven to work, a bread-and-butter smile, money in the bank.

"No," he said.

"What do you want the money for?" I asked.

"Nintendo."

"Oh." He has family. I felt foolish for my fantasy.

"What's your name?" he asked.

"Sarah."

"What's yours?" I asked.

"Eddy."

Eddy and I were rooted to our spots like fence posts about fifteen feet apart and connected by the signals of arousal our bodies had revealed.

"Sarah," he said.

"Yes, Eddy," I said.

"Sarah," he said.

"Yes, Eddy."

He walked over to me, slowly, saying my name with each step. "Sarah. Sarah ..." He was close enough that I could smell the cedar smoke in his shirt and the potato chips on his breath.

"You're bleeding," I said.

"Fuckin' thorns'll do that," he said.

"By your temple."

"Yeah?"

As he rubbed it, the tiny ruby of blood broke and trickled down the side of his face. Spontaneously, I reached out and wiped it away. Struck by another attack of S.F.s I quickly withdrew my bloodstained hand and suspended it like a beacon in the twilight. I stared; my molecules of skin were mixing with his molecules of blood.

Eddy, reassuringly, pressed my hand to his chest and mopped the blood onto his T-shirt. I kept my hand there. Now a reckless Land Rover, it traversed the terrain of his pectoral muscles, over the ridge of his jaw to the final crest of his cheek-bone. And it filled my palm.

Reaching up, he took my hand in his and placed it by my side. Then, with the back of his hands and nails he slowly began to graze—featherlike—the inner skin of my forearms. I shivered and thrust them forward for more. Over and over. I arched my neck up and back, and it was next—over and over—then my face, my hair, his fingers, his nails—over and over.

He paused for a moment and stepped away. Eddy took off his clothes—his T-shirt, his boots, his jeans. Lit by the moon, the contours of muscle, highlight and shadow, were hills and valleys, relief on a map. He was a journey waiting to be taken. He would guide me to new sensations, a prospector mining me, vein by vein until we struck the motherlode.

I took off my clothes, my tentlike dress, my sandals, my panties. He made a nest amid the rosebushes with our clothes, and we lay down, watching the moon as it reached its zenith in the sky. I wondered where I would be at its descent. Eddy leaned over, resting on his arm. He removed the elastic band holding his ponytail and let his black hair fall loosely over his shoulders. On all fours he straddled me, dropping his head, and his hair fell over my breasts. Like a whisk of down, his hair swept my body from head to toe, tickling my skin to the next plateau. I arched my back to meet him and met his lips skimming mine. Gliding over the surface of my skin, his warm lips teased the ache that craved him. Skimming like a schooner, gliding like a clipper over my rippling body, the ache became me. I undulated in the breeze, yearning for the hurricane.

I felt the power he could wield as he raised my torso off the ground with one hand under my back and the other nearly encircling my throat. He could have snapped my neck like a twig. I looked him in the eye, his equal, not his prey. He raised his hand from around my neck and placed it on my cheek, raising me like a platter to his lips. He kissed me. Harder and longer, harder and deeper, stronger and longer his mouth enveloped mine.

The moon like a spotlight opened our eyes, his riveting on

mine, diving deeper and deeper. We grabbed hold closer and closer, gripping, licking, rubbing, squeezing, kneading skin into flesh. Crablike I clutched him, and we rolled like tumbleweed out of our nest onto the earth. Tumbling under the roses he filled me. Again and again. A mold of my buttocks in the earth. Again and again. Deeper and deeper into the lode. And the molecules of earth mixed with the molecules of flesh. And the moon became his eyes, the roses his hair, my hand his shoulder, my breasts his chest, my thighs his thighs, and he became me and I became him. Ravished.

AUTHOR'S NOTE

I wrote the story because I think, as I believe most women do, if we're really straight with ourselves, that, instinctively, on a primal level, we want to be ravished. It is tricky politically, but ravishment, as the story explores it, is not rape. It is a fine line, but the line is there and Sarah draws it.

I believe a woman can acknowledge her desire for ravishment and be a feminist. In fact, I think that a denial of these powerful instincts of female sexuality is a denial of the principles of feminism as I understand them.

THE WAGER

❥❥❥❥❥❥

by Sara Davidson

*Like the heroine of the previous story, Sara Davidson's Lucy is
ravished. A sexual challenge, issued in the mutual excitement
of new lovemaking, presents her with an excuse to indulge in the
passivity for which she knows she has secretly longed. It's obvious that this self-censorship alluded to is another way many
women today are forced to police themselves for an impossibly
elusive correctness, caught between the exigencies of sexual politics and the actual sensations of the flesh. Although some will
argue that "The Wager" and stories like it cause us to continue
to believe too susceptibly in the myth of the master lover, personally, I can think of no greater barrier to fulfilled desire than
any use of the word "should" and whatever lie it leads us to.*

It was like falling through a chute; they sped down and
around past darkened houses and moist night lawns with
sprinklers running until they came out on the Pacific Coast
Highway, the beach. The sand was gray and damp, the parking
lots closed up. Joe shifted gears impatiently when they hit the
light at Sunset Boulevard. There was tension in the car, the

accelerating tension of sexual possibility, and the sweet scent of Thai grass. Lucy guided him along the foggy streets that led to her house. He put on the hand brake, opened the door of the Porsche, and helped her out.

They had the house to themselves. Pam was staying with Henry and would not be back until Sunday. Lucy poured amaretto into glasses and told Joe to pick out an album. She heard familiar chords, then Mick Jagger.

Wonderful party, Lucy thought. Her pockets were crammed with phone numbers written on scraps of paper and matchbook covers. Elated at the appearance of so many prospects after a dry few months, she slipped out of her shoes and sat down on the rug, facing Joe.

They knew little about each other. He was from Los Angeles, she from New York. Both had made films for television and had been married.

"How long have you been separated?" Joe asked.

"Two years."

"What was he like?"

"Want to see a picture?"

"Sure." He lit another joint.

She went into her study and brought back a photo she had always liked. Her former husband's face was split by shadow, so that the right half appeared sunlit and ingenuous, the left half withdrawn and dark.

Joe studied it, then frowned. "I don't like him. I'm sorry."

Lucy took the picture back. "No one feels neutral about Jerry."

"How long were you married?"

"Seven years. And you?"

He stretched his arms over his head. "Ten months. I'm afraid it wasn't serious."

"What's the longest you've been with someone?"

"Few years." He smiled, dimples coming to his cheeks. He was tall, athletic, with dark blond hair and a beard that, together with his close-set eyes, gave his face a soulful cast. "Can I help it if all the women in America are screwed up?"

"Funny, they only say wonderful things about you."

He laughed, as if to say, your point. They talked some more and listened to music, and it was 3:00 A.M.

"Want to go upstairs?" Lucy said.

He shook his head no.

Pity.

"Not yet."

"Hmm?"

In a casual tone, Joe said, "I think we should prolong this through the evening. I'm going to arouse you one small step at a time."

"What are you talking about."

He moved closer, picking up the amaretto bottle. "The rest of the evening is in my hands. You don't have to do anything. You're not going to do anything."

Something prickled in her.

"I know it won't be easy, you're the kind of woman who likes taking charge." He tilted his chin, as if to say, come on, I dare you.

Who do you think you are ...

"I bet if you're with four people trying to decide on a restaurant, you can never just sit back and go along."

"That's true."

He set down his drink, moved toward her, and kissed her. She was aroused, he was aroused, she thought they were going to lie right back on the floor, but he broke away, leaving her beached and breathless.

"I don't like this," she said.

"Too bad." He smiled.

She threw a shoe at him. She could feel that crazy, instant intimacy—the almost palpable sense of closeness—induced by the Thai grass. He turned over the record. "I wish you had some Sting. He's the only guy around still saying something. Course, the reason I like the Stones is that they don't want to say anything, except fuck me."

"They've had some good lyrics."

"It's all fuck me, all just one lyric."

"'Jumping Jack Flash.'"

"I can shake it good, fuck me."

"'Brown Sugar,' no, that's obvious."

"Fuck me, black woman."

"'Street Fighting Man.' That was about something."

"Yeah, I'm a street fighting man. When I get home from the riot, fuck me."

Lucy laughed. There had to be one. "What about that song ... oh, what was it called? It was on 'Between the Buttons.'"

"'Ruby Tuesday'?"

"No, that's not on 'Between the Buttons.'"

"Sure it is."

"No it's not."

"You're wrong."

"I have the album, I'm positive."

"So am I."

"What do you want to bet?"

"Let's make it juicy."

"Okay."

She lay down on her back to think. He slid over, lifted her blouse, and moved his lips slowly across the smooth, taut hollow of her stomach. She sighed, and reached up to run her hand along his back, but he took the hand off and set it on the floor.

"I can't touch you?"

"Nope. You can't do anything." He went to the record cabinet to look for "Between the Buttons."

"This is stupid."

"You'll come around."

"What shall we bet?" Lucy said. His arrogance was galling.

"Dinner at the restaurant of one's choice."

"In Paris."

"It's not here," Joe said.

"Might be upstairs."

He got to his feet, she started up after him, but he turned, pointing at her. "Sit down." She did. He walked behind her, lifted the long dark hair and kissed the nape of her neck. "Nice try."

"I'm not going to throw this."

He began unbuttoning her blouse. "You hold still."

She did.

He set her blouse on a table and sat about six feet from her. "You look better with your clothes off."

"You're blowing this, you know. When you want to, I'll have cooled."

"I'm not worried." He sipped his drink. He was wearing a blue shirt with the cuffs rolled up, and she could not help staring at his arms. They were tan, smooth, with muscles rippling under the skin and a covering of fine blond hair. She felt a shock of desire so strong it was like pain.

"Lucy, it's an act of almost superhuman control for me not to jump on you right now, but I'm not going to. Because delaying it will make the pleasure even more intense."

"No!" She twisted in frustration. "You're playing with me, and I don't like it."

"I'm not."

"Yes you are, and I want you to stop."

He crawled across the floor and put his face up to hers.

"Can you tell me exactly what you want me to stop?"

She considered how to phrase it.

"No."

They laughed. Joe rolled with her to the floor, kissing her again and again in the crook of her bare neck, but then he stopped himself.

"Let's decide what the bet will be," he said, returning to his chair.

"The loser has to be the other's slave. See how you like it."

"For how long?"

"Twenty-four hours."

"Okay, if you want to prolong the agony. Where's the album?" He started for the stairs.

"Not up there."

He turned.

"In the bookcase. Bottom shelf."

When Joe found the album, a smile came to his face.

"I'm right, aren't I," she said.

He slid the record out of the jacket, cued it on the

turntable, and paused. "Still want that bet? I'm willing to let you off now, because I'm such a nice guy."

He was bluffing. "Play it."

Lucy's hands flew in the air, she was certain she had won, but at the first chord she was slumped in defeat. How could this be? She had believed with all her soul that she was right, and she wasn't. She walked to the window.

"Here are the terms. Tonight doesn't count. You'll be my slave on any day I choose."

"You really want to humiliate me, don't you."

He came up, took her by the shoulders with a gentleness that surprised her, and kissed her, a kiss like those she had dreamed of at thirteen: walking down a dappled lane in a far-away place with a strange new boy. When Joe pulled away, she burst into tears. "I'm scared."

She saw a look of alarm. He walked closer, and when his face was next to hers, the pouting, hurt look in her eyes turned to merriment. He grabbed her. "You're fantastic." Then he put one arm under her legs, the other under her arms, and, hoisting her sideways, headed for the stairs.

For the next several hours, she was not permitted to move a hand, she could not tell him where or when to touch her, but he knew.

She was not fighting anymore, she was nearly out of her mind with pleasure. It was every fantasy she had ever day-dreamed. Foreplay that had no end. Lovemaking that had no objective but to tantalize and please. This was going to last all night—nights and nights and nights—and it was all being done *to* her.

She was on her back, and Joe was above her, balanced on his arms. "I want you to be my slave now. Tell me I'm better than everyone."

"You think you're better than me?"

"I'm not saying that. Tell me I'm better than everyone."

"You ain't better than me."

He slid out. "You're my slave, you have to." He began to stroke her with his finger.

"I can't say something I don't ..."

"Is that right?"

" ... believe, and have it be ... credible."

She loved what he was doing, she loved him, she wanted it to last forever. The finger stopped.

Looking at him earnestly, she said, "You're better than *everyone.*"

The finger resumed. "Big deal." He burst out laughing. He slid down between her legs, homing in with the same instinctive accuracy he had shown all night. She could feel the climax now, swishing its tail like a fish. He was pulling it up and out of her. Up and up it came, big, this fish was going to set records, they were going to weigh it, they would pose beside it for photographs. You could see its powerful form rising up through the water, navy blue.

"Let me now, Joe," she said, "please, let me ..."

It broke the surface, shooting into the air with spray.

She was jelly, she could not stop laughing. He plunged into her as she lay, arms flopped above her head. "Move a little," he said. "Okay, stop now." She lay still, the way she had always, secretly, wanted to lie. It felt good, oh it was good like this, she loved lying back passively with her arms flung up, but as he went on, she began to move, involuntarily at first. Her small rump began to bounce, then she was matching his movements, pulling on him, squeezing.

"Oh sweetheart."

"Give it to me ..."

"Yes."

"Now."

"So fucking good!"

It was seven in the morning. They had been making love for almost four hours. She had not kissed him or touched him with her hands, and he had been hard the entire time.

"Have you done this before?" she said.

"No."

They stared at each other, awed and a little scared, until the room became a bubble of heightened feeling and the world outside—the people in their apartments, sleeping, eating corn-flakes, turning on the television—seemed to exist on another plane that was shallow and dull.

They tried to sleep, but kept thinking of things they wanted to say and arousing each other unwittingly as they tossed.

"We've got to sleep," Joe said. "I wish I had a Valium."

She went to the bathroom and returned with two yellow pills.

Joe swallowed his, took a swig from the amaretto bottle, and kissed her, sweetness on his lips.

AUTHOR'S NOTE

I wrote this during the six-month period when, pregnant with my second child, I was forced to lie in bed and abstain from sex of any kind to avoid a premature birth. During this interlude of forced abstinence, I found myself writing the most erotic passages I've done before or since, and having a wonderful time with it.

I've always felt that the most exciting sex comes not from technical virtuosity but from the play of fantasy and emotion. The fantasy in this piece is that archetypal one best dramatized in *The Taming of the Shrew*—where a strong woman resists with everything in her arsenal and yet is overcome by the cunning of the male.

THE STORY OF NO

❧❧❧❧❧❧❧

By Lisa Tuttle

Lisa Tuttle, a much-published writer in several genres, here shows that she's as capable of being perverse as she is of being original. Naturally, any editor's concern, when introducing such a blink-if-you-dare story, is not to reveal too much, but there are a few things I feel it's safe to mention. In "The Story of No" you will encounter a wife, a husband, a memory, and a surprise, and, oh yes, there is *a copy of a certain book by Pauline Réage.*

A t first sight I thought I knew him and felt my blood heat, my muscles loosen, the breath evaporate from my lungs.

The imprint of his touch rose like stigmata on my skin, and the memory of his tongue hungry in my mouth aroused a need I hadn't admitted to myself for a long time, a desire for the forbidden.

"What is it?" asked my husband. Startled, I looked across the restaurant table at the well-known face and remembered who and where I was: a wife in her forties staying in an elegant, expensive English country house hotel with her husband,

the vacation our anniversary present to each other. "See someone you know?"

"No." For that was in another country, and besides … "He
wouldn't be that young, if it was who I thought. He was that
age *then*." The man I remembered would be my age still and
maybe would still find me attractive. That young man couldn't
be much past twenty. If he looked at me, he'd see someone old
enough to be his mother, someone not worth noticing, sexually
invisible. He turned his head, and his clear green gaze fell on
me with a shock like cold water, and he smiled.

"You're blushing," said my husband with interest. "Was he
an old boyfriend?"

"No. Oh, no. Just someone I met once in Houston. Do you
want to taste my salmon mousse?"

Once. A single night. Yet the memory of it was with me
always. Many a dull or sleepless night I had pulled it out to
comfort myself. I had used it so often it had come to seem like a
story I'd read somewhere, and not something that had really
happened to me. As a fantasy, I'd even shared it with my husband some nights in bed. But it was real — or had been, once.

I first saw him in a Montrose bar, drinking by himself. He
had a tumble of black curls surrounding a long, clean-shaven
face, with a sensuous mouth and startling green eyes. Only the
overlarge, slightly crooked nose kept him from beauty, but his
was a striking face and mine were not the only eyes drawn to
stare at it. Nor was it only his face that attracted. He had a
physical presence as disturbing as some rare perfume. His was
not an outstanding body — nobody would have picked him to
model for a centerfold — but it was long and slim and wiry. My
husband, handsome, tall, and well-muscled, was certainly more
attractive by objective standards, but I wasn't thinking of my
husband as I admired the fit of the stranger's jeans.

I took a seat and ordered a drink. I wasn't looking for trouble. I hadn't been planning adultery. I was content, I thought,
to look and not touch. I liked the way his lips curled around a
cigarette and his eyes narrowed against the smoke. I liked his
slender fingers, and the way he moved, shifting his weight or

rolling the stiffness out of his neck and shoulders as unself-con-
sciously as an animal.

I gazed for a time at his intriguing, less-than-classical profile, then shifted my stare, let it fall in a caress on his shoulders,
his back, down to the ass which so nicely filled his tight, faded
jeans. He turned his head lazily toward me as if he'd felt, and
liked, my touch. I moved my eyes back up his body to meet his
eyes, and I didn't smile. He was the first to look away. Then I
did smile, but only to myself.

Someone else, a man, approached him, cigarette in hand,
and he gave him a light and responded to his conversational
ventures absently, his attention hooked by me. I could feel his
senses straining in my direction even when his back was
turned, his eyes fixed elsewhere, his ears assaulted by the blan-
dishments of the cigarette smoker—who eventually gave up
and took his need to someone else. Which was when my prey
turned around and looked at me again.

I had to hide a smile of triumph. That I retained the ability
to make a man desire me was reassuring. I had been feeling
mired in marriage, as if my wedding ring had conferred invisi-
bility, and his look sent a surge of well-being through me. As he
straightened, flexing his shoulders and the muscles of his long
back before moving away from the bar with an easy, loose-
jointed motion, I imagined him naked and aroused and felt a
tightening of my internal muscles.

He bought me a drink and then I bought him one. We sat
and looked at each other. There were few words, none of
importance. The conversation that mattered was conducted
between our bodies, in minute shifts in posture and attitude, in
the crossing and uncrossing of my legs as I leaned toward him
and then back, in the way he stroked his own face with his
long, slender fingers. He never touched me. I think he didn't
dare. I tried to make it easy for him, resting my hand on the
tabletop near his, moving my legs beneath the table. With
every move I made I aroused myself more until finally, quite
breathless and unthinking with desire, I reached out my hand
beneath the table and put it on his denimed thigh.

The pupils of his strange green eyes widened, and I smiled. He put his warm hand on top of mine and squeezed.

"Can we go to your place?" he asked, his voice very low.

Confronted with reality, I lost my smile. What was I playing at? I pulled my hand away and stood up. He followed me so quickly that he nearly overturned the table.

"No," I said, but he followed me out of the dim, air-conditioned bar, into the parking lot. The hot, tropical night embraced us like a sweaty lover. Someone, in a book I'd once read, had compared the smell of Houston to the aroma of a woman, sexually aroused and none too clean. I drew a deep breath; spilled beer, gasoline, car exhaust, cooking fumes, perfume, after-shave, rotting vegetation, garbage, and, beneath it all, a briny tang that might have been a breeze wafted in from the Gulf of Mexico.

He was right behind me, following, and as I turned to tell him off, somehow instead I fell against him. And then we were clutching each other, breast to breast, mouth to mouth, kissing greedily. The need I felt when he first touched me, the intensity with which it rushed all through me was so powerful I thought I would faint. Then, slowly, resting in his embrace, I came back to myself, back to him. I had never known anything as sensually beautiful as his mouth; the soft, warm lips that parted against mine, dryness opening into wetness, a moist cave where the sly, clever animal that was his tongue lived and came out to nuzzle and suck at me greedily. His breath was smoky and dark, tasting of desirable sins, of whisky and sugar and cigarettes.

His hands, long-fingered, strong and clever, moved over my body as we kissed, at first shy, but then, as I clung to him fiercely, making no attempt to push him off, becoming bolder. He was quickly impatient with the barriers of my clothes, which were little enough: a cotton blouse, a short summer skirt and underwear, my legs bare, naked feet strapped into leather sandals. One of his hands, which had returned again and again to cup and trace lazy patterns of arousal on my bound and covered breasts, now began swiftly and without fumbling to unbutton my blouse, while his other hand, behind me, was pushing up my skirt and tugging at the elastic of my panties. In a matter of minutes, maybe seconds, he could have me stripped naked.

I wanted nothing better than to be naked in his capable hands, but not here, in public, surrounded by strangers—was he crazy? "No," I gasped and pushed him off and pulled away, struggling to refasten my buttons.

He reached for me again, and I slapped at his hands. He looked stricken. "I want you. Don't you—?"

I laughed. "Not here, be reasonable!" There were people all around us, getting in and out of cars, overflow customers from the bar and people from the neighborhood out for a breath of air, drinking beer from six-packs purchased at the convenience store across the street. This parking lot and the whole street was like a fair or a carnival, an impromptu, open-air party to celebrate summer in the city. I waved a hand to indicate the crowd passion had temporarily hidden from us, and as if I'd waved away smoke we both saw, at the same time, a man and woman locked in a fervent embrace just yards away from us. As I stared, I realized that the woman had one hand inside the front of the man's trousers.

My stranger grinned at me, a wide, white, wolfish smile. He put his hands on my hips and pulled me tightly to him. His erection felt enormous. His breath hot in my ear, he whispered, "Nobody's going to notice. Nobody'll care."

It was true nobody else seemed to notice the passionate couple, or, if they did, they politely pretended not to see. Other people had their own concerns; why should they care? Nor would it have been different if the lovers had been of the same sex. The Montrose was the most Bohemian and most sexually tolerant area of Houston, which was why I had chosen it for my escape that night. It provided a place where I could temporarily forget who and where I was and become a stranger, pretending I was a free woman at large in San Francisco, New Orleans, or Paris.

The smoky, spicy, sweaty smell of this other stranger, his

body's heat and solid mass against me, the hands that caressed my hips and thighs and breasts, all wore away at my hesitation, as did his low voice, telling me a story:

"I was at a rock concert one time, thousands of people packed in close together, all standing up to see better, and moving, kind of dancing in place because there wasn't room to do anything else. I was with this girl ... she had on a really short skirt, like yours, and one time when she dropped her purse and bent over to pick it up I saw she wasn't wearing any underpants. So ... I got her to stand in front of me, and I unzipped, and slipped it in, and slowly, easily, pumped away. Nobody knew what we were doing. Even when we both came nobody noticed, because everybody was yelling and hopping around." He had pushed up my skirt at the back again and now snagged the elastic of my underpants—soaking wet by now—and began to ease them down.

"No."

Half of me wanted him to ignore my refusal, not to stop, to take me there among the crowds, even to be seen by disapproving, envious strangers—the other half of me was horrified. What if somebody who knew me came by, somebody I worked with, or one of my neighbors? So I said no again more fiercely, and when I pulled away he let me go.

"You're driving me crazy."

"What do you think you're doing to me?"

"Nothing, compared to what I'd like to do."

We stared at each other, hot and itchy with frustration. I grabbed his hand. "We'll find somewhere not so public. Come on."

I had nowhere in mind except to get away from the crowds. We walked away from the laughter and talk, away from the blare of amplified music and the bright blur of neon signs toward the quieter streets where there were no bars or all-night service stations, no massage parlors or convenience stores; quieter streets lined with trees where the buildings housed beauty parlors and dentists, small businesses that closed up at nightfall. On one such half-deserted street he pulled me suddenly into the embrasure of a darkened antique shop and pushed me up against the wall.

"No." I whispered the word, soft as a caress. I wasn't even sure he heard. His hands were swift and urgent. My blouse was unbuttoned, my bra undone, my breasts out, nipples teased and kneaded to an aching stiffness. I surrendered, undone, melting, and then quite suddenly I saw myself from the outside: some slut, half undressed in a public place with a stranger, letting a stranger do that to her—I woke up with a sickening shock. That couldn't be me. I'd always been a good girl, even before I married I'd only had two steady boyfriends; I'd never picked up strange men. Now that I was a married woman this sort of behavior was unthinkable. Sex was something that happened at home, in bed, not in a shop doorway.

I tensed and fought off his hands. I twisted to one side and struggled to push him away, but he pinned my wrists together effortlessly, one-handed, and stared at me, a faint smile twitching his lips.

"No," I said weakly, not meaning it. I suddenly wanted more than anything to be overpowered, to be made to do what I wanted to do, to have the guilt taken away. He gazed into my eyes and read there what I wanted as he rolled an erect nipple between thumb and forefinger. I felt fixed by his gaze, unable to fight. I stood very still, quivering. He let go my hands and tugged my skirt up to my waist.

"Take off your pants and spread your legs," he said.

I felt dizzy with desire. "No," I whispered. I didn't mean I didn't want to, and I didn't mean I did. By my word I meant a different kind of yes; meant make me do it, do it to me, I'm helpless now.

His eyes were unwavering on mine, but for a moment I was afraid he wouldn't understand. Then he said, "Try and stop me." He tugged at the waistband of my panties, and then gently peeled them down my legs. When they reached my ankles, I stepped out of them and stood passively, my sex exposed to his view.

A little sigh of pleasure escaped his lips as he looked at me.

Then he became stern again. "Up against the wall and spread your legs."

I swallowed hard, then found my voice and the only word I had left. "No."

He laughed. "No? No? What does that mean? Your body's saying something else." He slipped his hand between my legs. I gasped and quivered as he found my wetness. "Your body doesn't lie. Your body says yes." His touch was as soft as his voice, delicate and perfectly judged. I moaned and closed my eyes, unable to watch him watching me as he stroked my clitoris. I let him continue until his touch was too teasing, his fingering too delicate for my much harsher desire, and then I reached down to push his hand harder against me and his fingers inside me. He gasped as if he were the one penetrated, and I cried out with pleasure, a loud and violent "No!"

The wall was hard against my back. My thighs ached with strain as I rode his hand, the clever, stranger's fingers that knew me better, it seemed, than I knew myself, knowing just how to stroke and to probe together, knowing when a teasing gentleness should become more brutal. All this time he watched me, watched my face contort and read my desire as he murmured obscenities and endearments, commands and compliments alternating with a purpose like the hard-soft touch of his hand.

And then his other hand was on my ass, fingers probing the crack, and I moaned as he began to work me with both hands, back and front, and I cried out for more, still more.

Without taking his hands away, hardly faltering, he went down on his knees and began tonguing my clitoris, breathing hard with his own excitement. The warm, wet touch of his mouth was gentle, exact, and excruciating, and it was more than I could bear. Like lightning, white-hot, jagged, and intense, the orgasm flashed as I cried and yelled and clutched his curly head. "No," I cried, and "No" again, as if I must, in my last, desperate moments of pleasure, deny the force of that pleasure, or the reality of it—as if that word would keep it from being real to anyone but me.

Later, but still too soon, while I was rocked in the afterglow, unwilling to be disturbed, he caught my hand and carried it to his crotch, pressed it against the hard, warm bulge of his cock.

"No."

I have often wondered what I meant by that. Never in my life before that night had I said no meaning yes, but that night no was my word, my only word, and he had seemed to understand.

I pulled my hand away. "No."

Maybe I'd forgotten how to say yes. Maybe I wanted him to force me. Maybe I'd just had enough and wanted to send him away. Maybe, my own desire sated, I simply wasn't interested in his. Later, when I wanted more, I couldn't believe I'd meant I'd had enough then. I didn't want to believe I'd been selfish enough to send him away unsatisfied simply because my own immediate need had been met. Most of the time I preferred to believe that when I said no at the end I still meant yes, and that it was his understanding that failed him, and me.

Whatever I might have meant, whatever I'd wanted it to mean, he heard me say no, and took me at my word and left, and I made no effort to call him back.

I never saw him again, although there were nights when I went looking, and there has scarcely been a night since then that I haven't thought of him and longed for another chance.

After dinner, my husband and I took coffee in the large, yet cozy library, seated on one of the couches upholstered in leather as soft and supple as living skin, near the fire crackling in the hearth. We didn't talk to any of the other guests—we were being more English than the English on that trip—but we didn't have much to say to each other. Maybe we'd been married too long, maybe we were inhibited by the company. Certainly I was memory-haunted, aroused by the presence of the young man who looked so much like my long-ago stranger. Guilt made me uneasy in my husband's company, made me flinch when he touched me. My eyes kept sneaking across to him, and I pretended it was the books in the floor-to-ceiling bookcases that interested me. I felt him watching me, too, usually just as I looked away, but occasionally our glances would intersect, meeting for one highly charged instant before we both hastily looked away. Was it possible that this boy found me as desirable as had his look-alike of nearly twenty years ago? I hoped my husband wouldn't notice, but maybe it wouldn't be such a bad thing for him to know that another man wanted me.

It grew late, and we left the library, passed through the great hall, and mounted the grand staircase, our feet silent on the thick, pile carpet. I gazed up at the Pre-Raphaelite beauties who adorned the brilliant stained-glass windows but hardly saw them through my memories of warm, sensuous lips, long, clever fingers, and the cock I had never known.

I undressed slowly and dreamily in our luxurious room. I was down to the black silk teddy he'd surprised me with on Valentine's Day when my husband came up behind me and pulled me to him, his hands on my breasts, his breath warm in my ear. I could feel his erection, and I was as aroused as he was, but by the memory of someone else.

Guilt, or something else, made me whisper, "No."

He kissed me gently on my neck, and I moved my silk-clad bottom teasingly. His hands tightened on my breasts while his lips sought out the pulse in my neck. Caught up by rising excitement, again guilt mingled with desire and I breathed, "No," and he let go.

I remained rooted to the spot for a few moments in astonished disappointment, feeling the chill of his departure, hearing him sigh as he got into bed.

But what else could I expect?

No had never meant yes in our shared vocabulary. I had never wanted it to until now, just this moment, when I longed for a little telepathy.

Tingling with frustration, I peeled off my useless sexy underwear and climbed naked into bed.

"Goodnight, my darling," he said, and the chaste kiss he gave me forestalled my chance of letting him know, with my mouth on his, how I really felt. Of course I could have done something more obvious, or simply told him in words, but I couldn't think of the right words. I was in a mood to be taken, not to take, so all I could do was lie there wide awake, sulking about being misunderstood and horny, while he fell asleep with insulting ease. Surely, if he'd *really* wanted me he wouldn't have been able to sleep. Surely, if he'd really wanted me, he would not have walked away.

Time in darkness alone passes slowly. I thought again about that long-ago night and imagined I hadn't said no, but yes. Or that he had ignored my token protest, had pushed me against the wall and taken me, willingly against my will. Pleasure without guilt; I didn't want to, I couldn't help it, he made me.... The game I had to play if I were to remain a happily married woman. Finally I got up. I thought I'd seen a copy of *The Story of O* on the bookshelves downstairs. With a little help from my hand, it might help me to sleep. I wrapped a silk kimono around my nakedness and left my sleeping husband.

The great house was silent, although not dark. Electric lights in the form of candles burned on the walls of the hallways, illuminating all the closed bedroom doors. I imagined all the other guests paired in pleasure except the solitary stranger, who might be lying awake now, as horny as I was, and for the same reason. I wished I knew which was his door.

In the library the fire still burned, casting enough light to show me that someone was there before me.

He must have had the same reason as I did for coming here. As I entered the room he turned in surprise from the bookcase, a book in one hand. He wore a short, flimsy robe, tied with a sash. Under it, I knew, he was naked.

We stared at each other without speaking for what seemed a long time. There aren't many times in life that you get a second chance. I knew I'd never forgive myself if I didn't take this one. I closed the door firmly behind me and walked into the room. When I was only a few feet away from him, standing in the full glow of the fire, I stopped, untied my kimono, and shrugged it off, enjoying the sensation as it slithered silkily down my naked body and settled on the floor, enjoying also the gleam of his eyes as he stared at me without speaking.

He made no voluntary motion, but I saw the rising of his

heavy cock, and the blood-flushed, rounded head parted the silken curtain of his dressing gown, roused by my nakedness. I had never seen it before, and it was bigger and more solid than any of my fantasies.

I smiled and licked my lips. A few steps more, and I sank to my knees before him.

"No," he said. He caught me by the shoulders and raised me up. "I'm going to fuck you—the way I should have done years ago. You won't get away from me this time."

I was stunned. It wasn't possible that this was the same young man I'd picked up in a bar almost twenty years before— he wasn't old enough, and he spoke with an English accent. But if he wasn't the same man, how did he *know?*

His hands were on me, rougher than I remembered, and greedier as he felt and fondled my nakedness. Then he pulled me hard against him, the silk of his robe like the cool fall of water against my skin. His warm, firm cock butted at my sex, and he kissed me. How I could remember such a thing with any certainty after so long a time, I don't know, but his lips felt like the same lips, and his mouth tasted still of desirable sins: of whiskey and sugar and, very faintly, cigarettes. I nearly swooned with pleasure as his tongue moved in my mouth and his hands, gripping my hips, moved to caress and explore my buttocks and finally between my legs.

He laughed, finding me so wet and ready for his probing fingers. "You're hot, aren't you? Can't pretend you don't want me."

"No," I murmured into his mouth, agreeing. I wanted him, now, hard, fast, slow, any way at all.

Without letting go of me, his mouth fastened firmly, devouringly, on mine, his cock prodding me, he walked me backward and pushed me down on my back on the very same leather couch where I'd sat drinking coffee with my husband a few hours earlier.

The shock of memory, of sudden guilt, made me struggle up and exclaim, "No—I can't—"

"Oh, yes you can."

"No." I said it reluctantly as I struggled to rise, sorry that he wasn't stopping me, outraged that I wasn't stopping myself. But my freedom was an illusion. As soon as I had regained my feet he caught me in his arms and picked me up with a strength I had not known he possessed. Ignoring my feeble efforts to escape, he turned me around and pushed me down, face first on the couch. It was warm and solid, both yielding and supporting, covered in leather so fine that I had the sensation of having been pressed down on top of some other person. Before I could even catch my breath he was lifting me by the ass, a cheek in each hand, and then I felt his lips on my labia, his hot, clever tongue raking my clitoris.

All protest, all urge to flight, rushed out of me in a low moan of pleasure. He drew his head away with a low laugh. "Yes, you'd like that, wouldn't you? Let me do anything but fuck you.... But that's what I'm going to do, and nothing you say can stop me."

I said nothing. I didn't think about what I wanted, or what was right. I lay still and let him position me for his pleasure. I was lying nearly flat, facedown on the broad leather-cushioned couch, my legs dangling over the edge. He lifted my ass and parted my legs and the head of his cock nudged at the slick lips of my cunt. I couldn't see him anyway, this stranger my lover behind me, so I closed my eyes and gave myself up to physical sensation.

He was very big and greedy in his lust. Although I was very wet and willing, he spared me no tenderness but thrust himself inside me hard and fast, using his hands to part the cheeks of my ass at the same time, as if he wanted to split me in two. Even as I welcomed and wanted this penetration, at the same time the sensation of being forced was strong, and I cried out, half fainting with the shock of it.

"No ... oh, no ..."

He laughed and thrust again, this time burying himself to the hilt in me. Withdrawing slightly, he thrust again. "No?" With each thrust he repeated the word which came out sometimes as a croon, sometimes as a gasp, and I echoed him.

"No ... no ... no ..."

Our denials came closer and closer together as he found a hard, driving rhythm that satisfied both of us. I lost all sense of place and time and even of self as he drove into me and drove himself, and me, finally, over the brink into a fierce, all-consuming orgasm, with a final shout in which our two voices mingled.

A little while later I felt him withdraw. I made a small sound of protest but no move, too exhausted and happy where I was, sprawled facedown and legs spread on the couch. Until I heard the door to the library open.

Annoyed that he could leave me this way, I opened my eyes and raised my head just as the lights came on. There in the doorway, coolly surveying me and my lover, was my husband.

He looked at me, lying naked and flushed, and then at the man, also naked, his still-rampant penis glistening with our mingled juices. It was very quiet. And then, shockingly, he smiled.

"Happy anniversary, darling," he said. "I hope you enjoyed yourself?"

I began to push myself up, my mind whirling.

"Oh, no," he said. "Stay there, please. Or shall I ask our friend to hold you down?"

My erstwhile lover was beside me at once, his hands on my shoulders firmly keeping me from changing my position.

"I certainly hope you enjoyed yourself, because now it's my turn," my husband continued. There was a note in his voice that I had not heard in a very long time, and I suddenly realized that he had set this up, a sexual game of a sort I had never imagined he would want to play, an unexpected anniversary gift for both of us, and suddenly I felt more excited than I would have thought possible.

"You've been a naughty girl," said my husband. "So I've asked our friend to stay.... I'm going to have to punish you first, before we can kiss and make up."

I began an ineffective struggle to get away, but the stranger had no trouble restraining me. "No," I whimpered. "Please. No."

AUTHOR'S NOTE

It seems like it was only a few years ago (although I suppose it must have been ten or fifteen) that I frequently came across articles purporting to detail the differences between male and female sexuality, ones which declared that women tended to be less interested in, less likely to be turned on by, pornography, whether visual or written, than men. Maddeningly, we were supposed to accept such statements as reasoned, scientific conclusions! Yet a more sensible, sensitive response to the tests and surveys that yielded this rarely questioned generalization would have been that as pornography (a term meaning, literally, writings or drawings depicting whores) was always intended to appeal to a masculine audience, women's relative indifference, or repulsion, to it was unsurprising. Whether women are actually less, more, or equally responsive to pictures and texts that aim to arouse is a question that can't begin to be answered until women have had more opportunities to create and enjoy our own erotogenic stories.

It'll be fun, but it won't be easy getting there; we're laying the groundwork now for women not yet born. Though I myself would love to find a new way of writing about sex, and a new approach to sexual fantasy, "The Story of No" is not that breakthrough. As the title suggests, it's a response to other people's stories, its inspiration literary rather than personal.

REASONS NOT TO GO TO FORT LAUDERDALE

❖❖❖❖❖❖

By Liz Clarke

The exuberance of Liz Clarke's story was extremely heartening to come across, after seeing so many submissions by older, wiser—and more depressed—women closer to my own age who either lack for opportunity or who've pretty much, for the usual reasons, given up on dancing (or "scrumping") the night away. The sexuality of such nineties students as Clarke depicts, shadowed as it is by AIDS, perhaps is more highly charged, more polymorphous because of that mortal threat. But I can't say that I felt anything other than grateful after encountering this not quite sophisticated—yet not quite innocent, either—example of their youthful energy, optimism, and zest for romance.

So you have multiple lovers. How exciting." Joel was starting to get on my nerves. He was also lying through his teeth; he was jealous as hell.

I just smiled at him. My feet were starting to freeze. I'd taken my shoes off to run through the mud in the cornfield, but now the wind was picking up. We'd just gotten back from spring break. Or rather, he'd gotten back; I'd stayed on campus.

"Who is it?" he asked.

"We agreed not to tell. You know how people gossip around here."

"Don't you trust me?"

Not a sno-cone's chance in hell. "I'm sorry, Joel, I promised."

He sulked. Several hundred yards away, at the edge where the field and woods met, there was another het couple rolling around. I looked out across the field at Mt. Jasmine and the Gourami Range.

"Tell me about your break. How was LA?" I said. That distracted him for a while. He told me about all the parties he'd gone to.

"I missed you," he said. "You're the sexiest girl I know." Translated, that meant I wasn't beautiful but he considered me worth fucking anyway.

"Woman," I corrected automatically.

We walked back to Amphlett Place.

"Who was it?" he persisted, reaching to touch the bite-mark on my throat, which was what had tipped him off.

"Joel. I really can't tell. Don't take it personally."

"Was it Elliot?"

"*Please!*"

"Gabe or Cat?"

"What makes you think that?" I said, very very casually.

"You said you spent break in your apartment bonding with them."

I laughed. "It wasn't Gabriel or Cat." It was Gabriel *and* Cat.

Joel went back to his apartment. I went back to my apartment. As far as I was concerned, after the way he'd dissed me before break, he'd better consider himself lucky to ever see the inside of my room again.

I'd gone over to his place the night before he left to say good-bye. He was scrubbing the bathroom sinks, and he had a Crockpot of beef stew going. It was like walking into the Twilight Zone. I have hideous psychic scars from childhood Crockpot meals.

"What are you doing?" I climbed onto the counter beside where he was scraping at several semesters' worth of smeg.

"Cleaning. I mopped the bathroom floor and cleaned the kitchen and did all the dishes everybody left."

Oh, Lord. The problem was, he was rabidly attractive. He had Bambi eyes and long dark curls, and he smelled sweetly of clove cigarettes and reefer. Twenty years from now I'll catch a whiff of cloves, and it'll knock me to my knees. I reached out and traced my finger along the curve of his ear. He had his hair back in a faded ribbon ponytail holder. Stop cleaning that damn sink! I hadn't *intended* to jump him when I went over, but maybe it was the challenge, or the cloves, or something. He put the sponge down. Progress. I pulled him over and locked my legs around him, slid my tongue up from his collar to the notch behind his ear.

"I'm cooking dinner for Katya. She's coming over in about half an hour," he said.

I took hold of his hair and kissed him good and slow, grinding my hips into him. Oh, yes. That ought to get his attention. When I slid off the counter to press my whole self against him, my knees were syrupy.

"How long?" I pulled him into me, my back against the doorframe of his room. My hand down his belly to a firm hold on his crotch.

"Half an hour."

"Mmm …"

His head went down to the space between my breasts, and he unbuttoned the top of my shirt. Half an hour was realistic, knowing him. I could manage with half an hour. I wanted to drag him into his room and throw him down. I could hardly breathe. God, what *was* it about him?

He squeezed my thighs and pulled away from me. "Katya'll be here soon. You'd better go."

You've got to be kidding. The smells of Crockpot *au boeuf* and Comet cloaked the scene. He turned back to the sink and picked up the sponge. He wasn't kidding.

I buttoned my shirt. "Have a good break," I said, heading for the couch where I'd dropped my leather jacket.

He followed, sponge in hand. He had a lot in common with sponges. "You too."

"Have a good dinner." Die of botulism. I pulled on my jacket. My knees still felt shaky, and my cunt was screaming in frustration. Which person in this picture has the warped sex drive?

"Thanks."

I paused in the doorway, holding it open. "Tell Katya hi."

"Maybe you can come over later tonight."

"Maybe." Maybe, as in, maybe you fully deserve to eat Crockpot beef stew. He'd seen the last of that shirt I borrowed from him.

Outside the stars were ice chips. I glanced toward my apartment. Patricia had materialized and suction-cupped herself to Gabriel as soon as Alan and Sarah had left together. I wasn't in the mood to deal with that; not right this second. I wasn't in the mood to do anything except fuck. All lubed up and no place to go, I thought sourly.

Except that wasn't entirely true. Cassie had come over a couple of days earlier and told me she'd changed her mind about our ban on exchanging fluids—as we romantically phrased it. Actually, it was her ban. I failed to see the difference between her exchanging fluids with me and with the men she was fucking. If anything, my fluids were safer.

At the moment I certainly had a surplus of fluids, so I turned around and went to Cassie's. The Goddess was smiling on me; she was home.

When she'd come to see me on Thursday, Cassie had also had a suggestion involving Gabriel. And her. And me. I didn't know what kind of revelation she'd had, but I wasn't going to complain. Maybe it had to do with what was going on among the group in the apartment already. Gabe had of course expressed interest when I informed him of Cassie's little proposition. Anything sexual caught Gabe's interest. But, he said, he wasn't too into it. Mainly he didn't know Cassie all that well.

And I knew Cassie all that well, but I wasn't really into the specific nature of her idea. We needed to talk about it.

It was as good a pretense as any.

Warning: this part of the story reinforces the notion of bisexuals as promiscuous scum who view same-sex recreation as a substitute for the Real Thing. If you believe that stupidity already, nothing I can say is going to change your mind and you'll get offended in a few paragraphs.

"That dipwad threw me out!" I snatched off my jacket and dropped down on her bed. Like most Serling College students, she didn't have a bedframe, just a mattress on the floor.

"He's such an asshole," she said. I didn't even have to tell her who I was talking about.

We thoroughly trashed Joel, which took a while because we wanted to extract every bit of pleasure we could from the task. When he'd been reduced to a gob of wombat slobber drying to a crust on a rock somewhere in the Australian outback, I said, "I mentioned your proposition to Gabe."

"Yeah? What did he say?"

I filled her in. She already knew my reservations.

"Well, actually, I've reconsidered that too." Apparently this was the week for Cass to totally reorder her cosmology. "What if I was more actively participating?"

"Define more."

"Everything but exchanging fluids."

"Whose fluids?"

"His."

"Hm. Okay, yeah, I'd be more comfortable with that. I'll talk to him again." All semester I kept expecting Ricardo Montalban to step out from behind some piece of furniture and hand me a drink in a hollowed-out pineapple. "Where'd you get this idea?"

She made her eyes even more huge and innocent and chocolate-brown. "Weeellll ... Gabriel is very attractive." This was true. "And you're very beautiful." This was debatable. Cassie snuggled closer to me. "I thought it'd be fun."

"That's it?"

"Yeah."

"Okay." Gabriel saw an ulterior motive in everything.

I kissed her neck. She was lying on her back, and I was curled up beside her, her arms around me. For some reason we wound up that way a lot. I kissed her some more, and she didn't tell me to stop. I didn't stop.

"Why, Liz," she said with delight as I nibbled her earlobe, afraid to move below her neck for fear she'd tell me to cut it out, "I do believe you're horny."

I hate that word, especially in reference to me, so as a matter of course I deny any connection with it. But I didn't stop kissing her either.

"Ooh, that feels nice." *Nice?* I was about to come just kissing her above the shoulders. "I think living in that apartment has been good for you."

"Yeah? How?"

She sat up. I sat up. "Mm, more comfortable with your body. You've gotten a lot more aggressive," she said.

To prove her right, I lunged at her.

"Oh, Natasha," Cassie giggled in her sexy Russian accent. "You do such things to me!"

This is the way things were with Cass: I never knew what, if anything, was going to happen until it was in progress. It was always slow, cautious. Which made it almost painfully hot. I was afraid she'd change her mind any second. Cassie asked, "Are you okay? Are you sure?" every five minutes. Making love to her was like finding my way along the edge of a cliff in the dark. Like falling over the edge. Like spreading purple wings and catching an updraft. All at the same time.

"Hey, Natasha, want to exchange fluids with me?"

"Well, Anastasia … if you insist …"

And as I said, this was the first time we'd done more than kiss and nibble and roll around.

"You probably won't be able to make me come," Cassie said.

Ha! She obviously didn't know who she was dealing with. She'd told me, of course, that she almost never had an orgasm during het intercourse—it had been a while since she'd scrumped with a woman. Clearly her memory needed refreshing.

The first kiss on the mouth always sent a few pebbles skittering over the cliff edge. Her skin was butter-soft. She liked her nipples sucked so hard I was always afraid of hurting her. My shirt got unbuttoned and stripped off; her loose green dress and the wool leggings underneath; we struggled me out of my jeans. It's a scientific fact that women's underwear is more appetizing than men's. Anyone who's ever had a hard time keeping a straight face (or concealing disappointment) at ratty semiwhite Fruit of the Looms knows it. Of course Cassie never wore a bra—she had Teflon Tits worthy of Ripley's "Believe It or Not." Not being so blessed, my personal lingerie collection ran toward black and purple lace bras, and bikini underwear flowered like Hawaiian shirts.

Maybe it was the uncertainty of it, the feeling of being bad and getting away with it—unless I got caught. Maybe it was the unexpectedness of her deciding it was okay. For some crazy reason it reminded me of those old Impulse cologne commercials: "If a man you've never met before suddenly gives you flowers ..." That close to orgasm, any wild thing might fly across my mind. Usually in a matrix of purple swirls, thick flocks of birds, or bursts of exploding color ... it's very depressing to me as a writer that I have such clichéd mental images during sex.

Cunts are most often compared to flowers, to butterflies, to seashells. I'm guilty of doing it myself. You can compare labia to petals, clitori to pearls from here until next Tuesday, but trust me, kids, when you're up close and personal a cunt is a cunt. The Goddess be praised.

Everywhere she touched drew fire to the surface. I was shaking. My hands and mouth grasping—

"Oh *my*," she said, giggling.

"Shut up."

She had on a Cocteau Twins tape and three candles burning on her dresser. Oh my Lord, she felt good. She pushed my thighs open, and her tongue was hot although not as hot as the flesh it was touching. Colors and colors. How sad it would be to have orgasms in black and white.

"You taste so good," Cass said, grinning over my belly.

That had been called to my attention before.

After my eyes uncrossed I kissed my way down her stomach and up her thighs, and she reminded me again that it would
take an act of God or Congress to make her come. I had a mental image of a mechanic spitting into her palms and pushing up
her sleeves, a pianist cracking her knuckles with a flourish.
Two fingers, tongue, and she shrieked up the scale as she came.
Nine minutes flat by the clock on the dresser, at the head of the
bed with the candles and box trilling *The Pink Opaque.*

"Oh, God, stop, stop." She sat up, gasping, eyes saucered.

I'm sure I looked smug.

"Oh, my God. How did you *do* that?"

I sat up and wiped my mouth on my shoulder. "I've been
worshiping at the Shrine of Cat."

"Thank her for me." She curried her fingers through her
hair. It made utterly no difference. Her hair was a soft bowl-
shape, the same brown as her eyes. "I can't believe you did
that. Oh my God." She hooked her arms around me and kissed
me with markedly more respect.

I felt like calling the *Enquirer.*

"Living with that group *has* been good for you."

"Certainly educational." I neglected to mention the oral art
I had performed on Patricia when she joined Gabriel and me in
bed the morning after the last dance party in our apartment. It
occurred to me that Cassie had deliberately waited until I
wasn't a blushing baby dyke paralyzed at the very thought of
initiating sex.

When the phone rang at 1:30 that morning I was in the
kitchen, gathered with Gabe and Patricia around a bubbling
vat of chickpeas like the three witches in *Macbeth.* We were
making hummus. *Knowing* it was Joel, I let Gabe answer.

I listened to Joel with the steam from the pot saunaing
my face. "...and we had dinner and then we got really really
stoned and watched *2001* on the VCR ..." No more first year
students, I vowed. No way. And Lord, no one else from Los
Angeles. "...it was really really fun. She just left. So can you
come over now?"

"No, I don't think so." We Southerners have politeness knocked into us from the womb. Fortunately for him. "It's late."

"I could come over there."

"Joel. It's 1:30 in the morning. I'm going to bed." Total lie. "Have a good break."

"Will you write to me?"

"Right, sure." *Please.*

I did, in fact, go to bed around three, after pounding out my aggressions into the mush of chickpeas, tahini, lemon juice, and way too much garlic, gleefully fantasizing Joel's brain squipping through the octagonal holes in the potato masher. Gabe and Patricia accompanied me, and none of us got much sleep—but despite that morning's educational and entertainment value, I'm taking the liberty here of substituting another event from later in the week. With those two I always felt like I'd been conked over the head and woken up in a bad porno movie. Also, I promised Cat she'd be in this story.

Monday and Tuesday, Gabriel and Patricia went to visit Doug in Plymouth and Alan in Boston, Gabriel oozing garlic from every pore after all the hummus he'd consumed in the intervening thirty-six hours. Wednesday I sat in the kitchen windowseat reading *Interview with the Vampire* and watching the entrance to the Amphlett Place parking lot for his return. Just as I was positive the only thing I wanted for the rest of eternity was to be a vampire, I realized I'd deliberately sought out the sunniest spot in the apartment to read. The view of the parking lot was a factor too, of course. But naturally I didn't see him drive up. He must have walked from Greenvalley Village, where Patricia lived; they'd taken her car.

"Hi."

"Hi."

"How was it?"

"Okay." The apartment door closed behind him, and he checked the message board before hauling his stuff to his room. I put down my book and followed him.

He dropped his duffel bag and backpack onto the floor, turned, and put his arms around me. We didn't have the kind of thing where I could call him baby and tell him I'd missed him. I did it anyway.

"I missed you too," he said, looking faintly surprised.

Standing on my toes and stretching, I just barely reached his shoulder. For that reason I generally stood on his bed when I was in his room—when I wasn't lying on it. Gabriel's room tended to be a gathering place and most evenings saw at least one and up to five bodies sprawled on his mattress (no frame, and he'd added a foam pad). What form of entertainment said bodies engaged in varied. I kissed his neck, still vaguely garlicky—amazing how bodies get so familiar so fast. Much easier to get to know a body than the person living inside it. It could have been just a consequence of the living conditions that I knew Gabriel liked the web of his thumb and first finger bitten before I knew the names of his brothers and sister.

After—what, a month and a half?—I knew him by taste, smell, the texture of his skin. I knew the way he kissed and the weight of his hands. The pattern of his breathing. I could identify his step on the stairs.

Knowing the parts of him that were covered with more than clothes was a different story altogether.

Of course Gabriel had groupies on twenty-four hour call, snatching each others' hair out for the chance to kiss and bite and fuck and suck and give him backrubs. He didn't think it was at all amusing when Alexa or Cat or I suggested he put a sign-up sheet on his door.

When standing-up kissing got old, he scooped me up as easily as picking up the cat (admittedly the cat, Gandalf, was the biggest, baddest beast this side of the Pecos), carried me down the hall to my room, and threw me down on my futon—more room than his bed. One-oh-one Amphlett Place, where fantasies come true. Sometimes, at least.

"Missed me, huh?" I said, grinning up at him.

Gabe dropped to his knees beside me on the futon. "God-damn, you are so hot."

"Why, thank you."

One arm plunked down by my left shoulder; him half bridged over me. "No problem." Slowly his face came down until our lips brushed. Just barely touched. That one point of light friction, more a tease than a kiss. I raised my head and hooked my arms around his neck to draw him to me, lips and tongue, tasted him deep as his hands at the small of my back pulled me to sitting up.

He had on that look, the one that could scrape electric fingers across the back of my neck from the other side of the room with Sarah and Alexa chopping veggies for burritos, Kyle reading aloud from a chemistry book, and Alan blasting his music from upstairs. I could never hold that gaze for long. Predatory, feline; eyes hardening from blue to green. Stone cherub's mouth. Gabriel knew how to ride the thin edge of fear, push back the borders. No one had ever done that to me before.

Slow hand outlining cheek, lips, neck. The curve of his smile. His hand rounded my shoulder as if he were drawing me in silhouette. I took one of his hands and carefully circled the index-finger joints with my tongue, the webbing of his palm, sucked his fingers. He practically purred.

"Lock your door," he said.

This struck me as mildly insane. "Nobody's going to come in the apartment except for Cat," I said, getting up to humor him, "and we'd invite her in anyway."

When my room was locked I knelt behind him, pushed aside his mane to kiss the sweet nape of his neck and rub his back, working his shirttail out and my hands underneath to warm skin. We rarely made love in the daylight. My room glowed white with sun reflecting off the snow outside.

Gabe, I had discovered, had not actually reached a Buddhalike state of Sensitive New Age Guy-dom. He merely channeled that macho energy into socially acceptable directions. Like ... sex. He bit, he grabbed, he said "fuck." All endearing traits. Fucking Gabriel was being sucked into a cyclone headed for an Oz where Glinda is a drag queen and the Wicked Witch of the West is a hot Top in tight black leather. (Remember when all the Munchkins prostrated themselves before her?) And they don't sing that dippy "Ding-Dong the Witch is Dead" bullshit. The soundtrack is by Prince—and the Yellow Brick Road leads to Erotic City.

Like they say, getting there is half the fun. This was a cyclone of hot breath in hair, open mouths, arched back, wet fingers. Tell me you want it. Hands held over my head—

"Don't move," he murmured roughly and kissed me soft as a baby's mouth, licked the salt from my eyelids.

Cyclone of blood draining, drawing to the center. Falling in a spiral. Tell me you want it. Pulse in my cunt; when we finally stripped all my pores opened their mouths and greedily tasted air and skin. Ah, the joys of sensitive nipples.

His teeth locked firm on the side of my neck, the skin of his stomach against my back. Condoms in the top desk drawer. Gabriel could (did) pick me up and move me like a doll. As far as I was concerned, he was jungle gym, roller coaster, water-slide, and concession stand all in one.

"Oh, my God, let me look at you." His hands on my hips. I was on top of him, not minding that my right foot was starting to fall asleep.

I grinned. Struck a Madonna pose with my hands behind backtossed head.

"Very hot."

I rolled my hips in that way that popped his eyes out of their sockets, and he stopped laughing.

We were sprawled in a sweaty postcoital tangle and the light had faded some when we heard the outer door open, followed by a knock at my room. Gabriel whipped a blanket over himself so fast it created a sonic boom.

"Chill, it's locked. Who is it?" I sang in my most Little Red Riding Hood-innocent voice.

"It's Cat."

"Just a min-ute!" I got up and pulled my robe off its hook on the back of the door. It was a black rayon deal from East-West Gifts, with a red and orange dragon across the back.

"I can go away if you and Gabe are busy."

"No, we're done," I said, opening the door. "Come on in."

"Aw, I missed it?" She dropped her backpack, closed the door, and joined us on the futon.

"Mmmm, not necessarily," Gabriel said, kissing her neck. I

wondered why the hell he'd bothered to make himself decent—
like Cat had never seen him naked before?

I kissed the places on her neck Gabe was missing.

"Goodness!" Expressions got passed around like hickeys. I
believe that one originated with Alan.

"How was work?" I asked between kisses.

"Oh, sucky," Cat said cheerfully. "I like this, though."

Gabe had said before that Cat reminded him of a snake, all
sinew and grace. She could have been carved out of pearl. At
Serling, if you were asked to describe a specific dyke and you
said, "She's got short brown hair," the querant was likely to
slap you because 95 percent of them had short brown hair. Cat,
however, defied the standard kd lang DA. Her crewcut spiked
naturally, without the aid of gel or Butch Wax. The three of
us—as we had all commented—made a beautiful physical contrast: me an inch shy of five feet, short red curls with a green
Krazy Kolor streak, pale gold skin, and curves galore. Cat perfectly lithe and androgynous, at least until you saw her naked
at which point you became aware that she had killer hips and
breasts; delicate Celtic features. Gabriel somehow androgynous
too despite his height, broad shoulders, and perpetual three
days' worth of beard; sweet soft skin, fine hair to his shoulders.

With Gabriel and Cat I wished I could observe the scene at
a distance, to see those bodies fully. The two of them together
was ... Gabe had described Cat and me as live MTV, the video
to "Lesbians of the Congo, in D Minor." Cat and I also agreed
that watching Gabe and Alan was hot enough to make us want
to be men for a couple of days. Gabe and Cat together just
made me want both of them more—maybe I was the most inse-
cure person of our circle, but when there were three of us I
could never shake the fear that the other two would find each
other far more interesting than they found me. We tried so
hard to be all liberal and liberated.

"I think you need to take your clothes off," I suggested to
Cat. She thought so too. Gabriel thought so too. We assisted
her. My Chinese robe got shed as well.

"Guys," Gabe said when Cat and I were pretzeled, "I'm

tired. Do you mind if I just observe?" We were his favorite spectator sport. The price of being bisexual is that sometimes all the sleazy stereotyped things about it actually happen. What makes this qualitatively different from Cassie wanting to watch me fuck Gabriel? Don't confuse the issue by trying to insert logic into it. "The two of you, goddamn ...."

Cat laughed into the valley between my breasts where she was kissing. We knew Gabriel well enough to translate. As long as we were scrumping anyway, it was no big deal being his live MTV. Cat's lower lip just begged to be bitten. Come to think of it, I would have sold my blood to bite any part of Cat. In my modified Land of Oz, she got the part of the Witch of the West. She was working magic on my cunt, drawing blue streaks of sparks with her tongue, when somewhere back in Kansas Gabriel groaned as he came and fell back on the bed. He stayed to watch until I sizzled and melted, and then he kissed us both and put his clothes on.

"I'm going to take a shower. You guys are amazing."

"We know," I said.

Cat, still between my legs, propped on her elbows, laughed and kissed my belly. "*You* are amazing."

Affirmation time! Everybody empower and validate the person to your left — it's group therapy with orgasms!

Gabriel left; Cat and I stayed. Weeks earlier, Elliot, accosting me outside Rogers-Nelson Hall after my 9:00 A.M. class, had suggested that I install a turnstile at my door. No wonder we broke up; the boy couldn't even come up with a creative insult.

Of course Gabriel was kidding when at the end of the week he suggested that the three of us move to Seattle and have a group marriage. Of course Alexa and Alan didn't think it was at all funny when they got home and found out. Sarah was mercifully spared, being the only resident not scrumping one or more of me, Gabriel, and/or Cat. (Except for Kyle, who'd had the sense not to get involved in the first place. Much to my and Cat's disappointment.)

Mr. Roarke never did show up with pineapple drinks, ordering everyone to smile. I don't think any of us ever got

hearts or brains or courage from the Wizard. A home, maybe—
the real kind, with a family you want to kill and at the same
time love powerfully enough to die for.

I didn't see much of Joel after that, but I didn't tell Elliot. I
let him think my turnstile was having its hinges spun off.

Also, Cassie's evening of debauchery never happened.

There's always next semester.

AUTHOR'S NOTE

The idea is, wouldn't it be fabulous to come to sex (no pun
intended) without cumbersome emotional baggage? Talk about
the ultimate fantasy! Even with the lovers I adore and who
adore me, we carry our histories, mutual and individual. We
have our issues. Of course, for a child of the age of AIDS,
codependency, and Oprah, it's just to be expected: latex and
therapy are facts of life.

The residents of this story have collectively survived abuse,
incest, rape, alcoholism, drug abuse, eating disorders, suicide
attempts, depression. In their circle, the line between "friend"
and "lover" tends to blur or not exist at all. They need the closeness, the intimacy. They're discovering, too, that sex can just be
fun and playful, and not such a big damn religious deal. Come
on, if you can't have sex with your friends, who on earth are
you supposed to have it with?

BLESSED IMMORTAL SELF: HOW THE JEWELS SHONE ON YOUR SKIN!

❧❧❧❧❧❧❧

By Susan Swan

If one thing is certain, it is that there are no certainties when it comes to sexual attraction. And, like so many aspects of erotic awakening, the possibility for surprise is always a factor. Here, Susan Swan makes us share the unexpected sensations of tenderness a woman might feel for a lover who fits into no previous category of imagined desire and who sneaks, unbidden, into her heart.

Blessed Sankara: *Om namah sivaya!*

You say you cannot live without me—that the taste has gone out of your morning tea and a sunset has no beauty because the next day will not have me in it (*Om shanti,* Sankara! Or have you forgotten the mantra, my master, Vishna, gave you?) Every day I pray you will attain God and the thrill of holy bliss. Instead you say we belong together and that you loved me from the first day you saw me standing on the ashram dock. You said you recognized me from Padma's old photographs in our retreat brochure. You said you'd never seen a sweeter yogi than this young woman with a dark braid down her back doing cartwheels on the beach.

Those pictures were taken more than a dozen years before you stepped off Chandrashekar's ferry with the other guests, still dressed in the clothes of northern cities, as pale and apprehensive as children sent to stay with relatives they didn't know. You said I still looked youthful, leaning over the railing to watch the procession troop ashore, but you were drawn to my mournful eyes. I seemed sad and perplexed for a woman hardly older than your own daughter. And then you noticed how I limped up the path by the yoga platform, lurching slowly past the upside down bodies of the other guests doing their morning headstands. Behind me trudged the giant Narayan, my faithful shadow, swearing to himself as he pushed the old cart stacked too full with suitcases.

You are always polite, Sankara, and have made no accusations, but I know you assume I'd been sleeping with Narayan before you arrived. Believe me, my darling, nothing much had transpired although naturally we were thrown together a great deal because we were preparing the new book of our master's letters for publication. (*Siranda Upanishad*—a universal scripture in my master's own handwriting.)

That first day you said you sensed Narayan's possessiveness, but I paid no attention to him or the foolish display he made of himself each morning, chinning himself on the exercise bar in the small courtyard of the ashram. The other women liked to watch the muscles wriggling like snakes in his upper arms. But not me, not your Shakti. Despite his height and physical prowess, to me, Narayan was just a spoiled boy not long out of high school with big hands and ears like Jughead in the old Archie comics. He was the pet of the camp, you see, because he was the swami's kid brother.

It is true I did enjoy discussing our project with him. Narayan does have a sardonic turn of mind, and he'd visited my master in India, and, oh Sankara—the amusing stories he can tell about forgetful old gurus meditating in Tibetan caves and getting frostbite because they never come out of their trances! Still, I didn't take Narayan seriously. And that first day, I paid no attention to you either, Sankara. I was carrying Vishna's forbidden stash of chocolate (which Narayan had just smuggled in) and hoping my master wouldn't scold me for being late.

Of course, you had noticed my sprained ankle because you coach basketball like my father, and you've trained yourself to spot an injury. I like to believe our meeting was preordained, a necessary form of incest, but I want to circumvent my nostalgia and tell you the truth. Who else at the Siranda ashram really worried over my foot? Oh yes, when it didn't heal, some of the staff gave me remedies, but it was only to hear themselves talk. It's ironic, isn't it, that we who serve others often can't serve ourselves.

So it was you who came to my small hut carrying your blue plastic box, the first aid kit you take everywhere, like a purse under your arm. You found the ice for it in the retreat's failing refrigerator and showed me how to elevate my ankle on pillows and then tape it tightly with a tensor bandage. R.I.C.E., you said in a fatherly tone—rest, ice, compression, elevation. When the swelling didn't go down, it was you who insisted on taking me to the hospital in the capital.

For that alone, I will always be grateful. But I haven't been fully honest, even here. Because I did notice you the first day. Later in meditation. As you slouched against the whitewashed wall of the temple, not bothering to sit cross-legged like the rest of us, while my master Vishna chanted his unending *bhajans* and mantras. It was the Easter our master grew lax and let those of us with bad backs lean against the temple wall. So I sat beside you, glad of the chance to rest, and found I couldn't take my eyes off you. What an ugly, ugly old man, I thought. It was your skin. You see, there is no point now hiding how you repulsed me. I was disgusted by the spidery web of wrinkles that crawled across your face, threatening to erase your features. You looked the way my father did during his last month in the hospital—distracted and restless, a withered mummy forced to stay alive against its wishes. But then I noticed the way you'd styled your hair in bangs that fell straight onto your forehead like a Roman senator. There's life in the old boy yet, I thought. And you turned to stretch and caught me staring, and I was taken aback by your clear hazel eyes glittering like Krishna's jewels in your aging face.

Sankara, I do not wish to hurt you. But I am trying to be as truthful as I can. So you will understand why I left you that morning. You didn't deserve such an unexpected leave taking, I know. It was several months later. We were old lovers by then, and you lay naked on my narrow cot, your fingers playing with the new black hair on your chest. Once again, you were shaving twice a day, and the white hair on your face and chest had started growing in dark. Because of me, you said. Because sex with me was making you young again. Now I am being unfair. You never said "sex." You always said "love." And you weren't greedy about your orgasms. You always pleased me first, as many times as I wanted, and then you pleased yourself.

Seven for me and one for you. Even steven, you'd say. No man has ever been so easy or gracious with me. Too often lovers want to please a woman out of anxiety or vanity. Not for the thrill of it, not like you.

I remember the sight of my hands in the bowl of milk cleaning the altar beads, made of real *rudrakshi,* the expensive wood my guru admired. I remember letting the beads spill off their plastic string into my palm. They were still damp, not sticky the way our sandalwood beads get if you clean them in milk.

I sat down on the bed beside you and with one hand began to stroke your forehead. I knew every inch of you by then, Sankara, and yet I still struggled to overcome my disgust before I touched you. And then when I did, I wondered why I had to struggle. I loved the feel of your skin. It wasn't dry the way I imagined old skin would be. It was slightly oily and surprisingly pliant for a man. Wait. I lie again. Your skin was as soft as foreskin.

As I began to place the slippery beads on your body, I saw Narayan doing his chin-ups outside the window. He couldn't

see me at first. How could he see in the glare of the morning
sun? It turned everything except the roiling green ocean a sul-
phurous yellow. I sensed Narayan was looking for me. Then he
swung down and heaved his knapsack onto his shoulders.
When he finished buckling up the straps, he walked over to my
hut, and just as I was putting the first two beads on the lids of
your closed eyes, he whispered my name. Then very softly, he
moved my shutter ajar. I looked up and he beckoned to me.

Frightened, I poured a bunch of beads into one of your ears
whose drooping lobes I'd so often nibbled. My clumsiness
made you giggle. And then I began, no longer slowly, to place
the beads deep in all the silky crevasses of your sun-baked
body. You were lightly brown like tulsi wood by then. I lined
up four, maybe five in the creases in either side of your groin
where the skin was still pale. And you accepted my little game
eagerly, eyes closed, smiling. You looked as beatific as Krishna
smiling on the temple altar in Visha's pictures. You know the
pictures I mean—the ones my master has me string with beads,
like the garlands on Christmas trees ... the very same beads I
was putting on you that morning, our last time together.

I smiled back down at you, and you started to run your
narrow tongue over your lips. Now when I think of us making
love, what I remember most is the slow, gratified way you
licked your lips when I sat astride you, as if you could taste me.

Tenderly, I took the biggest bead, the 109th bead of the
japamala, the bead that's bigger than all the others so you know
when you have come to the end of your mantra, and touched it
to the tip of your penis. And your penis swung upward, erect
again, and your glittering hazel eyes flew open, but you
couldn't see Narayan who stood silently watching us at the
window, only me. I placed the biggest bead in the sunken hole
of your belly button, where it nested like one of my master's
dark unblinking eyes.

My darling, you weren't the only one who thought I made
you young. Each time you penetrated me—stroke by stroke,
slowly at first and then faster and then slowly again, ah
Sankara, how I liked those slow strokes!—each time you

pushed into me, you lost months and then years, decades even! And by the time you came, you were younger than me. Yes, each time we made love I rescued from death the Methusaleh I'd noticed on the first day.

That morning, as you lay before me, splendid in my master's jewelry, not knowing that Narayan watched you too, I began to grow sleepy. I had been ill several times that last month, twice with a fever and sore throat and once with the flu. That was not usual for me. And I thought for a moment, my flu had returned so tired and sluggish did I feel. I yawned … once, twice, three times, my eyes fixed on you so I wouldn't look at the window where Narayan stood scowling at us. You didn't notice my fatigue. You groaned and pulled me down to you, whispering that I should sit on top of you again.

Naturally, I wanted to please you. And show the doubting Narayan that you were as virile as a young man in the bedroom! So I crouched down, excited by his jealousy and prepared myself to summon up in you all your gorgeous youth.

And then an exhaustion, like the exhaustion of age, rose up in me, and I knew I had to make a choice. I could be with you or with men like Narayan who'd lack the wisdom to love with full acceptance but wouldn't exact your price.

And so my beloved, I made my dreadful choice. I live now with Narayan in———, a new spiritual community Vishna, our master, has started near the capital of———. My guru forwards your letters to me, and I read them with great sadness. Narayan says if you loved me, you would release me and not write begging for my return. He says you are a vampire who doesn't have my real interests at heart. Narayan is young and doesn't choose words judiciously, but in one respect, he is right. I gave you back what I could of your youth. Now it is my turn, my love, to have the gift bestowed on me. *Om shanti,* Sankara! You who loved me the way nobody else has. Without limits or judgment. You'd never seen anyone so supple, you said, as this young woman in Padma's photographs. You admired her bare legs bending backward into a human wheel.

Thine own self, Shakti

AUTHOR'S NOTE

As far as I'm concerned, there's a confusion between erotic realism and erotic writing that focuses on sexual or sensual feelings. *The Last of the Golden Girls*, my novel about girls growing into women, faced obscenity charges, later dropped, because of this confusion. I was accused of promoting lesbianism because I wrote about two teenage girls pretending to make love as practice for the real thing with men. I'd be happy to promote any form of erotic love anywhere, any time, but in this case. I saw the girls' erotic awakening as part of my novelistic realism.

I'm glad to say I wrote this story primarily to describe and, I hope, evoke sensual feelings. I chose a spiritual retreat as the setting because I've spent time in these places and noticed a connection between the spiritual and the erotic. Deep erotic feelings, like spiritual feelings, are part of the mystery of the inner self. Despite what the gurus would have us believe, I think that the intense concentration that comes with meditation also heightens the awareness of the senses.

BLUE FEATHERS

❯❯❯❯❯❯❯

By Anne Rhyd

Chance encounters and sexy strangers are staple elements of erotic writing, and it is in this tradition of the literature that reality and fiction most clearly part company. However, it is for that very reason—that fiction can improve on reality by rewarding risk-taking only with perfect orgasms—that we get such pleasure from the inhibition-shedding of others in erotic fantasy-adventures. In "Blue Feathers," Anne Rhyd also recognizes that donning a mask in a carnival atmosphere will lend a sense of freedom and enhanced possibility to even the most staid among us, yet because her author's imagination is in complete control of the situation, the results of the ensuing indulgence can be sweet rather than sinister.

Josephine squeezed herself between a lamppost and a trash can as revelers pranced and paraded and even cartwheeled past her down Chartres Street. Her niece was nowhere to be seen—which meant that she truly was nowhere on the street, because even this boisterous crowd could not conceal the horde of children with Susan. Now Josephine had more than an hour to kill before three o'clock, the time they had agreed to meet after separating.

Only an hour before, she too had been caught up in the festive mood. They had been eating beignets and threading their way through the Vieux Carré from shop window to shop window when Susan had suddenly pulled her into a dark store. "Time to get our masks," she'd announced, and each child sprang first at one of the jeweled and sequined creations crowding the walls, then at one another, each convinced that the best mask was in someone else's possession. Josephine leaned against a brick wall out of the way. "You, too, Aunt Jo," Susan had said. She turned to the proprietor. "This is my aunt's first visit during Mardi Gras," she told her. "So she needs a very special mask."

The woman eyed Josephine through the dimness. She was tall, with elegant posture and languid movements, her hair piled and twisted on her head and interwoven with sparkles catching the light. Her mask was scarlet and decorated with feathers dyed to match, as was her satin dress—a magnificent creation whose strapless and feathered bodice clung to an equally magnificent figure before billowing into a full skirt. She reminded Josephine of a ripe strawberry dipped in chocolate. A white cat on the counter rubbed against its mistress, rumbling, and another cat wove itself around her legs.

Finally, the woman had smiled. "Yes, Queen Etta has a mask for your aunt," she said, pulling one from behind the counter. "There's only one other like this one in the world." The mask was a rich royal blue, the right eye outlined in blue feathers, the left, in blue rhinestones. Two strands of tiny blue beads dipped below the mask on one side. Josephine put it on. It smelled of sandalwood, and the lining was soft. The bead fringe brushed against her cheek caressingly with each breath. Josephine looked in the mirror, then fingered her dress ruefully. The mask made its navy knit and loose fit, which had seemed so practical that morning, look dowdy.

Etta had seen the gesture and pointed to a gown. "Try that one. It's like mine, only blue." Josephine shook her head quickly, afraid that the similarity would only emphasize the contrast between Etta's full body and her own more sticklike one. But, she thought, she didn't have to come out of the dressing room; she could just see how it looked. She eased its weight off the hook.

In the cubicle, merely a closet separated from the store by a rough burlap curtain, the silky fabric slipped over her head and slid down her body. As she fastened the long row of buttons up the front, she felt the softness hugging first her hips, then her waist, then her breasts. The skirt draped in soft folds that brushed her thighs. She lifted her eyes to the mirror and saw looking back at her a stranger, a woman strong enough to meet life's challenges, a woman brave enough to take risks, a woman daring enough to wear such a dress—in short, a woman unlike she had recently felt herself to be.

She pushed the curtain aside and asked, "Can I please leave my other clothes here until later?" The children stopped fighting over the masks to stare, and the littlest boy had started crying at seeing her so transformed. "Certainly," Etta replied. Then, as Josephine paid, she heard whispered, "Strong grisgris on that. My mother, she knew the voodoo, and her mother before her, and they taught me." Etta winked. "The dress is sure to bring you a real treat."

As they herded the children out of the store, Josephine had needed to shield her eyes from the sudden glare. The weather seemed more sultry than ever after the cool cavern of the store. "Good for you!" Susan offered her approval. "That's a beautiful dress."

"Queen Etta promises it'll bring me a treat."

"Well, you certainly deserve some joy in your life for a change," Susan told her, and then she and the children had melted into the crowd, leaving the older woman standing alone.

Now, after an hour's crowded wander, Josephine had found her way back to their meeting spot and at first thought she would just wait there. She had watched a boy try and balance steaming bowls of crawfish, then saw two yapping poodles rip each other's costumes off while their owners shrieked, then looked at a laughing woman, her dress open to the waist, tossing strands of beads from a wrought-iron balcony. So much activity, so much noise, yet Josephine felt as detached as if she were watching it all on TV. The smell of gumbo and étouffé wafting by increased her restlessness and made her stomach growl.

"Might as well get another beignet while I'm waiting," she thought. She turned and ran straight into a broad chest. A man's arms caught her. "Are you all right?" he asked.

"Oh, yes, but I'm very sorry." Embarrassed, she put up her hands to distance herself from him, but a clumsy unicyclist knocked the man toward her. He automatically grabbed her waist to keep from falling, she just as automatically leaned forward to balance his weight, and suddenly she was locked in an embrace with a total stranger. And enjoying it, too, she realized, feeling the comforting warmth of his body through their costumes and smelling his clean scent. The skin of his arms was warm and dry under her hands, and she found herself reluctant to let go. A blue feather drifted lazily between them, and she looked up.

He was wearing a mask that was the twin of her own. But how different it looked! What on her face had seemed so exuberantly feminine had the opposite effect on his; the contrast between the mask's baroque delicacy and his strong bones gave his face depth and drama and heightened his masculinity, like a pirate in bright silks and an earring, or a cavalier in lace and ruffles.

Between the mask and his pirate's costume, Josephine realized that all the clues to his identity were extinguished. She could not say whether he was young or old, professional or working class, conservative or liberal; she knew only that he had a solid body and a beautiful mouth, with lines that owed more to smiling than frowning. The idea that she could invent his identity for herself excited her, and she was embarrassed to find herself not only unable to let go of this stranger, but also wanting him, wanting to touch the cheekbones jutting from beneath the blue feathers and to pull the tightly curled hairs escaping from his shirt.

"You have excellent taste in masks," he said, his voice a rich baritone with an accent she could not place.

Reluctant to break the magic of the moment and be alone any sooner than she had to be, Josephine said nothing but continued to cling to his warmth.

Looking down at her left hand, the man let go of her waist and pulled back a little. "Aren't you afraid your husband will find us like this?" he teased her.

"My husband's dead," she responded, after a pause. The words sounded as harsh and ugly as the reality they represented. Then, she added, "I'm a little scared to take it off."

He looked at her for a long moment, then reached out hesitantly to stroke her hair. "Then that's a second thing we have in common," he said. Josephine could barely hear his words over the crowd and the thudding of her heart in her ears. "After my wife died in a car accident, I kept her toothbrush on the sink, her fuzzy slippers under the bed, everything just the way she left it. Finally, I sold it all and came down here to start over."

"That sounds pretty drastic."

"Yes."

"Was it the right thing to do?"

The man thought for a moment, then said, "I think so." He added, "It must have been. I never had mysterious and exotic strangers in slinky dresses falling into my arms before I came here." His words startled her. For the first time, she realized that when he looked at her, he was seeing the stranger who had looked back at her from the mirror at the mask store. Just as his mask and costume concealed his identity, so did hers. She could be anyone she wanted to be today. Suddenly she felt as mysterious and exotic as he saw her.

He reached up and touched his mask. "My wife loved this color. I chose this mask because it reminded me of her," he said. "Seeing it on you makes me realize I must look silly in something this feminine."

"No, it has quite the opposite effect on you," she assured him and was surprised to feel her face getting hot. She tried to gather the willpower to move away.

They stood there looking at each other until an exuberant accordion player whacked them as he pulled on his instrument. "Why don't we get out of here?" suggested the man. Josephine explained, "I have to meet my niece here at three." "Fine," he said, and she gave him her hand. The warmth of his smile made her stomach knot. He started to lead her away, then stopped and gently pulled her ring off and dropped it in her purse. "Just for now," he said softly.

Her hand snug and secure in his, she followed him away from the throng and through a maze of alleys and courtyards. The smell of food and spilled alcohol gave way to that of the flowered vines that tumbled down from balconies and clung to the crumbling walls. The modern world seemed far away, and it was easy to pretend he really was a pirate, perhaps Jean Laffite himself, newly arrived from the bayous to dispose of his booty. They would drink the most expensive port in the city to celebrate his luck, and he would give her a ruby necklace that had been intended for a Spanish noblewoman's neck. All her companion needed was a sword at his side to look the part completely.

Finally, he unlocked a door and led her down a cool dark hall and up some stairs. His room gave no more clues to his identity than his appearance; only a pair of blue jeans tossed over a chair marred its spartan neatness, and only a cuckoo clock on the wall gave it any character. The windows, bright and barely draped with white gauze that the cool breeze alternately puffed up and sucked out, looked out onto a shady courtyard.

Josephine was suddenly aware of the absence of the din. She heard no laughing, no bottles clanking, no dogs barking, only a small fountain tinkling water, and a faraway phonograph playing a scratchy record, the voice barely discernible as a twangy Cajun French, and her host's breath in her ear, warm and tickly. The contrast between his warmth as he held her and the cool of the air playing around her legs and rising between them made her shiver. The sudden chill of her underwear made her realize that she was dripping wet already, just standing in his arms.

They kissed, gingerly, masks bumping. She reached up to take her mask off, but he stayed her hand. He backed her onto the sofa and bent over her when she sat. She opened her mouth in anticipation of his kiss, but his mouth landed instead on her mask. His teeth gently plucked a feather from her mask and traced its outline on her face. He encircled her face with downy caresses, finally brushing the corner of her mouth over and over. When the wind blew that feather away, he pulled out another one, this time running it over and in her ear so very softly that she only knew she really felt it by the increased rasping of her breath. Again, the wind took his feather, and this time he pulled out two and stroked her neck and chest with them, down to the edge of her dress.

Finally, there were no more feathers in the mask. He looked at the feathers over her breasts and smiled. Kneeling in front of her, he leaned forward ever so slowly and grasped a feather—and her nipple—with his teeth. He took his time plucking some feathers, chewing more than pulling, the soft fabric bunching and twisting under his teeth, gentling their points and spreading the caress over her whole breast with his every movement.

Kneeling, he no longer needed his hands to support his weight, and he used them instead to unbutton the top button of her dress and to bury his face there with his feathers. He unbuttoned another button, then another, and spread the bodice wide. Pulling the points of the fabric taut away from her breasts, he circled one breast with the feathers, spiraling in tighter and tighter circles until the feathers were concentrated on her nipple. He stroked her nipple around and around with the fuzzy stubs until she clenched his hair in her fists and wrapped her legs around his waist.

Pulling free of her, he continued unbuttoning her dress. Finally, he had her exposed from neck to knee, and he gently tugged at her underwear until it, too, was at her knees. Spitting out his mouthful of feathers, he pulled some longer, stiffer ones from her dress and slowly worked his way down her abdomen. Then his head was between her legs and he was stroking her with the feathers. Every so often, he would paint slow, warm, wet lines down the inside her thighs, then return to the source of the moisture. An occasional feather fell from his mask, grazing her stomach before being tossed by the wind onto her arm or face. Finally, she was sobbing and bucking, and he buried his fingers in her as she came.

After a minute, she was able to loosen her fingers from his hair, and she pulled his shirt off. His skin was tan and taut over his muscles, and the curly hairs waved slightly in the breeze. An appendicitis scar—or perhaps a souvenir of a duel—peeked from under his pants. She picked up several feathers from the floor and slowly traced the white line with one, pausing to loosen his pants to follow the scar to its source.

Quickly but gracefully he kicked off his shoes and pulled off his pants, jumping a little when his bare feet stepped on a feather. Josephine's breath quickened as she looked at him, and it pleased her to hear him struggling to master the raggedness of his own breathing. She ran the handful of feathers slowly and deliberately down the inside of his thigh and calf, up the other leg, then back down again. The barbs of the feathers snagged in the hairs of his legs and resisted her pull. Trying not to tickle him, she carefully drew the feathers between and around his toes. Now it was his turn to clutch at her hair.

Twining her arms and legs around him, enveloping him, Josephine closed her eyes. Suspended from him, she felt as if she were bobbing weightless in the ocean. His thrusts would push her one way, then the sofa cushions would gently bounce her back in the opposite direction, and soon she lost all sense of time and gravity, knowing only the movement and the blackness. Finally he collapsed on her, and in the stillness she felt her awareness of her body return to her. He stroked her hair gently and whispered things she couldn't hear.

They both jumped when the cuckoo clock signaled the hour. He sighed and leaned back on his heels. "Your niece will be waiting for you," he said, and he carefully and slowly buttoned all the buttons on her dress and adjusted her mask straight on her face before putting his own clothes on. "I'll take you back where I found you."

Josephine was not at the lamppost long before she saw Susan. As they got closer, Josephine saw that all the children had lemonade, and Susan was sucking on one herself and holding out another to her. Condensation dripped down the side and splattered on the sidewalk.

"Sorry, we got separated," Susan said. As Josephine reached for her drink, Susan noticed her left hand.

"Aunt Jo, you've lost your wedding ring!" she exclaimed.

"Don't worry, I've got it right here in my purse." Josephine reached inside for her ring, hesitated, then slipped it on.

Susan now had gotten a good look at Josephine, and she eyed Josephine's denuded mask and dress. Josephine resisted the urge to check whether her buttons were evenly buttoned. Finally, Susan said, "I hope you didn't just stand here the whole time."

"Oh, I wouldn't do that," Josephine replied.

"Oh, yes, you would!" said Susan. Then she looked at Josephine's mask again with puzzlement and pulled a small blue souvenir from Josephine's hair. "I've been thinking that maybe you should stay down here with us forever. There's no sense in you going back to an empty house and all that snow."

"That sounds pretty drastic," said Josephine.

"Desperate measures for desperate times," said Susan.

Josephine sucked on her straw as she considered Susan's offer. "I'll think about it," she said. "But I doubt I'll stay." Contemplating another stray blue feather, she paused. "But who knows? Anything may happen."

AUTHOR'S NOTE

Pieces of this story grew out of several elements of my life about the time I started writing it—planning for an upcoming move to New Orleans, grieving over being forced by an illness to leave a writing job at a magazine, even having a conversation about how best to incorporate beads and feathers into a stained-glass panel of Mardi Gras masks. Also, I wanted to portray sexual attraction in a way different from that in men's magazines and romance novels, in which the heroine is usually young, beautiful, and rather simpleminded, and in which an essential element is that the hero establishes his dominance over the heroine and she accepts it.

THE AMERICAN WOMAN IN THE CHINESE HAT

❥❥❥❥❥❥❥

By Carole Maso

If there existed a world atlas of sensuality, France would occupy at least a continent, and it is probably true that this story by Carole Maso, which unfolds with such purposeful indolence, would lose a great deal were it set, say, in Indiana. Another point, wittily made here, is that language really is just a different mode of touching and that words, whether familiar or teasingly strange to the ear, can be an important element of foreplay.

A woman, x, and a man, y, plan to meet at the prearranged coordinate, z, a fountain on the Place Antony Mars in the south of France, in some late afternoon in summer at the end of the twentieth century.

Both walk slowly, inevitably to z, embracing their common fate and now as they stop and turn, each other. Y, a man with *cheveux longs*, clearly French, kisses x twice on the cheeks. It is as if he has stepped out of some unmade film of the dead Truffaut. She looks to be German or Scandinavian, possibly English or American and is wearing a Chinese hat. The sun is very bright, so bright in fact that sometimes one or the other, and sometimes both, seem to disappear in it. He circles her slowly. She sits stationary at a white plastic table, the kind that have become "*la mode*" in France in the last few years. He circles the fountain, the periphery of z, slowly, looking at her with some exasperation.

"*Il fait chaud,*" he says.

"*Non, il fait beau.*"

"*Il fait chaud.*"

"Such bright, white light."

"*Oui, la lumière.* Speak French."

"*Oui, la lumière.*"

She conjugates *vouloir. Vouloir* is to want.

She watches him appear and disappear, appear, disappear.

"This reminds me of another savage and beautiful afternoon."

"*Encore?*"

"In the savage and beautiful afternoon we tried to speak. You said: 'Where do you live?' I said: 'New York.' It was a time when I was still hoping you might save me."

"*Oui,*" he says, "*comme un prince charmant, sur son cheval blanc.*" He laughs.

She claps her hands. "Are you ready? *Vous-êtes prêt?* Are you ready now?"

She stands up. "*La première position,*" she says and arranges his arms and legs into the first position of ballet. He's so beautiful.

"*La deuxième.*"

He holds the position for a moment and then breaks it.

"You thought I could save you," he says. "You wrote it in that notebook.

"*La troisième. Parfait!*" He holds the pose.

"Already, you knew there was nothing I could do for you." He moves away.

"I asked: 'Where do you live?' You said: 'Near the cemetery.' I asked: 'Where were you born?' You said: 'The most beautiful coast in the world.'"

"No one understands why you have come to my country," he says." "'*L'étrangère*,' they all say."

She cries. "But I remember the beautiful forever of the perfect afternoon. The beauty by the fountain. And *les cheveux longs*."

"*La femme qui pleure*," he says. "*Chante avec moi*." He begins in English the song she has taught him.

> Row, row, row your boat.
> Gently down the stream,
> Merrily, merrily, merrily, merrily
> Life is but a dream.

"I was already trembling then," she says.

"Crying."

"Yes, for joy. In grief."

"'*J'ai peur*,' you said."

"Yes. Already that first day there was *une chambre blanche* ... a black and white film. *Un ange*."

"You were expecting maybe a miracle." He smiles.

There is a close-up of the young Frenchman. A profile. And then the slow motion turn of his head. A panoramic gaze.

"You are an angel," she says.

He laughs. Takes her Chinese hat.

She takes it back.

"She remembers the dazzling, the catastrophic afternoon."

He tries to remember that first day. "Already," he says, "you knew you were doomed."

"Stop," she says, running her finger down his arm, his chest. She skims the beautiful surface of his skin.

"*La dernière position*," she says.

"*Non*," he says, "*pas encore*."

He offers his hand, and she steps into the gesture.

"I love you," she says, entering the illusion like almost everyone.

He shakes his head. "It is only a dream," he says. "A lie. I thought you were different."

He takes her hand and holds it under the rushing, brilliant stream of water and then releases it, and they stand like that.

She in her Chinese hat.

He with his *cheveux longs*.

Not touching, not saying one word.

Unaccountably there is a dizzying movement of the camera, and they are suddenly seen from high above. The camera hovers. Something else hovers. It is, we see, one of the beautiful angels of France. The angel weeps. It begins to rain.

"I thought you said it never rained in summer."

He laughs.

It is night now. They turn and walk toward the cemetery. He guides her up the steep stairway placing the palm of his left hand on her back. He moves the other arm around her waist and presses the palm of the right hand against her heart. He applies the smallest pressure to her chest and whispers *"arrête."*

"Stop," he says, in a heavily accented French.

"Ouvrez la porte," she says, giggling. The man opens the door.

In the room there is a bed, a lamp, a black book next to the bed. A strange white light shines through the window. Light the cemetery gives. It reminds her slightly of night in the great illuminated city. "Home," she says, but of course that is not it.

She thinks of her city—silent now, very dark. Inconceivably tragic. She can't imagine.

"J'ai peur," the woman says to the man, digging her fingers into his upper arm and doing a quick little pirouette so that now she suddenly faces him. There is terror in the eyes of the woman who stands on tiptoe and searches his face for some sort of explanation. *"Je ne comprends pas,"* she says.

"Tu ne comprends rien," the man smiles. She releases him. He directs her to the bed.

"Yes, this I still understand," she says.

He hovers above her. Her arms encircle him. She feels the metal of his belt buckle against her lips.

"Non." He pulls away, gets down on his knees and watches her, observes her face, the two lines in her forehead that mean she is tired, the slightly open mouth. He holds her ankles in his hands and slowly moves them apart.

"Il fait chaud ce soir," she says and lies back on the bed. Slowly, everything is slowly, he undoes the six straps of her sandals. He pulls the straps tight and then loose. Six times on one foot. Six times on the other foot. He glimpses the golden brown pubic hair beneath her skirt.

She sits up and sweeps her hair to the top of her head and then tilts the head back. He studies her carefully, intently, her forehead, nose, chin, throat. She lets her hair fall and then says again, *"Il fait chaud."* She asks him to bring—what is the word?—her pocketbook. "Where?" She flexes her dazzling body. *"Là,"* she points, and he crawls to it on all fours.

From her bag she takes a small round box of hairpins which she hands to him. She turns so that she is facing the wall. He pulls the hair to the top of her head as he has watched her do and attempts to fasten it there. Long curling tendrils escape his every effort, and he sighs.

"Do not give up so easily," she says.

"Comment?"

She unbuttons her blouse and neatly folds it. Then her brassiere. It opens in the front, the back shaped vaguely like a heart. Her breasts, released from the elastic and bone and lace, swell.

She sings the birthday song, softly, off-key. "Today is my birthday," she says. Though it is not true.

He sees that the edges of her ears are red and that she has a slight heat rash along the back of her neck. Alternately he feels tender, then hostile, then indifferent toward her.

She raises her arms to check her hair, and he takes this opportunity to place his nose under her arm, breathing deeply. He runs his mouth along the slightly roughened skin of the American, cleanly shaven. He bites her, but gently. She wants him to bite her harder, hurt her somehow—make her feel something. But he won't.

She takes a small mirror from the leather bag and fingers

the curls he has fashioned with the hairpins, approving of the job he has done. "Perhaps you are *un coiffeur,*" she says, laughing. He moves his mouth to her rose nipple. She observes him in the mirror, a ravenous and fragile child. When she has had enough she nudges him away with her elbow. He goes around her back over to the other breast, and it is the same thing. She watches him and then brushes him away tenderly with one white wing. She turns to face him. She tries to tie his hair in a ponytail.

"*Non,*" he says.

"*Mais, il fait chaud.*" She tries again.

"*Non.*"

Slowly, she unbuttons his shirt, she counts each button: *un, deux, trois, quatre, cinq, six, sept.* "You are like a child." She outlines the rib cage with her mouth, presses where she imagines the heart to be.

She unfastens the familiar belt now and slips his penis from his pants. It has a life of its own. It is at a particularly lovely angle from his body, she thinks. "*L'explorateur,*" she calls it.

Pushing her down, he pins her hands to the bed. He is more erect now, harder. He straddles her, kneeling, putting his knees under her arms. He raises himself, slowly above her so that he is just out of her reach. Her tongue is barely able to graze his underside and then not. He sways rocking back and forth, back and forth. She struggles to get free. She tries to raise herself on an elbow. "*Non.*" He watches her. She struggles to meet him. She is so wet. "Let me go," she says.

"*Non.*"

"I want you."

"*Non.*"

"Please."

"Speak French." And with that he releases her hands, leans back, and thrusts himself into her mouth. There's a funny dipping motion. It's getting hard to describe this anymore. It's getting more and more difficult. He takes himself out of her mouth and with one hand pulls her skirt up around her waist and begins to touch her gently. He smiles and shakes his head at her wetness. His long hair hangs over her. *"Tu es comme un petit cheval,"* she says.

She bends her knees, throwing him off balance, and he topples in mock defeat. "Do not give up," she says, "so easily." Parting her legs, muttering in French, he enters her, and she is laughing and asking, "What are you saying?" He covers her mouth with his hand.

He moves his hand down to her throat as he thrusts harder and harder. "You're choking me," she says. "You're choking me." Then nothing. And I would like to help her, but I can't.

The black book falls to the floor, and she looks up terrified. *"Non.* It has no meaning," he says in English.

He sits up, and he is deep inside her, and he is now swearing and sweating, and asking for something. She doesn't know what. She tells him, she keeps telling him what she wants. What she needs. She wants to be on top now.

"Speak French."

She finds a way to say it.

"Bon."

He watches as slowly the strands of her hair escape the pins with the violence of her motions. She takes his small surrender and rides—somewhere far away, with him. *"Tu es comme un petit cheval."*

Her dazzling body falls forward onto him. She covers him with a veil of hair and tears. She is afraid. She wants something that doesn't change. Something permanent.

She'll never go far enough.

He turns her over and with an eerie precision. Takes one foot and then the other and places them on his shoulders. He holds her ankles and steers her so that her head is touching the floor. Off the edge of the bed, beheaded as she is, only a torso now, he drives into her with new ferocity.

She tries to speak, but it is useless.

"My God," he says in English, laughing.

She curls into herself on the floor. He looks at her from the bed. Her body divides into two perfect shapes: the back, the buttocks.

She seems to be floating.

I go over to them and pick up hairpins from the floor, the drenched bed. I examine the black book.

"Look," I say to him. "She is dreaming her way home."

AUTHOR'S NOTE

This is an excerpt from my latest novel. It chronicles the decline of a young American writer who has come to France to live. In her desperate efforts to slow her own disintegration she clings to sex as some last resort. In this section she entertains the possibility of romantic love for a moment—but only for a moment. The clinical, detached claustrophobic feel to it is in part an *hommage* to Claude Simon, Robbe-Grillet, and the French *nouveau roman*, as the narrator tries to hold on to some literary identity, even if it is a borrowed one.

In the novel's many sexual scenes there is an eerie splitting-off of personality as she becomes both observer and observed. "And I would like to help her, but I can't," the one who watches says. The deliberate choice not to exploit the potentialities of language, sex, or the imagination—hallmarks of my earlier fiction—made this an extremely frightening book to write. It was written from a dark, cynical, lost place in me and confronts one of my greatest fears: the catastrophic loss of feeling.

WINDOWS

➤➤➤➤➤➤

By Idious Buguise

Idious Buguise, like Barbara Gowdy and Carole Maso, finds herself writing about watching and being watched. And presented with this frustrated and harrowingly articulate narrator, we recognize her as something of a passive-aggressive voyeuse who does, in fact, realize that the act of simply opening her psyche, even to a silent shrink, might be a way of letting in some light. At the same time, one will surely have split seconds of uneasy identification with such a character—a woman who is clamorously certain that much that is owed her is being denied.

Every day I sit down in this artsy-fartsy, really-not-very-comfortable raffia palm chair, and you sit behind that glass and metal hi-tech desk. I talk and you listen with your eyes closed or staring out the window, and I wonder what you can see that I can't see. I talk about sex, and you shift position. I stare at you, and you squirm a bit. Are you excited when I talk about sex and sticky cunts and throbbing penises, or do you just pretend I'm reading you some trashy-fiction subplot and not rambling on about the real-life thoughts in my own flesh and blood brain? And how many of these words are really my thoughts, and how many of them are just some soft-core porn I'm inventing as a game to excite you? Do you know which is which? This can't possibly be therapeutic. I don't even tell you my dreams. I just make it up as I go along, and you, with your shoes on the desk, never looking at me, suck up the money, day after day.

Ramble time!

Today, on the way here I sat next to a man on the Number 12 bus, and he had the most beautiful hands. No rings, no hair. No hangnails or torn cuticles. And, of course, those hands reminded me of the imaginary fingers I carry with me all the time.

Oh, my God. It really wasn't so very long ago, you know— three, three and a half years ago he left me for her. I bet they do it in every room in their house. Yeah. I know it's a long time without sex. But what the fuck do you expect me to do? I can't go out and sell myself. I can't go up to just anyone—or even a special someone—and say "put your arms around me, your lips on mine, and play softly with my crotch." I mean that just isn't done anymore. At least I can't do it.

It was so much easier in the sixties. I wasn't obsessed with checking out hands and fingers and trying to mentally place them on my crotch. Back then everyone just sort of melted into everyone else, and there was no threat of herpes, pregnancy, or AIDS. Herpes wasn't even considered. We all took the pill. And HIV was unknown. We did it everywhere, in every imaginable position. Oral sex, gentle sex, harsh sex. Hammocks, floors, bathtubs! And I loved all of it. The kissing and touching and sucking and fucking, and I never demanded anything, and I did everything, and I was lost in a decade of dope and sticky bed sheets for hours at a time. And the person I was then really did love it and walked around with a buzz in her crotch for any guy who'd play games with her. Fingerfucking was only something you did on the way to losing your virginity. It wasn't the prize at the end of the day. What I want now is the good old-fashioned lying in the back seat of his parents' car, crotches touching, hands everywhere soft and stroking, and just learning how to touch and please. All that adolescence, innocence, and steamy windows: I don't want to grow old. I don't want to die.

Did you have orgies in the sixties? Or were you just getting paid to hear about the orgies? Why do I even bother to ask you questions? You never answer me. You know sometimes I hate you. 'Cause I'm having problems with my fantasies and you have such a store of other people's, you could so easily point me in the most satisfying and orgasmic way with some of those stories, and you don't. I must be a masochist, continuing to come here.

Okay, so I have to accept the present and stop living in the past. I'm almost fifty, divorced with three grown-up kids, and I can't stop the aging process. You've told me that. That's the one thing you have actually said. Words do flow from your mouth. What you haven't said is that I'm also sagging, have crow's feet around my eyes, look haggard, and probably should consider hormone replacement therapy.

I know. I'm not that girl anymore. I'm a woman now with different needs and wants and not very generous and not very caring and sharing and certainly not a child of the sixties any more. I'm divorced, bitter, distanced from and jealous of my spring-chicken kids, unable to talk to my friends, and I want to have a sweep-me-off-my-feet-affair. But I don't want to give. I'm a "gimme girl" of the eighties—gimme this, gimme that! And now it's the nineties, and I want to be satisfied. I mean really satisfied. You know what I mean. I-don't-want-it-to-end-satisfaction! Is that so terrible?

I'm so useless I can't even masturbate. I've tried, but the rhythm isn't right. I just can't seem to get the right mixture of fantasy, motion, stroking, and wetness. It all gets so dry and useless. And anyway I don't want to do the work. I want it done to me.

Before getting on the bus today I walked past the sex shops in Soho and saw all these gadgets for "quick, self-contained, easy, safe sex." How do people use them? And how could they possibly be any better than human flesh—even my own? Nope. I can't use gadgets. I want flesh. Masturbation isn't really for

me, anyway. Are you a wanker? Do you do it? Do you rub
your penis hard and rough until it explodes? Or do you do it
softly and let it all dribble out? Do you wipe it right up with a
wad of Kleenex? Or do you not do it 'cause you think it's all
too sticky and smelly and you don't want to deal with it. And,
in your secret mind, do you call it juice, or cum, or spermato-
zoa? Well, what do you call it? You're squirming again. Who's
weirder? Me talking like this and paying you, or you getting
paid to listen to it all?

Sometimes I think about the guy across the street. And I
can see myself lying naked with him. But these thoughts are
sterile: they get me nowhere. I can't see him sticking his penis
in me or getting sweaty. He's got the kind of skin that doesn't
sweat. It probably doesn't even tingle. As usual, I've probably
picked the wrong man for a fantasy. We are always lying naked
side by side in the grass behind a bush. There is no moaning or
grunting, just soft stroking and lots of deep kisses with some
spit dribbling out—okay—so the kisses get a bit too wet! He
plays genteelly with my breasts, and I seem to spend most of
my time with my eyelids half closed in a state of ecstasy. But it
isn't real. And anyway I don't really have such excitable nipples. My husband used to talk about an old girlfriend who had
whistling tits. He'd only to look at them, and they'd stand up
and whistle "God Save the Queen." Mine just sort of roll back
along my middle-aged flabby sides and wait for my crotch to
wake up and sing an Otis Redding song. This guy—he's got
nice hands. Not great hands, but okay hands. I think if they
were just a bit better, I'd be more satisfied with my neighborly
fantasies.

Really, this analysis isn't getting anywhere. I share my sexual fantasies with you, and you sit there saying "ah, ah, ah ha."
I don't get any satisfaction, and I don't think you do. Although
I must admit I can't see your hands, and they could be working
away, jerking off left, right, and center. If that's true, then I'm
paying you to jerk off. Seems a bit unbalanced. Don't you
think? You know, if I had an affair, I bet I'd stop coming here.

Right now I know what I want, and I know how it should
feel. Do you want to know? Don't really have any choice. Got

to listen, don't you? I don't really want any more kisses and stale breath and too-hard hugs and big fat penises pushing their way inside me. A finger—the middle one with short fingernails—must run ticklingly down my naked side and around my armpits over and over and just brush the edge of my crotch and occasionally almost by accident stray into my pubic hair and then immediately move off and start again. This has to happen for about five minutes, and each time the accidental brush with the pubic hair lasts two seconds more. Over and over this occurs until the side and the armpits are forgotten and only my crotch starts to move on its own. It takes off from the rest of my body and arches, strays, and moans with each soft stroke of this one finger. Sometimes this finger actually moves in and out of me and circles my ass, but mostly it just strokes—not rubs. I keep whispering to this finger "Don't stop, don't stop." I just want this finger to go on and on forever. No rough stuff. No heavy-handed movements, pushing or throbbing stuff. Funny that. You men all think and talk about throbbing, pushing, explosions—none of that interests me. I just want softness and tenderness and an unconnectedness. You probably underrate the mouth also. I want to lie back and kiss for hours.

I don't really want to be a part of the action. I want it done to me, and I want others—the unknown others—to watch. You know, even when I talk to you and I try to shake you out of that stupor you inhabit, I talk about throbbing and juicy and use words like "cunt" and "penis." But that isn't really what I'm thinking. I don't think you could ever really know what I'm feeling when I see myself, our mouths, and this finger in a soft gray-lit room with shadows dancing outside the windows. Nope. You and I, man and woman, inhabit two different sexual spaces. We need each other, but we can't really see into each other's ecstasies. How do you do it? Do you take my stories home at night? Does my rambling help you in bed?

Take these magic fingers I'm telling you about. Unfortunately, they have personalities attached to them, and sooner or later the finger is replaced by a word or a tongue or a penis, and the rhythm is interrupted and I lose it. Everything gets mundane. Stroke one, two, three. Lick one, two, three. Suck one, two, three. And, again. Repeat. As soon as the personalities enter the scene, I dry up and pleasure rapidly changes to boredom. I start to create shopping lists, listen to the radio, hear the voices next door. I don't want to give pleasure. I don't want someone sticking their tongues and penises in me. I just want to sail away on this wet island of a soft middle finger playing with my crotch.

I suppose even better than doing this with my neighbor is to do it with a stranger in a hotel in Manchester and have the bed next to an open window so that the people (whom I don't know) living across the way can actually see what is going on. Yeah! I would like to give them pleasure so they could watch us—without my knowing they are watching me—and they start doing it also. And after a few minutes this would spread up and down the street until every window is steamy and every woman is getting a tender middle finger stroking her crotch and every bed is wet with vaginal—I bet you don't like that word—drippings. And, even now, telling you about it, I feel this drop in my stomach and whimper in my throat, my eyelids drop, and my crotch does it own version of a banged funny bone jerk, and I want to have you come over here, from behind that goddamn fucking pretentious desk of yours, clip your fingernails, and take your beautifully manicured and buffed middle finger and start to get to work and earn your money.

AUTHOR'S NOTE

I always wanted to get a job as a window cleaner but am afraid of scaffolding, so I became an anthropologist: it's the same thing without the heights. I recently thought about becoming a marriage counselor but decided it was too restricting. So now I sit alone creating my own clients and their marital problems and trying to solve them. "Windows" is one chapter out of my first client's life. She is a fifty-year-old divorcee crying out for love. She can't accept her aging body, her divorce, and her need for sex.

THE MANGO TREE

❧❧❧❧❧❧❧

By Sabina Faye

Like other contributors to Slow Hand, *Sabina Faye uses geography as an aid to stimulation. Additionally, as anyone who has ever eaten a ripe mango knows, there are few experiences more deliciously sensuous. So, having let herself be initiated into one sort of tropical ritual, Faye's heroine is definitely ready for others. And, thanks to the author's lush imagery, this story of erotic adventure far from home could just as easily be termed armchair travel into the realm of the senses.*

Of all my senses, touch is the one that operates strongest; steering a course through my life from some deep primitive place and moving my hands to feel even before my brain registers sight. Nothing is real to me until I touch it. I choose my clothes by the feel against my skin. I recoil at nylon and have near orgasms over certain silks. At home I eat with my fingers, for nothing tastes the same off a fork—a utensil as thin and cold as its name. I think I was meant to live in caveman days, with my bed a pile of skins on rock, my feet bare to the ground, and a haunch of fire-roasted beast in my hand. I walk into a room and cannot settle anywhere until I have swept around touching each thing, the wood of the table, the fabric of the draperies. Art galleries make me nervous. Museums don't exist for me, with everything cased and distant.

But I was born in the waning 20th century, into a world of shrink-wrapped produce and climate control, in the most untouchable country on the planet, England. I came to Australia looking for wind. Free-falling into the far tropical north, I was not disapointed. I found a land where the air was plump and the ground vibrated under my feet; where it rained in heavy drops and the night sky stung my face, and there I found a man of the most incredible skin.

I cannot think of him even now without a shudder, without this sensation like butterflies in the back of my heart. I had never felt skin like this before. It was soft as a newborn's tongue, smooth as a pond. It was like chocolate and moss, violas and black ice. He was a dark-haired Swede and rarely wore more than shorts and a silver ring on one toe. Beyond that, if asked what he looked like exactly, I could not tell you, so lost was I in his pure glorious flesh. I could touch him anywhere, his arm, his foot, the back of his hand, and feel my juices start to flow. There was a current beneath the softness. I had never been so aroused by simple touch before.

I had come from England to work on a distant relative's boat, a job arranged in the proper British manner, through family connections, as a way to deal with an unruly daughter of nineteen who intended not to go on to a respectable university or at least secretarial school, but hitchhike to Istanbul or anywhere. But my family was burdened with the lingering bondage of a respectable name in society (although like most such families, an inversely respectable fortune), and it would have meant tiresome scandal. So it was decided that father's second cousin, from the seafaring side of the family (which now consisted mostly of shipping clerks), who skippered a charter yacht on the Coral Sea, should take me on as cook.

And that is how I came to be squeezing mangoes one Saturday in the farmer's market in Cairns. It was my first attempt at provisioning the boat, and I had already finished with the

ordinary. Bags of potatoes, onions, cabbages, carrots sat waiting, but now I was lost in the fruit. I had never seen half the
fruits offered here, not personally I mean, and I was a little
delirious with the smell and feel of them. There were whole
pineapples, with their tantalizing patterns of prickles. There
were hard hairy coconuts and furry kiwi fruit. There were
papayas, one cut open on each stack to show the fleshy orange-
pink inside.

I picked up a mango. It was a soft heavy weight, the skin
like glove leather, mostly green with a deep scarlet blush on
one end. I turned it over a few times.

"What is this?" I asked the woman behind the stall.

"What IS it?" She squinted at me and stepped a little closer
as if looking for signs of antennae or something. "It's a mango.
You never seen a mango, luv?"

I shook my head. "What's it taste like?"

She shrugged. "Like a mango! Tastes like a mango." She
laughed and picked one off the stack, stabbed a side tooth
through the skin and peeled it back, exposing a bright orange
pulp. "G'wan, try it," she nodded toward the mango in my
hand. "Y're a pom, eh?"

I had only been in Australia three days, I didn't know what
a pom was, but she looked friendly enough that it couldn't have
been too insulting, so I nodded. I brought the mango up to my
mouth when I felt a touch on my arm. "Not that end," a man's
voice said. But I hardly heard him because I was immediately
taken by his touch. It was the softest touch, as if a small bird
had brushed its chest against my wrist. I turned and saw the
man who belonged to the touch.

"This way," he said, and I felt his fingers curve around
mine as he turned the mango in my hand. The softness of the
two skins around my hand sent my poor brain spinning.

"The tree sap drips down on the stem end and stays on the
skin," he told me. "If you bite the wrong end it can make your
lips swell and sting." As he withdrew his hand my fingers
clutched harder around the fruit, and as I punctured the skin
with my tooth, warm sweet juice squirted out and ran down my
chin. The man laughed as drops of it landed on his chest. I

reached instinctively to wipe it off and had my first real touch of Deyan's skin. It was hot but dry, smooth as the moon, like suede and caramels. He did not move away but looked at my bold palm on his chest, then I noticed my hand was covered with sticky juice and pulled it back.

"They say the best way is just to take off your clothes and eat them in the bathtub." His voice was also rich, deep, and melodic. "Come on, there's a tap over here." He led me through the stalls to a faucet on the outside of the building, and we rinsed our hands. He took off his shirt, which, in the manner of most men in this tropical place, was light cotton and hung unbuttoned, soaked it under the tap, rang it out, and put it back on.

I am not usually struck dumb with men or anybody else, but I was having trouble getting any words out through the sensory storm in my brain. All I wanted was to touch him again, to stroke that flesh, to rub my face against that skin, to lick it, touch it, anywhere. I had never felt skin like this. Out there in the light I could see that he was older, in his thirties at least. He was slim and muscular, of average height, or maybe even less, but he had a smooth tall way of moving.

The sun was hot, shimmering through the dust of the parking lot as we sat on some milk crates and I finished the mango, leaning over to let the juice fall. We had told our names, but little else when my cousin pulled up in the truck to load the groceries.

It was a long week at sea as I learned to cook in the tiny galley, handle the sails, and chat with the guests. I swam every day in the clear tropical sea. The water was so salty I could float effortlessly, feeling the warm sun on my face and the soft water lapping against my skin, and remembering Deyan's skin. I thought of him often, gently rocking on the boat at night, or feeling the warm sun on my body. One night I sat alone on deck, eating a mango, the sweet juice dripping on my leg. I thought about what he had said, about eating the fruit naked in the bathtub. I sucked one finger clean and wiped the juice off my thigh. What did his thighs feel like?

The night breeze was cool, and I lay back and spread my

legs a little, lightly stroking the soft skin between my own thighs, slowly easing my fingers up under the shorts to stroke my softest place, as the memory of Deyan's skin grew too overwhelming.

As we sailed into view of the harbor at the end of the week, I stood at the bow of the yacht and felt the warm breeze on my face. It was soft and all-surrounding, soft as Deyan's skin. A shudder of anticipation rippled down my back. I had two days off, and I would die if I did not feel him. I did not know where he lived, except on the beach north of Cairns.

I walked down the esplanade, wearing only a cotton sarong with no underwear, licking an ice cream cone—another supreme sensory pleasure. Pelicans glided in low over the mud flats as the clouds edged with the first gilt of sunset. After a week at sea I loved the feel of solid ground and cool grass, the strange buzz in my head from the windless silence—these were land pleasures.

It was late spring and the frangipani bushes along the esplanade were in full bloom, the air heavy with the scent. I sat on a bench, spread my legs a little to cool myself off, closed my eyes, and smelled. It was a unique smell, sweet but urgent, like the perfume on a gown, discarded but still warm. The ice cream was cool, and I licked it as slowly as I could, boldly imagining it was not a double scoop of strawberry but the velvet skin of Deyan's cock I was wrapping my tongue around. I was jolted from thought as a brilliant storm of lorikeets rose up from the trees, chattering and shrieking.

I opened my eyes and there he was.

"Miss Mango. I saw your boat come in," Deyan said, a hint of amusement on his face at my posture. He sat down next to me, some inches away where I could barely feel the heat of his body.

"How was it? Did you get seasick?" He still had a slight Swedish accent, and a deep rich voice. The voice matched the skin, resonant, like a drum.

"No," I laughed. "Just lonely." We sat in a comfortable silence for a while. A dog left its jogger and ran up to our bench for a petting. Our hands rummaged his ears and each other.

Our legs were touching with the movement. When the dog bounded off again, Deyan made no move away, but the thin cotton of my sarong was still a maddening separation. He asked me about the trip, and I learned he was a biologist working mostly up north in the rain forest. He had to come to town today to mail off some spore samples.

"Is a rain forest the same as a jungle?" I wondered. "I mean people are always talking about the *rain forest* now, whatever happened to jungles?"

Deyan considered the question. "I think you need wild animals to be a jungle. A tiger at least, maybe a few gorillas."

"I'd like to see one."

"Which?" He smiled. "Tiger or gorilla?"

"All of them."

"I'll take you if you like," he promptly offered. I made a mental note of thanks to all those teen advice columnists who were always telling me to find out his interests. Although I actually had always wanted to see a jungle.

"Are you staying on the boat?" he asked casually. "Do you have to watch it or something?"

"I was going to, but I don't have to." A mosquito bit my knee, and I pulled the cloth up to scratch it. Why didn't I think of that before! Now I could enjoy the velvet of his knee against mine. "It's locked up." I felt a twitch in my groin. I could feel my wetness soaking through the sarong.

"I'm having a few friends over to the house for a barby if you'd like to come out." It was an easy invitation with none of the bumbling I was used to from younger men. "I could bring you back if you need to," he continued. "But there's lots of extra room to sleep if you want. And we could go up to the forest tomorrow. It's best to go in the early morning before it gets too hot."

It was already too hot as far as I was concerned. Wild animals aside—it was *jungle* drums I was feeling now.

Deyan drove with his legs apart. Everything about him seemed completely relaxed, but I knew it was a coiled repose. We turned onto the highway to Macon's beach. Deyan settled in the seat and stretched his head back, told me of an octopus he had found near Fitzroy Island that week. During the tourist season he picked up extra cash by leading nature trips for the resorts.

"They change colors so fast, you know. When everybody starts crowding in to look, it gets very excited and goes from pink to dark red, a brownish red." As I listened I wondered what colors we would be if our skin reacted to emotion like an octopus.

The beach house was a cool retreat; a small frame house right by the breakwater thickly shaded by ancient mango trees. Inside the house was sparse and clean with shabby comfortable furniture and lots of plants. There were stacks of books, mostly on plants and bugs, and underwater color photos on the walls.

"That's a clownfish," Deyan answered my thought as he came up behind me and handed me a glass of wine. "They live in those anemones."

"It looks like it would feel nice," I mused aloud as I looked at the wavy arms of the anemone.

"Only to the clownfish," he explained. "Everything else gets stung." As I took the glass I noticed a large branching scar on the inside of his elbow. Instinctively I reached to touch it.

"It's a jellyfish sting," Deyan said.

"Nasty." My hand lingered on his arm, drew back slowly, my fingers hungry for the touch. The hair on his arm was silky and fine. As I reached his palm he caught my hand and pulled me toward him. We kissed suddenly and deeply, and I could feel the bulge in his shorts pressed against my easily accessible sex. I think he knew there was nothing under the thin cloth. I ran my hand up under his shirt, drinking in the feel of him. That skin, soft as a butterfly's breath, smooth as port and twice as intoxicating; I could drown in this skin. I would gladly die tomorrow if my shroud would be so soft and warm.

I bent a little and began to kiss whatever skin I could reach. I ran my tongue around the little indentation where the collarbones meet. I felt his hands exploring my body, one finger exploring the rolled waistband of the sarong. Then a car turned into the driveway, and two guys appeared on the front porch with a case of beer and the party was under way.

The night turned into a swirl of people and music, cold margaritas and hot coals. Our eyes would meet, or he would come to me as I sat talking with his friends and put a casual hand on my back for a moment. We touched at the sink, or passing in the crowded doorway, accidental but prolonged. There were other women there with obvious interest in Deyan, but I didn't care, except that I wanted to touch him so badly. I was after his skin, not his fidelity. I was nineteen, loose in a new hemisphere, breathing the tropical night.

Soon the party would be over, soon they would all leave, and we could slip into the little bedroom, with its soft cotton sheets and louvered windows open to the sea. But at 1:00 A.M. everyone was still going strong, and I was about to collapse. I had been up since four that morning and had had plenty of margaritas. Somewhere around two, I fell asleep on a comfortable saggy couch on the back porch.

I dreamed I was diving under the water through a forest of soft anemones. I felt soft caresses. I opened my eyes and found Deyan stroking my arm.

"Do you still want to go?" he whispered, his hand still resting on my arm. I was wide awake at once. I could see a faint band of red over the sea where the sun was about to rise. We crept over other sleeping bodies, out the back door to his truck. By the time we got to the forest the sun was just starting to break through the canopy, but already the ground was steaming with heat. We walked for an hour, stopping often so Deyan could show me something. I felt delirious. So much texture! The fat-leaved plants, the mossy tree trunks, smooth shelf fungi, even the air felt unique, damp but sort of sparkly.

The trail was narrow and became more and more overgrown the higher we climbed. Suddenly my leg began to sting. I thought it was an insect bite and scratched it. A few more steps, and the pain spread and grew more intense. It was an odd terrible sting that hurt worse than it looked like it ought to. The skin turned splotchy red, and Deyan bent to look.

"You hit a stinging tree," he explained. "It must have been tiny, I've been looking out for them." It was a crazifying sting, a fierce irrational pain that made me want to stamp and cry. "It's like a stinging nettle," he went on. "But about a hundred times worse. Plus it will last a long time and hurt every time you get it wet."

"Great," I tried to be noble.

"There's another plant that will help if I can find it," he said. "Wait here."

As he rustled in the bushes I stayed on the narrow path, still amazed at the amount of pain from the sting. I could see him in the woods, his body bronzed and shiny against the sharp rays of morning sun. He was silent and engrossed with the search, moving unafraid in the thick underbrush. I was still a little shy of these woods; besides stinging trees there were deadly spiders and poisonous serpents.

But Deyan was at home here. He searched farther in. His bare shoulders glowed in the filtered light, and suddenly I had to touch him. I picked my way to his side, and rested my hand on his bare back. I felt new blood surging through my body. I stroked him lightly, with some fascinated fear, as a child might stroke a beautiful snake for the first time. He was bending to look at a plant that grew by a fallen tree. There was a huge wild frangipani bush between us, and as he turned to show me the plant his body stirred the branches.

They were still wet with dew, and the odor burst up like a cloud. Suddenly we were in a wave of perfume. "Oh, smell …," I cried and forgot the pain of the sting as the fragrance rushed in a cloud around us.

"Ummmm …" He closed his eyes and drank the scent. I also liked Deyan because he didn't talk much in the forest. He stepped around the bush and showed me the plant so I might recognize it again if I ever needed it.

"Nothing really cures the sting," he informed me as he pulled the leaves off and began to crush them in the palm of his hand. "But this will help a little."

He squatted down and began to rub the juice on my leg. The friction made it hurt worse at first, and I bent toward the frangipani for distraction, running my hands through the blooms. The dewy blossoms cooled my skin as the juice began to work. It was cool and tingly. Deyan's hands were warm, the palms calloused, the only interruption in that velvet skin.

Glancing down I saw his thigh muscles strong and steady as he squatted on the jungle floor, the skin brown and shiny with sweat. Our eyes met for a second, and then Deyan leaned forward and licked the back of my knee.

I shifted my feet a little, spreading my legs. The sting was on one ankle but his hands caressed both, then began to rub higher. I shivered as the sap cooled the inside of my thighs. Deyan stood slowly, sliding his hands up along my legs.

He leaned against me slightly and kissed the side of my neck. Then he caught me with one hand around the waist and began to play the other around the inside of my leg. My knees felt suddenly weak, and I stumbled a half-step into the frangipani bush. Overbloomed petals shook loose and stuck to my skin. I felt Deyan's hand firm on my hip, and he steadied me. I felt the lightest touch then as he reached smooth fingers up between me and began to stroke the sensitive skin there.

Deyan bent his knees slightly so I felt his thighs firm against my own, and rubbed himself like a cat against me from behind. I could feel him, aroused and hard, rubbing slowly against my ass.

We stood there in the heavy silence, rubbing luxuriously like bears. The sun grew hotter, and the thick forest was gray with haze. Deyan ran his hands up inside my wet garment. I leaned into him, reaching my arms over my head to touch the soft skin on the back of his neck.

Moleskin, silk, marble, honey, wind in the palm trees, cello concertos; I stroked his skin. I felt him peel off his shorts, then felt his legs pressing between my own, easing them farther apart, as he pushed me toward the fallen tree.

The trunk was covered with moss, soft against my breasts, almost tickling, until he pushed me harder down against the tree, the weight of his chest pinning me. The frangipani bush was half crushed beneath me.

The light cloth fell away, and I was naked in the rain forest. Deyan ran his hands down my body, digging his fingers into my ribs, pushing me almost harshly in the moss.

I felt his hard curved cock against my swollen sex, the tip probing up and down, ready but still teasing. I was going crazy, not wanting it to ever stop but hungry to feel him inside me.

He leaned back, slipped one hand around the front of my waist, down between my naked belly and the mossy tree trunk and found my hot wet pussy. He probed between the swollen lips, caressed the most sensitive spot between two fingers. I pushed off the tree trunk, crazed with the stimulation but not wanting to climax this way. His hands were great, but I liked to feel a hard cock deep inside — that full, steely pressure.

I tried to turn but he stopped me. He held his hand there, cupped around my sex but barely touching, leaving me on the very edge of orgasm. Then suddenly he turned me around, boosting me and leaning me back so I lay across the huge trunk. I was startled by his strength, and by this new roughness. He moved closer, and I could feel his cock huge and hard against me, like a mahogany log, sliding down the juicy slope. My ache spread like thunder across the plains.

My body began to tremble. I felt the blunt weight of his teeth against my neck, then finally, the tip of his cock slowly probing, slipping just an inch inside me. I groaned and raised up higher to swallow him deeper, but he held back, teasing. It seemed like forever, Deyan sliding, probing, just barely entering, as he continued to play with my clit until I couldn't hold back. Then suddenly I felt his legs tense, and he slammed in all the way. He thrust so deep, so fast, that marvelous curved rod churning into me, his hands pressing down on my arms, pinning me to the tree as he began to thrust. I felt a convulsive orgasm sweep through my body.

I was so wet I could hear him moving, and with every stroke another quiver stabbed through me. He came seconds after I did. Deyan's sounds were small, a catch far down in his throat, a small note on the breath, animal noises. I could feel each pulse as he came inside me.

We slipped together to the forest floor, drowning in the new scents — the smell of the moss and the jungle and our own juices, the ashy smells of sex clinging low around us, pressed down by the rising heat. He wrapped both arms around my waist, catching the frangipani branches, pressing the twigs into my skin.

The silence of morning had vanished, and the forest was full of soft twittering bird noise. Deyan pulled me gently off the tree trunk and brushed the moss and broken leaf bits from my skin. I thought he might speak and so kissed him. His bronzed body was covered with the pale petals, and I brushed them away, just wanting to touch that skin.

"Let me go—," I whispered. "—I have to feel you."

He looked puzzled, but leaned back and let me feel him. It was an intoxicating greedy touch, as I felt every inch of skin on his body, carefully, completely. We sat there until we had strength enough to walk, then slowly, we started back down the trail.

My season at sea passed too quickly. Cyclone season came, and the boats were put to harbor. What I remember of the water is the silken ripples over the coral, the warm straight rain of a passing storm. What I remember of the boat is the feel of the sailcloth and ropes, the sun-warmed deck, the smooth varnished helm. And what I remember between voyages are the nights with Deyan.

I was drunk on his skin. Lying next to him I grew dense with desire, reeling with the fascination of touch as if it were a new sense, an accidental gift from the gods, a momentary secret that would be snatched away when they discovered it missing.

We made love in the wooden house, with ripe mangoes falling on the roof and Deyan's small black cat walking soft-pawed across our bodies, as we lay exhausted in the dark, sweaty, but still touching.

Touching somewhere, even just fingertips, with the waves washing over the breakwater just outside and the night wind blowing in cool off the sea. Moonlight bounced off the water, slipped between the louvers, and sparkled on his skin.

It was a suspended, flooded feeling; like morning in the jungle as the sun first penetrates the canopy and steams away the night. On the forest floor, in that pocket of heat, everything seems halted, swollen, and ready to burst. Fat-leaved plants give off their must, and the ferns tremble. The rising heat has a noise—a huge soft invisible noise.

AUTHOR'S NOTE

I discovered erotic literature in my Catholic high school English class (probably unbeknownst to the nuns) in Keats's wonderful poem, "The Eve of St. Agnes." It is a delicious story of dreaming, longing, and awakening desire. Although the closest the two lovers get to physical contact is a little hot breath on her ear, the erotic images are overwhelming.

> Anon his heart revives: her vespers done,
> Of all its wreathed pearls her hair she frees:
> Unclasps her warmed jewels one by one;
> Loosens her fragrant bodice; by degrees
> Her rich attire creeps rustling to her knees.

Eroticism, I believe, is about imagination and the power of creativity. Sadly, for many people, imagination in general is quashed early, and sexual imagination is never even allowed to blossom. Creativity, though, is the one growing thing that does not benefit from pruning.

We are sensual creatures from birth. Eroticism is just an expression, a magnification of our senses. Fantasies enhance reality by making us more alive, more creative. At five we were allowed to have imaginary friends—why, at thirty-five, can we not have imaginary lovers?

Having said all this, however, I must confess that this story is less fantasy than most of my work. I did, in fact, once have such a lover, a dark-haired Swede with skin like velvet. Even today, when I think about touching him, I get a deep hollow pain, like a drop of water had just fallen in the cave of my heart. But that was years ago and a hemisphere away. I do not long for him, I cannot really remember much about him. Instead, I have taken one small bit of reality—a man with delicious skin— and explored the sensual fantasies made possible by the creative power of my own imagination.

EROS IN OVERTIME

❧❧❧❧❧❧❧

By Kay Kemp

*There really do seem to be two distinct strains that run through
any group of erotic stories, that play off either the warmth of
the familiar or the heat of the strange. But what happens, asks
Kay Kemp, when the familiar* becomes *the strange? "Eros in
Overtime" is a marvelous title for the portrayal of an all-too
real, all-too poignant situation, when two people make love in a
time warp of their own devising.*

SHE

He parks in front of the fire hydrant to prove he won't stay.
She waves through the window. She offered him the
driveway, but when she sees the red of his eyes as he rounds
the front fender, she shrugs, as you wish.

Eleven years they were together; in three cities, four houses
they tamed, or tried to, two children. Roughly forty thousand
nights (she counted). Countless fights. Now it's finished. Bliss-
fully, terrifyingly over. The lawyers are poised for their take.
But first, tonight. It seems an opportunity, a rarity. A night outside of regular life; between lives, they could be strangers on a
train.

The long loose arms, the rangy body cross the doorframe. It's as if he is a transparency; the corner is visible through him, their house. His body is different now, separate. He seems so big. Once that large animal was alert to her every move, attuned to her smaller tension. Now he is bones on hinges, a puppet without strings. A husband, once removed. Her life, the visible part, the part she could cut off.

That's what I married, she thinks, objective to the last. I just wanted to tell you, she says. I loved you.

I can't take this up and down, he says. I can't bounce back like this. Head in hands, he is crying. She watches in awe. That was her territory, the tears. She heaved and sobbed; he went grim, like a killer.

Maybe it's not a bounce, she says, maybe it's a corner. I saw what was ahead, and I don't want to go that way. Not yet.

CHORUS

For a while they sit like that, him across the room. The pained silences of all their years gather and swell the room, threaten to crush them against opposite walls. It's like some organ, dwelling there in the marital house, inflated, throbbing. What a clamor. The cruelties uttered, the dumb competing.

They sit and peer at each other over all this. It is where they sat before, dumb kids at thirty. They bought the house while the market was going up. It had thirteen rental rooms and a lock on every door. They worked so hard, the woodwork shines now, the floors are sanded. They dug holes in the doors to take out the locks, then mended them so you can hardly see. But something ugly got in anyway.

Oh sure, there were times. She had sat in that rocker so pregnant and he at her feet, his head on her stomach, listening. They lay on that rug in front of that fire as the wind came down the chimney, and it was the best place in the world to be. But, overall, marriage was a poison they took in. They leaned together, faint with the dread chore of it, being all in all.

Now he sits across the room a free man, made strange by

that, and alive. The line of his cheek is leaner, he's suffered. That's attractive. Her feet are under her; she sinks into the couch. They talk of banalities, the same old story—work, money, time, lack of it.

Then.

I'm going to try to tell you how I feel, he says. She can feel the immensity, the effort, granite cracking. He finds a new language, a new place to speak from.

He is crying, between the words, getting maudlin, he says but doesn't stop.

She loves to see a man cry.

Now he is in her arms, the tattered male in all his glory. She grows moist, it's so good, the great cage of his ribs, the braid of sinews in his arms. She's pulled into a spell of his remembered scent (what is it? half-clean shirt—soap—sweat—some damp shade plant). The fine light scratch of evening whiskers on her neck.

Stay tonight, she says. I know you're tired. We don't have to make love, just sleep with me.

Oh we'd make love, he says in the conditional, if—he puts his hand on hers and guides it to his cock, obvious, ready, and strange. The part she knew so well, she thought she owned it.

Go out and move the car, she says. You can't leave it there overnight.

HE

He crosses the doorframe again, lopes down the lawn to the car, and starts it up. There's a ticket already on the windshield, forty dollars. Still smiling he hears on the radio in the ninth the Blue Jays' Alomar hits a solo homer on a 1–2 pitch to tie it up with the White Sox 2–2. This is happening in the thirty seconds it takes to put the car in the driveway. He cheers.

He's upstairs now in the bedroom, the one she walked out of a year ago telling him she had walked away from his bed for the very last time. He steps out of new clothes he's bought since. She's already under the sheets.

It's been so long since I've done this, he says, stay overnight
at somebody's house.

Your house, she says.

SHE

Those clothes were different, she had nothing to do with
them. But naked he is himself. They wrap together, such
hunger. He's thinner, a new hardness against his belly, and the
great hands cup the globes of her buttocks, cup and separate.
She's so wet, she drips over him, and can't wait.

You want it now, he says, so soon? His laughter against her
breast.

I want to wait 'cause it's better, but I can't, she says. She
twists away, and for a while they touch, nose, rub against each
other. The wanting is as big now as the pain before. She guides
the warm missile out of its fur and over her skin, feeling the
purplish velvet, sucking water from his pores. His hands
become fingers, probes, and openers.

CHORUS

Everything comes back now, even this. He fills her like
silence fills daydreams, like water fills a straw, flattens and lifts
her like a drenching rain. All the points where they met before,
nipple and neck, hip hollow and thigh, they meet again.
Reclaiming him reclaiming her. He lifts his head, mouth like a
bird's, to catch her hanging nipple, and the sweet surge goes
straight down her belly; he connects her poles, now the two of
them make the circuit complete.

Slower now, they breathe together, steadily rocking and
holding. It is new and remembered, all at once. The very best.
She notes a slight change in the way he rolls, a new use of the
side of his arm, a compensation, a trick, if you like. The gesture
is slight but warns her. Then another. He asks her to get on her
knees to crouch a new way. He's been with someone else, she
thinks. It only takes a one-minute alteration in their precise rit-
ualized passion, and all becomes clear.

If I know it, do you know it too? If you show it, do I show it too, in my dance, my newly revitalized waltz, my jive? An inspired turn: we have each tried someone else. And no, we did not want them. The words are never said, in this instant it is forgiven, even relished.

There is that moment, halfway along, when she starts talking. It's always like that. She bleeds words, crazy, ridiculous words, ones that don't bear repeating: help me take me hurt me, stop, don't stop, fuck, cunt, and more so. But that ends before long, and his animal sounds take over. Nothing but growls now, and heaves and grunting.

Here is some moment of truth. Freed from speech now another lexicon takes over her head. Fasten to me all your loving now, that once I unbuckled, in such grief and rage.

It is for this they had each other.

The rest was extra, in the way. All that depended on this one act they have shucked off. It stands by now, alert, an audience: the last dozen years, the two children, the parents, the grandparents, the house, the bank accounts. Now all that will be divided, as they will be. But not yet. Tomorrow, each will take what is fair, what he brought, and go. It's only goods.

HE

Riches are in the meat of this nearness. He has found her now. It goes and goes, the desperate rocking, bone against bone. She becomes a vast hot channel split from the waist down, he pressing up between.

SHE

She calls out to him, every cell and pore, the old furry body, her brother, her old man, the one who seeded those children, the one who tasted her milk, who wished to nurse his children. Somewhere in all that she lost him, lost the man in him, the valued other.

CHORUS

Who's to sing the praise of this practiced love, this rewarmed corpse, who ever did? The woman novelists always cleaved desire and duty, made the passionate heroine accept the drowsy sputters of married sex. Who will discover it, claim it, the rich depth you can charge again and again with the booty of years?

In the morning the children try the bedroom door. What are you doing here, Daddy?

HE

It was only for last night.

CHORUS

The children bounce on the bed. Alomar tried it again in the eleventh, his third homer, tying the Jays up again with the Sox at 3–3. It was a form of heroism, but he couldn't do it alone. Sosa homered in the twelfth to make it White Sox 5, Blue Jays 3.

AUTHOR'S NOTE

I've always been in awe of prepositions. "Before," "after," "between", "behind": little words with huge power. They put us in the right place at the right time, or the wrong place at the wrong time—to be hit by a sniper's bullet, struck by lightning, miss the last boat. Fall in love.

I realize now that this preoccupation has the potential to turn me into an erotic writer. Placement and timing are what it's all about. This story takes something that is seldom written about—married sex—out of its place and time. Into the vacuum that is created rush memories and sensations, and the act of loving is recharged.

ANECDOTE
❧❧❧❧❧❧❧

By Catherine S.

Many of the women I know, if queried about the sexual fantasies their lovers or husbands have confided in them, would answer, I think, that men frequently dream of having two women available to them for an erotic interlude. But turn the tables and suggest back to them a single woman pleasured by a male pair, and some of these guys suddenly get a little huffy. Actually, of course, since any amorous combination offers the potential for considerable pleasure, it's going to be the one who crafts the scenario who gets to cast the supporting players. In this case: Catherine S.

I met Caldwell first. Not that it matters. Whichever one you met first, the other soon followed. They were a set, a unit. I have tried to remember what it was like, the brief time of knowing only Caldwell, of seeing him without expecting to see Mark nearby. I have no memory of it. But then, it truly was a brief time, perhaps two hours in all.

Caldwell had moved into the apartment below mine. We met on the fire escape, where he was trying to cook an entire chicken on a temperamental grill. He invited me to dinner when I lent him kosher salt for the rims of his margarita glasses. Mark came, too. Of course. This was how it had always been, and I quickly understood this was how it would continue to be. Caldwell and Mark. Mark and Caldwell. And me, Catherine. Sometimes. As long as I understood the rules.

They had been friends almost twenty years, since second grade. They did not remind me of other men I knew. They loved each other and were comfortable with this. If one went away for more than forty-eight hours, the other hugged him when he came back. Being with them was like being carried along by a warm breeze. I wanted to spend all my time with them. I wanted to be them.

Which one would I choose to be? Mark was tall and thin, with soft hands and the prettiest mouth. Words streamed out of that mouth, thousands of words about hundreds of things. Statistics carried out to inane conclusions. Ignominious deaths of famous people. Obscure laws and religious practices. State capitals. I called Mark when I wanted to be distracted or soothed. When I needed help with the crossword puzzle. Or when I wanted to lose control—drink too much, laugh too hard, drive too fast. I see him with a drink in his hand, his lanky height draped over a bar in some dive, making Caldwell and me laugh. I wanted to talk like Mark.

Words came easily to Caldwell, too, but so did work. He always had to be doing something. He could build a bicycle from components, tune up a car, get an eight-foot table into the trunk of a Toyota. He was broad-shouldered, with short, sturdy legs and bright eyes. I called him when things broke. I called him when I was restless. I called him to find out what had happened the night before. Caldwell was our collective memory, the one who filled in the blanks for Mark and me after a particularly hard night. Sometimes, he half carried me up the stairs to my apartment, putting me to bed. Mark trailed behind him, helpfully suggesting hangover cures.

They liked me because I shared their view that their friendship was their single best quality. I was an admirer, an audience. Unlike girlfriends, who came and went quickly, I didn't want to break them up, I wasn't enduring an evening with both in hopes of getting one. In fact, being with only one of them made me nervous and edgy. It seemed unnatural.

What I really wanted was their memories. To be in the team picture for the junior high school floor hockey team. To be there Halloween night in Madison, when they dressed as Marx and Engels, ate mushrooms, and got paranoid. To see the smoke the night they almost burned down their college apartment while trying to make a rack of lamb. Failing that, I wanted them to know me as well as they knew each other. One year passed, two years. I grew closer to them, true. But they grew closer still. It seemed I could not catch up.

It was spring, a time of heavy, drenching rains. My boss asked me to house-sit so he could go climb a mountain with some other executives. I liked the idea of living among fine things, even if they weren't mine, or to my taste. I liked the idea of being alone.

My boss lived in what had once been the guest house on a grand estate, in the rolling farm country north of the city. Developers had razed the main house and put a small subdivision on its site, leaving behind this shingled cottage in a grove of trees. Broken statues—one-armed Cupids, fawns with chipped ears, headless maidens—lined the rutted brick sidewalk that led through the trees. The house, mossy green with golden trim, was barely visible as you made your way up the path. The only sound was a small stream that ran behind the house. Polluted, my boss said, from the subdivision's runoff.

Inside, it was simple and spare, but not cold. Large, unshuttered windows stared back into the trees, leafy enough now to shut out the modern world just beyond the grove. It was a place of solid colors, inside and out: green trees, green chairs, blue sofa, red table, blue rugs, white crockery, cream walls. The effect was deliberate, I think, a way of forcing the eye to my boss's odd collections of things.

There were Mexican masks, for example. Not gourd masks, but larger, more delicate pieces, carved from soft wood. A woman's face peered anxiously from between butterfly's wings, caught at an awkward moment in her metamorphosis. A

mermaid stared stoically ahead as her tail—really a serpent—
swallowed her. A bird's face smiled with a woman's bow lips. A
jaguar had breasts and long, black hair, real hair, to judge by
the feel of it.

In the kitchen, bird cages and bird houses lined the walls
and counters. An egg had been placed in each. A Ukrainian
one in a pseudo-Victorian cage. A black glass egg in a cage
made of old coat hangers. A sugary diorama locked in a cage of
twigs. A real robin's egg in a house that was an exact replica of
the cottage. I was convinced there was yet another replica
within that bird house, and another within that, on and on to
infinity.

Finally, in every room, there were oil paintings, vivid can-
vases of women draped in veils, crouched behind walls, hidden
in courtyards, locked in towers. The women had purple faces,
red hands, green hair. It was unnerving, especially in the bedroom where there was no other color, just a white iron bed and
a white spread, and those women on every side of you.

I sat by the window in this lovely and disturbing place,
watching the rain come down, waiting. The idea of being alone
had been attractive. The practice was unbearable. I knew Caldwell and Mark would miss me eventually, would find me somehow. The odd little house would be my gift to them, one of my
ongoing bribes to keep in their good graces. Chocolates. Good
wine. My ears. My laugh, which is what they liked best,
spilling out at their weakest jokes and stories. I sipped brandy
and stared into the dense green leaves, casting a spell. I drew
them to me. It didn't take long. After all, I had left the directions on Caldwell's answering machine, along with promises of
expensive liquor and a large-screen TV set.

They were soaked to the skin by the time they found the
cottage's door. I watched them run up the curving path, laughing, in the middle of their never-ending conversation. Separated from them by the window, safe and dry within my cottage, I felt as if I were seeing them for the first time. Caldwell
and Mark. Mark and Caldwell. I couldn't imagine one without
the other, didn't want to. I wanted to be with them both, forever and ever. Even as I made my wish, I knew how impossible

it was. Others would claim us, one by one. Caldwell and Mark would manage to hold onto each other, I might manage to hold onto them. But it would not always be like this. Just the three of us. The perfect number in some ways.

I brought them coffee in white mugs, brandy in squat blue glasses. I brought them white towels for their hair, blue cotton blankets to wrap around their damp clothes. We sat cross-legged on the floor, wrapped in the blue and white light of an old-fashioned space heater. In front of us, the soundless television was turned to some out-of-town baseball game that no one cared about.

And, of course, we talked. They talked. Calculus class, in which Mark had cheated on the final and still flunked. Caldwell's chronic lateness, which kept them from a concert that turned into a riot. Trying to smoke. Learning to drink, a bad experience with Jack Daniels and orange juice that led straight to the emergency room. Story after story, joke after joke, with one constant. Caldwell and Mark. Mark and Caldwell. Caldwell's hands were like white lights rising and falling in the darkening room. Mark's stories ended with self-deprecating sighs, a cue for me to laugh, which I kept forgetting to do. I was too busy thinking of how they had looked, running up the path toward me, toward this house. Give me both of them, I asked the mermaid and the butterfly, the jaguar and the smiling bird. Just for now.

"The White Sox might actually amount to something this year," Caldwell said.

One man is easy, of course. We all know how to do one man—how to lean a little closer, how to touch a hand, or leave your fingers a moment too long on his arm. Every woman knows this. But if I touched one, the other would leave. Or perhaps, at best, wait and follow. That wasn't what I wanted. I thought of the bird house on the kitchen counter, the cottage within the cottage within the cottage.

Mark's voice now: "So this girl behind the counter, she repeats the order back very slowly, and gets everything wrong, absolutely everything ..."

I slid Caldwell's blanket from his shoulders, wrapped it

around myself, and laid down on the rug, as if I were going to sleep. They took no notice. So many times before, I had let their conversation be my lullaby, had faded away as they kept talking. Eyes shut, I listened to their voices—Caldwell's slow rumble, Mark's quicker, lighter rush of words. Beneath the blanket, I slipped off my clothes, touching myself. The wind moved in the trees outside, the rain-swollen stream rushed over the rocks, the purple-faced women whispered to me. They approved of me. I felt as if I were a solid color, too, as if my skin were changing from purple to blue to green to red to cream. I belonged in this house.

"No, what it said in the paper was that if the new law takes effect, it would be toothless, because there's absolutely no enforcement …"

I thought of how I had caught them, from time to time, appraising the curve of a hip or a thigh, judging the length of my neck. Men did this, of course, even with friends. Especially with friends. What is it like, Caldwell had asked me once, to be looked at when you walk down the street? It's like being a woman, I told him.

" … and she opened the car door, and there was this huge dog in there …"

Their voices now were indistinguishable. I couldn't make out words, or who was speaking. All I had was the sensation of warmth—from the space heater behind us, from the sounds moving between them. Their voices wrapped around me, familiar and beloved, endless and perfect. I didn't want them to stop. I took inventory of myself, noting how symmetrical the body was, how accommodating.

I sat up, the blanket falling to my waist. In the almost-dark room, my body absorbed all the light. It was shockingly white, the brightest thing in the room, I could no longer see their faces or their hands. And suddenly there was nothing to hear, except the rain, the wind, and the hiss of gas in the heater. They had stopped talking.

"Catherine—," Caldwell began, almost sorrowfully, as if I were drunk, as if he might have to carry me to bed as he had so many times before. He looked at me, looked away, looked at me again. He did not seem quite so sorrowful. Mark tried to pull the blanket back around my shoulders. But his hands kept shaking, and he gave up.

I wrapped my arms around myself, watching them watch me. The silence in the room was huge, deep, and wonderful. It was as if I were still watching them through a window, safe and dry, still waiting for them to find me. They still needed directions.

I kissed Caldwell, then Mark. Mark's kiss was as light as his voice, his pretty mouth worked well. Caldwell was earnest, as if he were trying out for something. I tasted brandy and amazement and something else. Competition, older than time, going all the way back to second grade. As I started kissing Caldwell again, Mark brought his arms around my hips and lifted me onto Caldwell's lap, so I was straddling him. Caldwell understood, began unzipping his jeans.

"It's okay," Mark said quietly to Caldwell, his hands cupping me, preparing to help me move up and down on Caldwell. He wanted Caldwell to go first, so he could best him, love me harder or longer. I knew this, somehow, and I knew I would not allow it.

Standing, I held a hand out to each of them and led them into the bedroom, into the center of the white-on-white bed. Stretched out between them, I undressed each of them, kissed each of them, held each of them. Naked, they were identical. They tasted the length of me, working from the ears to the shoulders, down to the breasts. But when their hands touched at the top of my thighs, they pulled away. They looked at me, almost angry, silently demanding I make it work, determined I make a choice.

Instead, I rolled toward Caldwell, fixing my mouth on his while reaching my arms back to Mark, opening myself to him. This was new to me, hot and tight. Mark stroked my belly and kissed my hair, reassuring us both, reassuring us all, even though he could barely move inside me. Caldwell's bright eyes shone brighter than ever. It was only when I brought him inside me that everything felt right, as if I were balanced between them.

They reached around me, holding on to each other's shoulders as if to steady themselves. Slowly, hesitantly, Mark started, gentle and easy within me, pushing in as far as he could, then pulling out again. Then Caldwell, picking up his rhythm exactly, did the same, stroking me gently and slowly, all the way in and out. Mark repeated himself. Caldwell answered back, deeper and more insistent, moving in as Mark moved out. They grew more sure of themselves, there was almost no lapse as they passed me back and forth. This, Mark seemed to say, pressing in until I cried out. No, this, Caldwell replied, thrusting deeper still. I could not tell them apart, could not tell us apart, could not separate one sensation from the other.

They quickened, as if they were arguing about something they cared about, became strident and passionate, their voices overlapping, interrupting. Yet the only sounds were the wind and the rain and the stream—and, for once, my voice, just my voice, until Mark groaned into my ear and Caldwell shouted into my breast, and one sensation ran through all of us and back again.

Silence. For a long time, no one moved and no one spoke. I had given them, given us, something new: a story we would never tell, not even to each other. We would leave the cottage and leave this behind, an intangible addition to my boss's collection of wild and beautiful things. Our best anecdote.

We fell asleep, still joined, but in sleep our bodies separated of their own accords. No longer entwined, we were too much for the bed. I ended up crawling away, making my bed on the pile of blankets we had left in the living room. In the morning, when I went to check on them, they were still asleep, clasping on another's hands, closer than ever. But this time, because of me.

AUTHOR'S NOTE

An old college friend gave me the basic elements of this story—two men, one woman, an isolated house. Everything else is invented. While I was writing it, I talked to my male friends, and they had little interest in such a combination. This attitude made me curious. I had to ask myself: how do you seduce two men simultaneously, instead of sequentially?

The traditional view of such situations is that they have to result in a choice—one lover over the other, or one before the other. Or neither. Or both, then suicide. Or murder. But given the right time and place, why shouldn't three people make love to one another? And why shouldn't they be two men and one woman?

I do find strong male friendships enormously sexy, all the more so because men ignore the sexual content of their friendships. Recently, one man was giving me a detailed description of going home to visit one of his closest friends.

"Landed at the airport, saw M., shook hands—," he began.

"Do you really shake hands when you see each other?" I asked.

"Well, we hugged," he admitted. "But I only do that with him."

TREATS

❧❧❧❧❧❧❧

By Rebecca Battle

In "Treats," Rebecca Battle takes a vivid, angry look at a sexually awakened teenager's unwillingness to play the demure role scripted for her by unseeing parents. As a narration, it reads like part-cinema verité, part-catharsis, and it seems to me calculated to remind us that in every household there are always several coexisting but very separate worlds.

It's always around midnight when you hear them doing it in the next room. You are usually into your second package of saltines by then, slopping on peanut butter and honey with reckless abandon. When you can't even force yourself to take another bite, your hunger—that other hunger—is finally, if temporarily, satiated.

You reach over to the bedside table, actually a light blue plastic crate with "Farmfresh" printed on the side, and push in the button to turn off the little black and white TV. The sounds from your parents' bedroom are much clearer now. With all the furtive whispers and frantic shuffling, they could be disposing of a body or hiding a stash of stolen money. But having discovered your father's dirty magazines some time ago, you know exactly what they are doing.

Pick up the sticky remains of your nighttime treat and walk toward the kitchen.

The hall is dark, and this makes you nervous, even though you are not alone in the house. It is midnight, the witching hour, and what good is your father or brother in the face of the evil that may be out there, that *must* be out there; otherwise why would you feel so unsafe? But it is a feeling you have gotten used to. Insecurity is the norm, and turning on a light would expose you. There is power in the dark and the quiet, as much as there is fear. You see others, but they do not see you.

It frees you to listen there by the door as your father and his wife stifle their moans. You stand on the balls of your feet, poised to dart into the kitchen if anyone should come out. You check for a light under the door of your brother's bedroom. Nothing. You turn back to the clandestine activity behind your parents' door, straining desperately for more sound, more stimulation. But usually the rustles and squeaks and murmurs are all you can grasp. Usually, they are enough. You feel the involuntary twitch between your legs, and the dull, low ache that begins in your crotch and twists a path into your gut.

Rush into the kitchen to hide the evidence of your binge. Quickly, so that you can get back to the cavern of your sheets and the treat waiting for you there. Once in bed, reach under the pillow and pull out the bottle of baby lotion. It is your teddy bear.

The lotion is cool as it touches your fingers, and you pause for a moment, anticipating the sensation when you reach between your legs. It is even colder there. It is wonderful. You spread it around eagerly between the folds of skin and over that one most sensitive spot. The clit, but you don't like calling it that. No, don't think. Right now, at long last, you don't have to think. Just let go, just imagine—*him.* Tall and athletic and a little dirty, always spitting tobacco juice by the side of the road at the bus stop. A hick, but they're all like that around here. What matters is that he pays attention to you. It makes going to school in this chicken farm, chicken shit county almost bearable. Just to greet him in the morning, perhaps bring him some cookies, have him sit with you at the back of the bus and reach up your skirt, between your knees.

Close your eyes and imagine him now, being with him in a way you have never been. Think what it would be like if he were swirling his tongue where his hand has been, and you clutching the sides of his head with your thighs, his shaggy brown hair wet against your skin. He is licking slowly from bottom to top, in long ice cream cone swipes. Your own tongue goes out to lick the air as you envision his, searching through every crevice. Your hand is his mouth, and then his lips, sucking around that unnamed spot, nibbling, seeking, devouring, around and around so warm and wet until you burst and writhe and whisper, almost too loud, "Fuck me! Yes, fuck me now!"

The distance from pleasure to pain is too short. First, the fear: that someone has heard your little outburst. Perhaps Lois, the stepmonster so adept at eavesdropping. Or worse, your father.

Then, the guilt. At having fantasized so recklessly. At not being normal. At not fitting in with anyone in this town. Your "new home," so they say, but really just another stop in a string of wanderings, of Dear-Old-Dad-Trying-to-Find-Himself-Wanderings. You don't know anyone, except your back of the bus buddy, and no one, especially not your parents, knows you. Knows what you do. The lotion and the food every night.

When did you learn to do this? A year ago? Two years? About when you learned to throw up. About when you learned to hate them.

It is a thrill to hide these treats. There they sit, in the very next room, as you sneak food from the kitchen to the bathroom, gorge on giant-sized Kit Kat bars or whatever it is, lean over the toilet, and then throw it all up. You know just when to flush so that it drowns out the sound as you gag on your own finger. Eating your cake but not having it.

You never know when you will get caught. When your father, grown sullen at the dinner table after too much to drink,

will say, "Come sit on my lap" in his all too friendly dirty old
man pathetic son of a bitch kind of way. And you will sit, to
avoid his anger. Then perhaps he will say, "I know what you've
been up to with the lotion." And he will look at you, rosy-eyed,
rosy-cheeked, with that mocking smile of his: "You know, the
Incas used to burn women at the stake who disgraced themselves that way." Or some other similar nonsense. But part of
you will believe it, or at least the implication that you are dirty
and deserving of a terrible death.

But you cannot give them up, your treats. They are the
only pleasure you know. They get you through these dinners,
for one thing, when you are forced to be with your father and
Lois. They get you through the exhaustion of pretending.

Sit up straight and wait for your father to take his first bite
before you begin. Then smell it and say, as genuinely as you
can, "Mmmmm."

Take a mouthful, and then another, as if you can't get
enough, and then: "Lois, this is really delicious."

"Well thanks. It's cassoulet, the national dish of France."

Your brother plays the game too: "What's this meat in
here? It's really good."

"That's goose."

"Mostly the gizzards," your father amends. He has decided
to take this opportunity to further your education. "This dish
originated with the French peasants. They couldn't afford to
waste, like some of us can" (a deliberate look to both kids), "so
they used every part of the bird. They ate the meat off, then
cooked the bones and the insides."

He takes another bite with hands made shaky from drink.
He is very self-conscious about it so you try not to stare. But it
is a natural attention grabber, the way he scoops up the beans
in the spoon and carries them painstakingly toward his mouth,
and all the while they are spilling back into the plate, so at the
end he must lurch forward to grasp the last few before they too
fall away.

He looks up, suddenly, as if he has caught everyone staring
at him. You purse your lips in expectation of his wrath. But he

says instead, "Lois and I have to go on a trip this weekend. Her father isn't feeling well, and we thought it best to look in on him. We figured it would be a drag" (he is always trying to use a "hip" expression for your benefit) "for you two, so if you promise to be good" (and here he looks at you and your brother both, one at a time, with a long meaningful glare) "then we'll let you take care of yourselves overnight."

Stay calm. Take care not to reveal your delight.

Smile and say okay, we'll be fine, I'm sorry for your father, Lois. Shall I clear the table now? Thanks again for dinner.

Go into the bathroom and vomit. It soothes your nerves, your excitement.

This is better than you ever hoped.

Finally! you think, as you flush the majestic national dish down the toilet.

You've got it all arranged. You will meet *him* at the end of the driveway the night your parents are gone. You will keep the porch light off so the neighbors don't see him and report back to your father. He may have asked them to spy. Your brother is going out at eight o'clock. He is planning to spend his night of freedom drinking Beam with his friends outside the Tastee Freeze. He is not so innocent either. You have agreed to stay home and cover the phone, among other things.

When you go to meet *him,* you are wearing your shortest dress, pantyhose, and heels. He knows what he is here for. Though you have not had the opportunity to take things further than the back of the bus, he has hinted from the beginning about his intentions. From the time when you first let him kiss you outside the rear exit door of the school. He had taken your breasts in his hands, as if it was the most natural thing in the world, as if they belonged to him. At first, you thought maybe you should object, but you didn't. You let him. You even let him reach down the front of your jeans as far as he could squeeze his fingers, where he took one slow circle with his hand and came up with a finger covered with wetness. You watched as he brought his hand up to his nostrils and breathed in, sniffing deeply and with relish.

He is older.

Now, as you approach him, walking carefully over the gravel, you hardly have time to make out his face in the dark before you feel his breath on your forehead, his hands clutching your buttocks, his penis thrusting out through the thin fabric of his shorts.

Make him wait. This is your night, your territory. You are not a woman, but for now you can pretend.

Take him by the zipper and lead him silently back into your bedroom. Make him stand apart from you, watching but not touching as you undress, staring him down with the bravado of a whore.

Make him get down on his knees and engulf your sex with his mouth.

Make him work hard, harder, not coming up for air. Keeping his head in place, forcing it to stay, both of you needing air, but holding on for more. This is so much more than you had imagined and almost too much all at once, so you push him away. He too seems a little off-balance. You stare at him shamelessly, there down between your legs, and you realize that maybe he hadn't done that before. That his finger smelling had been a bit of machismo which he wasn't planning to follow up on.

You have shaken him up.

You are the stronger one here.

Take his clothes off, slowly, so slowly, making him wait as you lightly brush each patch of skin with your lips. Stay a long time around his stomach, knowing he aches for you to go lower. You blow lightly on his penis, seeing it twitch uncontrollably in response.

The power.

Kneeling before him, you take him by the hips and spin him around, forcing him to his hands and knees. Before he can protest, you shove your tongue between his buttocks, all the way up, reaching for that bit of flesh behind the two sacs lying so helplessly there. That obscure, out of the way area you have seen in the pictures and have always been curious about.

Is he saying something now? It doesn't matter. Push him

down onto the bed and order him to wait there, on his back, as you walk slowly to the kitchen to retrieve the bottle of honey. There is something else you've always been curious about.

"What're you up to?" he asks, looking both a little afraid and a little thrilled.

You flip open the cap of the honey. It is a silly little plastic bottle shaped like a bear. You squeeze it hard, so the honey gushes out over his penis, onto his thighs, shining thick in the patches of hair. He has stopped questioning.

Keep his eyes locked to yours as you go down slowly, purposefully, and he groans in anticipation, much like the groans you have heard from that other room on so many nights.

You taste the slimy sweetness of the honey, and the salty flesh beneath. You grope messily around with your tongue, licking it all up. And suddenly you taste the rush of fluid escaping from him, along with his gasps. It comes half on your tongue and half on his stomach, swirling with the honey like saltwater taffy. You lick it up, all of it, with the ache between your legs growing more intense.

This you won't throw up. This is a treat all your own.

As you slurp the last of the liquid from his belly button, you reach behind and slap him hard, too hard, on the ass.

"Now," you say, "fuck me."

AUTHOR'S NOTE

There are few worlds as painful and isolated as that of adolescence. And many of us try to put it behind us as quickly as possible, by either forgetting or ignoring. However, sometimes such pain can be a springboard to anger, and anger, in turn, often fuels creativity and freedom. If it weren't for my own anger, I would not have been able to push past the inhibitions I continue to have about dealing so candidly with sexuality. As with the young girl in this story, it was anger that compelled me to decide for myself what I needed to say and, thus, to defy the image of a judgmental finger being wagged in my direction.

TOO TALL FOR GRACE

❧❧❧❧❧❧❧

By Susan J. Leonardi

"Too Tall for Grace" was the first story I accepted for Slow
Hand, *and, after you read it, it should be easy to understand
why it gave me an extra measure of confidence. Radiating
strength and careful originality, it is set in a community of
women whose everyday lives are spent in the sort of examination most of us prefer to avoid. The questions Susan Leonardi
raises are about love, about sexual desire, about body and
spirit, and she recognizes that in any human being conflict is
both natural and inevitable. Observing the serenity and the
pain inherent in difficult choices, Leonardi passes no judgment,
only showing us how lovers with different needs adjust to one
another, striving always to fine-tune their responses and
express their devotion.*

Karen had started to run on the day after the end of the
world. She ran even though only recently she had been
very ill, with a mysterious liver ailment, and almost died. She
ran even though she hadn't run since her last high school track
meet ten years before. She ran even though the mountain roads

knocked the breath out of her before she had gone a quarter of a mile. And she kept on running for five years, though not with the determination or desperation of the first day, the first week, the first month. She ran in the early seventies, before runners became (even in the mountains where you'd think just living would be exercise enough) familiar figures and before the books appeared telling you how to maximize your endorphin high and minimize the damage to your limbs. She ran until her right knee gave out, whether from the running itself or from what she heard as she ran by Lisa's open window, she didn't know.

What she did know was that half a mile into her run that day, her knee buckled and she fell. She limped home, cried — whether from the pain in her knee or from the pain of hearing what she heard as she ran by Lisa's open window, she wasn't sure, though she had a pretty good idea and she didn't like it — until her eyes were swollen shut. She was afraid to cry anymore, so she lay on her bed and willed away the pain so successfully that by morning she could walk without limping. The areas around the knee and around the heart, however, felt tenuous and sore, and her eyes were still swollen. The swelling was ugly and uncomfortable but hid the angry, disgusted, pleading looks she directed, against her will and better judgment, at Anne all through matins and lauds. She spent the afternoon alone, tending the flowers in the greenhouse, taking special care of the lavender roses, whose skins she touched, whose outer petals she blew gently, whose inner petals, though she could not see them, she sang to in a low quiet voice. Eventually she sang their favorites, "Lavender's Blue, Dilly, Dilly" and then "Purple People Eater" in reparation for the folksy laments she started with. They suited her mood but might, she feared, make the roses droop.

She skipped vespers and dinner again, telling herself aloud that she should lay off her knee as much as possible, not telling herself but knowing that she did not want to see Anne or Lisa. She wrapped the knee thickly in winter wools and wished she had hot water to soak it in. As she feared or as she hoped, Anne came knocking on her cabin door about seven. Karen didn't answer the first knock or the second. She knew Anne was there, of course; she knew Anne wouldn't come in unasked; she knew from the absence of footsteps that Anne was waiting and from the absence of any sound at all that Anne was waiting patiently, humbly, apologetically, wearily, and defiantly outside her door. She didn't get up from her reading chair ("I must stay off my knee," she said to herself by way of excuse) but called out, "Come in."

She hardened her heart when Anne hugged and held her. She said "What do you want?" When Anne didn't answer, she said, "Why, Anne, why?" and looked out the window so that she wouldn't cry again.

"Because I love her."

"You're infatuated with her."

"How do you know that"? Anne asked.

"Because she's not your type" was the first thing that Karen said, and then she said a lot of other things about Lisa — how loud she was, how obnoxious, how disruptive, how careless, how intrusive, how self-centered, how lacking in self-control, how immature, how ill-suited to life at Julian Pines — before she repeated the observation "She's not your type." Karen said all these things in a measured, calm voice, all the time looking out the window. She waited for Anne's explosion, hoped for it, longed for it in some part of herself (probably in the fat that lay around her left ventricle) she thought she had melted off running.

Anne reached her neck around Karen's face so that Karen had to look at her, but she didn't yell that it was none of her goddamn business and she didn't kick the desk and she didn't pound her fists on the wall, any or all of which Karen waited for, hoped for, longed for, expected. Instead she brushed her cheek against Karen's and so forced her to pull away for the second time. She said, "Who is my type, Karen? You?"

"Of course, me. Me. Me. I love you. I've loved you for seven years. I go out every day and run you off, and just when I think I might be getting somewhere, you pull this. My God, Anne, look what you've done to my knee."

✿ ✿ ✿

They talked late into the night, in and out of a circle the circumference of which was Anne's contention that they would be lovers still and always if Karen hadn't decided that their attachment was somehow inimical to the community life they were trying to lead and Karen's conviction that in spite of her unspeakable sorrow—it felt like the end of the world—Anne was, after all, right. Inside the circle was this new relationship which, Karen said, was equally inimical, which, Karen thought several times but only said once, was really much *more* inimical because Lisa was herself inimical to the whole spirit of Julian Pines Abbey, a place of silence, order, peace, prayer, and simple pleasures. Inside the circle, too, was Anne's desire for sex, which Anne wanted (but Karen didn't) to include among the simple pleasures, to make a congenial companion to or (when her argument became most intense and emphatic) a necessary component of silence, order, peace, and prayer. At that Karen snorted, but the conversation proceeded amicably and, it must be admitted, predictably, given the other conversations, theological, philosophical, literary, political, and psychological that Anne and Karen had had, usually late into the night, during those five years of daily runs. Conversations that were as often as not about lust, love, and community life.

Somewhere around 2:00 A.M. Anne advanced the theory (and Karen expressed skepticism of it, though later she began to think it had some merit) that the essence of life at Julian Pines, what made it different from other monasteries, what made it a place where women like she and Karen (and, yes, Lisa) could survive and flourish, was the blank pageness of it, the way you had to invent life every day and eschew the hierarchical assumption that peace is a higher good than passion or the clichéd assumption that peace and passion were mutually exclusive. Karen's refutation descended from these lofty heights to a more personal level at which point Anne accused her of seriously undervaluing Lisa, a brilliant and beautiful woman, and Karen charged Anne with so blatantly *over*valuing brilliance and beauty (Anne insisting here that "beautiful" referred not to any physical traits but to a wide spectrum of virtues) that they blinded her to the presence of serious defects.

Somewhere in the midst of all this heady (though Karen could feel it in her throbbing limb) talk, somewhere, that is, around three, came frantic knocking at the door, and, without waiting for Karen's response, Lisa threw the door open and stumbled in, face dirty and tearful, long hair wildly knotted, shoulders defeated, voice distraught. "Oh my God, Anne, where have you been? I'm a mess. I've looked everywhere. Do you have any idea what time it is? I was afraid you were lost in these fucking mountains." She took Anne in her arms. "Oh how could you do this to me? Anne, darling, what are you doing here in the middle of the night?" Karen, wondering at the extravagance of the drama, cynically admiring Lisa's convincing performance, and trying to figure out if Anne were so deeply deluded that she didn't detect the artifice, forbore repeating Lisa's question and said, quietly, calmly, as though soothing an overwrought child, "We were talking, Lisa, but we're finished now."

Anne looked a bit bewildered, from one woman to the other, then kissed Lisa on the cheek and said, "Go back home, dear one. I'm fine. Karen and I are talking, and we're *not* finished." This firmness reassured Karen that Anne smitten was still Anne, but she noted unhappily the longing in Anne's fingers as Lisa let go of them and left. "Quite a scene," Karen said.

"Did she ever tell you," Anne asked, "that her mother worked for the American Theatre Company?"

"No," Karen said, "she told me that her mother was a gypsy."

Although they talked until dawn, Karen didn't manage to convince Anne that Lisa's flamboyant immaturity was, in fact, flamboyant immaturity and hardly conducive to a decent, much less elevating, relationship. Nor did Anne manage to convince Karen that licking Lisa's labia did, in fact, contribute to her own growth, to the mission of the abbey community, to the spiritual renewal of the universe. Lisa left Julian Pines a month later that year (as Karen knew she would), wanting loudly and melodramatically to take Anne with her, but Anne, in spite of an anguish that she, too, expressed rather too vociferously for

Karen's taste, stayed and Karen's knee healed, slowly, over time. Although the conversations changed somewhat—Anne's rhetoric, for example, became a bit less grandiose, and Karen's dismissal of Anne's defense of lust and love a bit less adamant—they continued dense, long, loving, and repetitive. Karen had hopes, unspoken even to herself, that Anne would settle down, embrace celibacy, and cease in general to agitate quite so severely her, Karen's, life. Endorphin highs were nice, but running was dangerous.

The hopes persisted for years, seemed, in fact, fulfilled, until Teresa came. And then Karen let them go, because you couldn't make the same objections to Teresa that you made to Lisa. It was actually hard to make any objection at all except that she was sometimes vague and never raised her voice at the end of a question. She loved Teresa. Everyone loved Teresa. And Teresa's sexual relationship with Anne seemed so quiet, simple, and joyful that you almost, sometimes, might think that Anne was, at least partly, right about lust and love. You might even romanticize the relationship, you might say to yourself, well, Anne *has* settled down, to monogamy if not celibacy. Karen did all these things, and thought that she had finally come to terms with both the issues and personalities involved, when she, engaged one night with Anne in late talk and mutual comforting, felt desire, and Anne, too, wanted more than holding. And suddenly, though she walked away still longing, the hard edges of Karen's hardly won clarity blurred, and when that night she ran her hands down the inside of her thighs to stop the longing, she felt a certain blurriness there, too, and thought, for the first time in a long while, of running again.

By this time, though, Karen was the priest at Julian Pines (Beatrice had argued against using that word, so concretely did it conjure up a male human being, a hierarchy, a corrupt church, in the imaginations of all who heard it, but Anne had countered, cogently, most of them thought, and voted accordingly, that the very contrast between those expectations and the reality of *their* priest—a woman who conceived her priest part as just that, a part, no more or less important than other parts, she could play in the group—was itself salutary both for themselves and for their many visitors and correspondents) and spent the hours she wasn't painting and tending roses talking through troubles, fitting words to music and music to words, laying on hands. And in this way more time passed without Karen taking up again her weird and long-winded sport.

Late October in the Sierras can be starkly dry with pine needles and cones crunching underfoot, giving off the scent of mountain forest and holiday greens. Halloween day reached eighty-six degrees by midafternoon, was seventy at dusk, and plunged to forty by nine. As soon as it began to get dark, mountain friends brought children, theirs and neighbors', to the abbey's common house for tricks and treats. For treats, Jan made hot chocolate, Kathleen baked black-bottomed cupcakes, and Karen caramelized small apples from the orchard. For tricks there were witches' incantations. *Good* witches, the nuns carefully explained to the children (and hoped the parents would absorb, too), as most witches were, and are. Anne, Jan, Karen, Teresa, and Beatrice dressed the parts in costumes culled from twenty-five years' rummaging through used clothes sent, unsolicited, by supporters of the contemplative life. "Pray for me," said the letters accompanying the clothes, and so the community did, in their fashion, even as they pulled ruffled polyester blouses, barely wrinkled, out of bottomless boxes. Those they sent on, along with most of the skirts, coats, nightgowns, belts, dresses, and handbags, to local thrift stores and shelters. What they kept were jeans, wool and flannel shirts, fabric remnants, and occasionally attire suitable for dressing up, down, or different. Donna had discovered a gray bodysuit in a recent box which she wore this hallowed eve with oddly shaped corduroy ears. "Coyote," she whispered in response to a young questioner. Louise and Kathleen, having declared themselves weary of witches, wore, respectively, a dramatically colored and designed Renaissance gown, somewhat too large and badly stained, and a huge brown paper garment stuffed with cereal boxes collected from a neighbor's trash. "A bag of groceries, of course." Sharon came late and didn't dress, and Karen realized that probably no one had thought to warn the

relative newcomer of the coming chaos or to point out the cup-
board where accumulated costumes lay ready for play or party.

The children laughed gratifyingly at the cackling but not
particularly scary women and at the overexcited dog, Kiera,
who ran in circles and licked their sticky faces. They shifted in
their seats in the middle of Jan's ghost story, sign not so much,
Karen thought, of boredom as of longing for more convention-
ally sweet pastures of miniature Hershey bars and full-sized
Snickers. After they left, Karen sighed at the mess made in less
than an hour and took the largest broom to the common room
floor while Louise and Beatrice shook crumbs out of the rugs
and wiped up the brownish stains. Donna reported a puddle of
pee in one corner, and Kathleen seemed to remember a small
boy huddled there. "I'll bet his mother told him not to ask to
use the toilet," she said, "either because she thinks we don't
have one or because it seemed to her unseemly to mention such
an object in a house of prayer."

Jan drew the curtains, dimmed the lights, and chose carefully
from her collection of tapes. Before her arrival at Julian Pines,
the good nuns, under Louise's tutelage, did contra and Irish
folk dancing on Halloween and other celebratory occasions.
But Jan had brought rock music and amazing dance skills that
she insisted could be easily learned, and soon she had all but
Louise convinced of their cathartic capabilities. Louise she won
over by incorporating lower back exercises and learning with
great enthusiasm the folk steps for less raucous entertainment.
Karen was not, on either contra or rock nights, a very enthusi-
astic dancer, but some times, Halloween usually one of them,
she let herself be pulled, always by Anne, to the middle of the
floor, where she abandoned herself to the pounding rhythms
and lost for an hour or two that persistent sense of herself
(though it was, of course, less acute now, less pervasive than it
had been at seventeen) as too tall for grace.

She had used that phrase once, "too tall for grace"—it had
been her Aunt Pearl's pronouncement on Karen-at-fourteen-
years-and-almost-six-feet—when she and Anne were first
experimenting with sex. She had felt so, well, limby and jerky

next to Anne, who moved smoothly over Karen's stretched-out body and who, Karen had thought with awe and unstinting tenderness, moved like a dancer even when she came. "You may be," Anne had said, "too tall for Grace, but you're not too tall for me." In that sweet and silly pun (wordplay being one of Anne's many addictions and attractions) was, Karen recognized, the beginning of her long, slow, and sometimes painful process of standing up straight.

The witches left their costumes on and were the first to dance; Karen liked the long skirt at her calves and found softly erotic her circle of four—Beatrice seemed to have disappeared—black-outfitted women shaking, stretching, rolling, waving, and bending their witch-clothed bodies. "We look like nuns," Teresa shouted above the music, and they all laughed. Beatrice reappeared and joined the circle, which after a few minutes broke into a circle of three and a pair, Anne and Teresa. Damn them, Karen thought, oh, damn them both.

On another night she might have scolded the voice, called up her less belligerent spirits, repeated, incantationlike, the numerous virtues of the two witches dancing alone. But it was Halloween, there was mischief in the air, and she let the curse stand without censure, without comment, without even wondering what she meant by it. She just kept dancing. Both circles widened again, by the addition of the now uncostumed, though Donna left on her coyote ears. A weird woman, Karen thought, even weirder than the rest of us.

When she set out for her cabin, it was almost eleven, a late night for the good sisters. She flashed her light only when she needed it. Unlike Anne, who was night-blind, she saw well in the dark and didn't like to obscure the stars. She walked alone (having taken time to remove her witch's garb), fifty feet behind Anne and Teresa, engaged in some intense exchange that ended with a brief embrace when they reached Anne's rooms. A strange sight, Karen thought, two witches embracing in the dark, a small pool of light at their feet. She watched them. Teresa pulled away first and continued at a measured pace down toward her own cabin. The path to Karen's place diverged to the right from the road, about thirty feet before

Anne's. As she turned off, the remaining witch walked toward her. She wasn't crying—Anne almost never cried—but the veins stood out at her temples and her eyelids were red-rimmed, signs, Karen knew from many years' experience, of trouble.

"Turn off that flashlight," Karen said, in an effort to ignore what brewed. "Witches are supposed to be able to see in the dark." Anne looked down at her black clothes as though she had forgotten them and pressed the button. The two women stood there for a moment, in silence, under a moon that was not quite full and partly obscured by a small cloud. "I can't see your face," Anne said. "Can we talk inside?" She fumbled for a match to light the propane lamp in her entryway and let the lamp provide the light for the bedroom as well. Dim but suffi-cient. Karen sat cross-legged, as was her wont, on the bed and waited without speaking for Anne to initiate the inevitable rit-ual of sitting backward astride her desk chair as though she were going to plunge into conversation, then, before saying anything at all, turning back to the desk, opening the top drawer, taking out a cigarette, getting up and searching for matches, which were never in the porcelain ashtray where Karen would have kept them, were never, in fact, in any pre-dictable place. She ended up going back to the box in the entryway. After she lit the cigarette, she abandoned the chair and joined Karen on the bed, an action that would within a minute or two, Karen knew, necessitate getting up for the ash-tray, now out of reach. Karen liked knowing the moves ahead of time, liked knowing, for example, that there would be only one cigarette, to get them started, and that, once started, Anne would get right to the point.

"I'm a sex fiend."

Karen laughed. "You look like some sort of fiend in that outfit, but sex fiend wouldn't be my first guess."

"I'm not trying to be funny, Karen."

"Yes, you are, or you wouldn't have said that."

"I was trying to express, in a pithy but admittedly exagger-ated way, a serious problem. I mean, when I assess the situation rationally, I decide I'm just a normal woman with a normal sex drive. But here, among the saints, I feel like a nymphomaniac."

"Translation: Teresa doesn't want sex with you as often as you want sex with Teresa."

"Your translation," Anne said, "like most translations, is literally accurate but misses the subtle nuances."

"Like?"

"Like the fact that Teresa likes sex but doesn't seem to need it, like the fact that you liked sex once upon a time but seem to have transcended it, like the fact that Donna and Sharon and Louise and Jan and Kathleen and Beatrice do without it on a regular basis and never complain and never seem to fill the common space with erotic tension and never seem about to explode. What's wrong with *me?*"

Karen decided to be fair. "Maybe the question is what's wrong with the rest of us."

"I tell myself that sometimes," Anne said, "but it won't wash. You are all fine. You are affectionate and more or less sane and intelligent and fun and well, fine—not twisted by frustration, not anguished by erotic energy, not driven by the need to channel your sex drives into creative endeavors."

"You are affectionate and sane and intelligent and fun and fine, too, Anne, maybe even more so than the rest of us. Besides Beatrice."

"Then why do I feel like this? I love Teresa, I want her, I want her desperately, I want her to want me. She says yes, okay, fine, anytime, thanks, but she never *wants* me, and so mostly I've just stopped asking, and we haven't slept together in weeks."

"I'm sorry." Karen did feel sorry, rather to her surprise.

"Why should you be? You haven't slept with anyone for twenty years, and you never moan and groan about it."

"Never to you. I could hardly moan and groan about it to you, friend, when your answer would be—and it would be a fair answer—'you're the one who walked away.'"

"To whom, then?"

"Oh, to Beatrice."

"I bet you did it once, Karen, maybe fifteen years ago. Am I right?"

Karen laughed. "I think it was more like ten years ago, but yes, you're right. But ..."

"But you still have desires. You just breathe them into your roses, sing them into vespers, paint them into flowers, send sweet loving messages with them to us all, and maybe you even masturbate once in a while. Don't worry. I'm not asking. Damn it, Karen. I like my work, too, and I love vespers, and I feel close to my sisters, and I masturbate. But I want *sex*, with another living, breathing, panting human being. Who doesn't even have to be Teresa. Who could be Sojourner, who could be Jan, who could be that journalist who came—what was her name, Marta?—who could be you. Sometimes I even think about sex with Beatrice. I'm promiscuous as well as desperate.

"Do you understand what I'm saying, Karen? I live surrounded by women I love and I *want* them, and I don't understand why they don't all want each other."

Karen took a deep breath. She didn't know where to start. She lacked Anne's eloquence and perhaps her passion, but she, Karen, had things to say to this woman who mistook control for calm, who discarded effort, who, like the fisherman's wife, wanted castle for cottage and even then wasn't satisfied. She wanted to start five minutes back and say that if Teresa said yes, it was enough, take it, love her. It was greedy to want more than Teresa's yes. She wanted to say that Donna, good, kind, dependable Donna, preferred animals to humans and had who knows what kind of secret desires or secret holiness wrapped up in her silent ways. She wanted to say that Louise was single and celibate when she arrived at the monastery, in her thirties. What, if any repressions had brought her to them virginal were as incomprehensible to her, Karen, as to Anne. She wanted to say that Sharon hadn't been there very long but was, Karen strongly suspected, going to have a lot of trouble with this very desire and that Jan, Karen knew for a fact, though she wasn't at liberty to say so, had as much trouble with it as Anne; that Jan had actually, for over a year, had an enormous crush on

Anne, which she worked with touching diligence and ingenu-
ousness to overcome. She wanted to say that Kathleen and
Beatrice had desire beaten out of them at Mt. Carmel and that
Beatrice sometimes seemed to beat back desire still. Once, at
least, Karen thought she had seen it, alive and, yes, desperate,
in Beatrice's eyes—which were, at the time, looking at Anne.

She wanted to say that she, Karen, had times of calm and
times of chaos, that she *did*, when chaos came, breathe desire
into her roses and into her drawings, that she did love herself
with it and torture herself over it, that Beatrice had, in a most
passionate and un-Beatricelike way, said once that she must
never do it violence because without it this life was nothing.
She wanted to say that sometimes (maybe because she had
tried not to do it violence) she, Karen, wanted her, Anne, desperately and passionately, not often, but sometimes. Like,
Anne, like tonight when we were dancing, when you and
Teresa broke away from the circle and I said to myself, damn
them, damn them. I said that, Anne, because *I* wanted you, I
wanted to throw myself at you and rip off that witch's shirt
and—right there on the common room floor—suck your nipples through my teeth until they bled. That's what I wanted,
Anne (how do you like that?), that's what I *want*.

She wanted to say these things, and she did say them. She
said them all except for the part about Jan, which she knew
but couldn't say, and the part about Beatrice, which she didn't
know and couldn't say and was afraid of. She said them until
the tears were running down her cheeks and until Anne unbuttoned first the witch's shirt and then the witch's skirt and took
off the bra and pants underneath and came at Karen naked, her
nipples erect, and said in her huskiest voice, "Suck them,
Karen, until they bleed."

While Karen sucked, Anne stripped her, not gently, carefully, as she had so many years before (when that her tall, thin
body even breathed must have seemed to Anne a tenuous miracle), but quickly, roughly. Karen helped with her jeans, let go
of Anne long enough to light a candle to replace the dimming
propane lamp. "I want to *see* you," she said. She looked hard at
Anne's body, different from the memories but no less com-

pelling. She ran her hands down Anne's hips, felt Anne's hands grabbing her butt, pushed Anne to the bed. They struggled there, not for anything but the struggle itself, and Karen came out on top. She slid herself down until her mouth was again around Anne's breast, and she drew the nipples again through her teeth, in and out, in and out. At the same time she thrust three fingers inside of her and rubbed the ball of her hand firmly against Anne's pubic bone. Anne spread her legs far apart and danced wildly into Karen's hand, whispering, hoarsely, harshly, "Harder, harder," then moaning so loudly that young Karen would have let go at first sound of it, but this Karen didn't, couldn't. She only sucked and pushed and pulled harder until Anne came, almost shouting. She tasted blood.

Without transition, without letting up on the frantic pace, Anne flipped her over and took charge. Suddenly the moans were Karen's, and she felt with panicked pleasure the finger that had been aimlessly roaming her belly and cunt work its way slowly into her ass and Anne's thumb on her clitoris. And by the time Anne's mouth closed over her breast she had wrapped her legs around Anne's body and was using them to push her hips forward into the firm flesh of Anne's belly. "What *is* this," she said in a loud voice that seemed to be coming from across the room, "Oh God, what *is* this?" Anne slid her mouth down Karen's pumping body, and with her tongue traced circles in Karen's pubic hair while she pressed her thumb inside her. Karen writhed, trying to get herself into Anne's mouth, but Anne teased on. "Tell me what you want."

"You know what I want," Karen managed to say between breaths.

"Say it."

"Suck me."

"How?"

"Hard."

When she woke up at 4:30, Karen lay quietly beside the sleeping witch and wondered if what they had done at midnight was make love or do battle. She felt bruised, her thigh muscles ached. She remembered the way they had held each other down, pushed and pulled, teased and scratched, bit and shouted and dared. She remembered it as a dream and she the dreamer but not one of the breathless, violent women, teeth bared, rolling over in the bed, spitting blood out of their mouths. She wished it were light so she could see if she had broken the skin on Anne's breast. Surely not. She tried to say "Damn you" to the body at her side, but she couldn't. The words that came so easily last night were gone. And when she slid silently out of the bed and into her clothes, she longed for Anne's fingers on her flesh, not clawing but tracing. She took her shoes to the entryway, and as she bent over to pull them on, she noticed the objects on the table by the door. A glass of water, with a note taped to it: Always drink before running. Two pieces of chocolate on top of another note: Don't run away altogether. Anne must have written the notes, blind as she was, in the night, while Karen slept; Anne had known she would run, though she hadn't run for years; Anne, Anne, Anne. She loved her with every sore muscle in her body, with every drop of her blood, with every cell of her brain. She had loved her, not since the day they met, the two young newcomers, wary of the women, of each other, wondering, separately, about this strange step their lives seemed to have taken without them, not since then but since the day Anne appeared at the side of Karen's bed, though she had never nursed, and stayed through the long and frightening illness that so suddenly claimed her. Though the doctor had answered her questions patiently enough, her diagnosis of Karen's driving pain paled in explanatory power beside the dark, troubling pieces of her life that worked their way like shards of glass to the surface of her skin. It was Anne who took tweezers to them, held them up to the light for her, safely disposed of them when she was finished. Likewise the doctor's account of Karen's recovery bore too little resemblance to her own sense that cells healed under the tips of Anne's fingers, that every time Anne's hands rubbed her neck, her shoulders, her sides, they rubbed off death.

Outside Anne's door, Karen stretched and reached and fell without thinking into her old prerunning routine. It was dark and it was cold, but Karen thought that in a couple of miles it would begin to get light and she would begin, even sooner, to get warm. And so she ran, trying at first to ward off the cold by singing some of the songs, what she could remember of them, that Anne had sung to her during the weeks of nursing. Quiet, kind weeks. Anne had sung while she stroked Karen's face, blew cool breath on her hot forehead, traced soft circles on her cheeks. First there were folk songs—it was 1969—lullabies, labor songs, songs from the civil rights movement, songs from some long ago summer camp. "From the hills I gather courage / Visions of the days to be. / Strength to lead and strength to follow / All are given unto me." Karen looked out the window when Anne sang that one. "Nuns," Anne explained. "It was a camp run by the Sisters of Social Service. They wore gray wool and were into the inspirational stuff." But she sang it purely, and Karen's arms got goose bumps. They were so young.

"O gay is the garland and fresh are the roses / I've culled from the garden to bind on thy brow." Karen had liked the roses in that song. Some days she imagined them yellow and warm, other days, when her fever raged, lavender and cool. And then there was the song in a minor key, so slow and mournful. How did it go? "Come all ye fair and tender maidens / Be careful when you court young men / They're like a star on a summer morning / They'll come in view, then fade again."

"And, Sister Karen," Anne had said, after the first time she sang it, "let that be a lesson to you." Karen had been too sick to laugh. And there were days when she was so sick that she only wanted one song, but she never told Anne that, she just let her sing and hoped she'd come to it eventually. "When you wake, you will find / All the pretty little horses. Dappled and gray, pinto and bay / All the pretty little horses." Karen's mother had sung that song, but never the part about dappled and gray. Had Anne made it up?

She was already at the apple orchard when she remembered the Irish songs. Anne had thought of them late, when Karen was already mending, so she associated them with the best days of the illness, when she and Anne could talk and laugh, and she could eat, and Anne took such touching pleasure in bringing her food, always carefully arranged on the plate, trimmed with bits of parsley, accompanied by slices of apples in whose restorative properties Anne firmly believed. An apple a day.

"You may take the shamrock from your hat and cast it on the sod / But 'twill take root and flourish still though underfoot 'tis trod." Once Anne had figured out all the words, she sang it almost every day. A fighting song, she said to Karen, good for you. "And if the color we must wear is England's cruel red / Sure Ireland's folk will ne'er forget the blood that they have shed." Anne's English father hated that song, she said, so she sang it often, especially in March, especially when she couldn't get his attention any other way. He hated that song most, but he hated all Irish songs. Maybe, she said, maybe that's why she knew so many.

Anne used to say good-night with "Danny Boy," which, as often as not, she changed to "Annie Girl." After a while she'd make Karen sing the last two lines—while she kissed her: "For you will bend and tell me that you love me / And I shall sleep in peace until you come to me." The better she felt, the more lines she would sing, the more Anne would kiss her, her forehead, her cheeks, her ears, her neck. And, when the song was over, her lips. The kisses got longer, and one night they kissed so long and it was so dark and cold that Anne asked if she could stay. She could, oh yes, she could.

Karen picked up the pace, partly because she was running downhill, partly because she couldn't bear to remember what had happened that first night Anne stayed. The sweetness if it, the youthfulness of it, the carefulness of it, the wholeness of it. Whole and healed she had felt afterward, lying in Anne's arms. She didn't want to sleep because Anne was asleep, and she wanted to watch her, so small, so lovely, so delicate, so unlike the vigorous woman who had cared for her so competently, day after day, for almost three months. Sweet gum leaves were falling all around her, red and orange and yellow, she knew, though they all looked alike in the dark. She wanted to see a real fall someday, a Vermont fall, for example, a New Hampshire fall. Anne said that you had to see it to believe it but that

they deserved it, the New Englanders, compensation for the
cold and the dark.

By catching leaves and giving them colors—pomegranate,
persimmon, pumpkin, grape, mustard, ocher, olive, chestnut,
aubergine—Karen could stave off exhaustion for a while. She
stuffed them into her pockets so she could see, after sunrise, if
they lived up to their names. She ran and ran. It was still dark,
but you could feel dawn. She knew she should stop because
she'd been running an hour after years of not running and her
knee ached. She knew she should stop because she had gone
too far already, mostly downhill, and it would be a long hike
back. She knew she should stop because she was too old for
this, not the running but the running away. But she kept going
because Anne's taste was still in her mouth, Anne's smell in her
nose, Anne's fingers on her breasts, Anne's leg between her
legs, Anne's eyes everywhere. Run, Karen, run.

In the half light of this All Saints' morning Karen started to feel
her knee collapse. She cried out in irritation that her old injury
had recurred, that it was so cold, that she was so many miles
from Julian Pines, that she hadn't finished running. She
dragged herself to a tree and sat down against the trunk. After
a few minutes she had to shift her weight because her good leg
was falling asleep and her tailbone ached. She thought of
Anne's hands, generously covered with almond oil, cinnamon
scented, starting with her feet and massaging their way up,
every muscle, large and small, succumbing to their warm pressure. Thanks, she was convinced, to those daily rubs, her limbs
had worked admirably when she left her sickbed.

She leaned against the tree, almost warm on her back. She
listened for cars, heard nothing for a long time, thought again
about crawling to the nearest house, then fell, briefly, asleep.
She dreamed. A vague woman, a half seduction, a windowless
room, a cup of coffee she tried to smell but couldn't, a heart—
hers—beating fast, hard, loud. She caught herself before she
toppled over onto the ground, dream suspended. She was cold,
her bladder was full, her knee hurt. She wondered why no one
came.

Finally she heard a car approaching, more slowly than she would have expected, the curve around her tree. She was relieved that it didn't sound like a pick-up. She wouldn't ask a ride from a stranger, but there were, she reminded herself, friends in the mountains. It was, however, none of the Halloween guests, still sticky from her caramel apples, who was driving the car. It was one of the witches. "Anne," she shouted. "Anne." Anne parked the abbey Toyota in a small clearing on the other side of the road from Karen's tree. She got out slowly and walked, just as slowly, across the road. She sat down next to her. "Hi," she said. "Hi there."

"Hi there, yourself," Karen said.

"You forgot your chocolate." Anne held out the wrapped balls. Karen shook her head.

"I picked an apple on my way through the orchard."

"Looks like it's still in your pocket."

"It is," Karen said, "minus a bite." She took it out along with the leaves, most of them disappointingly brown, which she tossed in Anne's direction. Several landed in her hair. "Happy fall."

"Happy fall," Anne said, "oh happy, happy fall. When did you do it?"

"Do what?"

"Fall."

"How do you know I fell? Maybe I'm just resting. Waiting for the sun to rise over the mountain peak."

"You're facing in the wrong direction."

"And what are you doing in these parts, Sister Anne Stratford?"

"Looking for a runaway nun," Anne said. "Tall, thin, brown hair, wearing jeans and a green jacket. Early forties, very attractive, bum knee, answers to 'Karen.' There's a reward."

"What is it?"

"Oh, a cup of steaming hot coffee. Scones and boysenberry jam. Me."

Karen licked her lips. "I had a dream."

"Was she beautiful?"

"Very."

"Did she look like me?" Anne asked.

"Not a bit. She was tall, elegant, dressed in some sort of smoking jacket. When she was dressed."

"Nice dream. Did you run away?"

"No," Karen said, "I woke up. And I was cold and my knee hurt."

"That's the trouble with dreams," Anne said, reaching out to help Karen to the car.

"But maybe," Karen said, "maybe that's the trouble with sex."

And so the conversation went, predictably enough, all the way home, Anne wanting, it seemed, to go over every inch of the night's territory, describing the warmth of it, delineating the loveliness of it, dwelling on the usefulness of it. "We have been talking for twenty years," she said, "arguing away our lives. I feel as though we've settled something, come together, loved each other again in some significant way." Absorbed in the eloquence of one and skepticism of the other, they missed the sunrise.

"I tasted blood," Karen said.

"How did it taste?"

"Bitter," Karen said, "and strong."

Anne one-handedly unzipped her jacket and unbuttoned her shirt and lifted her breasts, one at a time, out of her bra. "Look," she said, "whole and pink. If you tasted blood it was your own. Maybe you bit your tongue." One at a time, Karen tucked the breasts (they were soft, smooth, tempting, unmarked by teeth) back into the cups; she buttoned the shirt; she zipped the jacket. She exaggeratedly examined her tongue in the visor mirror.

"Tongues heal quickly," Anne said, as she turned into the abbey entrance and drove slowly up the dry dirt road to the common house.

"Maybe breasts do, too," Karen said, "on the feast of saints. You know, a sort of miracle in honor of Agnes, who lopped off her breast to save her hymen. Or did the Roman lop it off?"

"The Romans. And it was Agatha. Or maybe you're thinking of Lucy who plucked out her eyes," Anne said, "or Apollonia who jumped into the fire. They were bloody and savage women, our virgin martyrs."

"I smell coffee," Karen said.

"Well," Anne said, "let's drink to them: St. Agnes, St. Lucy, St. Agatha, St. Perpetua, St. Felicitas, St. Apollonia, St. Cecilia, St. Anastasia, St. Catherine, St. Bibiana, St. Christina, St. Ursula, St. Dorothy, St. Barbara, St. Emerentiana, St. Margaret, St. Martina ..."

"Anne," Karen said, interrupting the litany, "sometimes you exhaust me."

AUTHOR'S NOTE

I have been thinking for a long time about Allan Sillitoe's story, "The Loneliness of the Long-Distance Runner" and Grace Paley's brilliant contribution to the conversation, "The Long-Distance Runner." It occurred to me that Paley accomplishes such interesting things by replacing the handsome male adolescent hero with an overweight middle-aged woman that I wondered what would happen if I replaced him with someone who differed not only in age, appearance, and gender but sexual orientation as well.

I then found a story by the English writer Sara Maitland called "The Loveliness of the Long-Distance Runner," in which the main characters are lesbian, but I didn't think the story worked very well. So, I wrote my own, using characters about whom I have been thinking and writing for several years—a group of offbeat nuns in a monastery in the Sierras. The original title was "The Nunliness of the Long-Distance Runner."

ABOUT THE AUTHORS
❥❥❥❥❥❥❥

Some of these names are real, some invented.

Carolyn Banks is the author of four novels, including *Mr. Right* and *Patchwork,* as well as many short stories. She and her husband raise horses on a farm near Austin, Texas.

Rebecca Battle works as an actress in Los Angeles and New York. This is her first published story. "Since I have a sublet, I had to type it at a public terminal, which turned out to be somewhat traumatic—writing about such things with all those people strolling behind you, discussing the latest fonts! Still, it definitely added to the excitement of the experience."

Idious Buguise lives in London near Paddington Station. "I have never been in therapy—except once for forty-five minutes when I was eleven years old—have two small children who know where babies come from, and hate people who wear fur coats."

Liz Clarke is a 1992 college graduate. A native North Carolinian, she wrote her first poem at age six and began her first novel two years later. She is an alumnus of the University of Virginia's Young Writers Workshop. "I'm fascinated by sex and sexuality these days because I spent so much of my life utterly out of touch with, and terrified by, my body, and so I'm making up for lost time."

Sara Davidson is the author of the bestselling novel *Loose Change*, which was turned into a miniseries. Her other books are *Real Property* and *Friends of the Opposite Sex* (from which "The Wager" was excerpted). Currently writing for television, she lives in Los Angeles with her two children.

Jenny Diski was born in London where she still lives and writes full-time. She has published five novels: *Nothing Natural, Rainforest, Like Mother, Then Again,* and *Happily Ever After.*

Susan Dooley is a writer living in a small New England village.

Sabina Faye is a mystery novelist who has lived in Australia, Nepal, and Switzerland; when not traveling, she makes her home in Washington, D.C. She has worked as an au pair, a manual laborer, a bartender, and as a dancing extra in an opera company.

Barbara Gowdy is the author of two novels, *Through the Green Valley* and *Falling Angels.* She lives with her cats, Jack and Emma, in Toronto, where she can be seen as one of the guest interviewers for the TV-Ontario book program "In Print."

Kay Kemp is a Canadian novelist and short-story writer.

Wendy Law-Yone was born in Mandalay, Burma, grew up in Rangoon, and lived in several countries of Southeast Asia before settling in the United States in 1973. Her first novel was *The Coffin Tree;* she is at work on a second. Her work has appeared in *The Atlantic* and in *Grand Street.* The mother of four, she is the recipient of a National Endowment for the Arts award.

Carol Lazare lives with her daughter, Lilly, in Toronto. Her work as an actress earned her two Canadian film awards; more recently, she has concentrated on writing for theater and film. "'Footpath' is one of a collection of short stories called *When the Cycle Ends* that I'm currently working on. All of the stories, of which there are now five, revolve in some way around the same characters, Sarah and Eddy; this one describes their first meeting and sets the tone for their obsessive relationship."

Susan J. Leonardi teaches literature and creative writing at the University of Maryland. She is the author of *Dangerous by Degrees: Women at Oxford and the Somerville College Novelists*. "Too Tall for Grace" will appear in a longer version in her collection *Nun Stories*. "I'm also working on a detective novel and collaborating on something more academic, a book called *To Have a Voice: The Politics of the Diva*. This is a project that perhaps suggests a secret longing to exchange the privacy of the page for the exhibition of the stage. In my next life, I'm going to be a performance artist."

Carole Maso is the author of the novels *Ghost Dance* and *The Art Lover*. She has recently completed a third, *The American Woman in the Chinese Hat*. She makes her home in New York City.

Anne Rhyd is a science and technology writer who has recently moved to New Orleans.

Catherine S. is a journalist. She is from a southern family that her sister has described as one part Tennessee Williams, one part Erskine Caldwell. "As a child, I read compulsively from a cache of books beneath my bed that included *Lolita, The Valley of the Dolls, Candy,* and *God's Little Acre*."

Susan Swan is a Toronto-based journalist, performance artist, and fiction writer. Her works include *Unfit For Paradise, The Biggest Modern Woman of the World,* and *The Last of the Golden*

Girls. Her new book, *Homage to America,* will examine the personification of ideas in the U.S. media.

Lisa Tuttle was born and raised in Houston, Texas, but now lives on the remote west coast of Scotland with her husband and baby daughter. She is the author of many short stories and several novels, the most recent of which is *Lost Futures,* as well as the nonfiction books *Encyclopedia of Feminism* and *Heroines: Women Inspired by Women.* She has also edited *Skin of the Soul,* a collection of original horror stories by women writers.

Bea Wilder has lived in Cambridge, Massachusetts, for the past twenty years, with the exception of a period when she taught in South America — "where I rediscovered my Peruvian roots." She has worked as a community activist, newspaper gossip columnist, and elementary school teacher. She is currently studying for a master's degree in counseling/psychology.

COPYRIGHT
ACKNOWLEDGMENTS
❧❧❧❧❧❧❧

ABOUT THE EDITOR

Michele Slung's works include *Crime on Her Mind,* a historical anthology of fictional women detectives; *The Absent-Minded Professor's Memory Book; The Only Child Book;* and the bestselling *Momilies*® books, *Momilies: As My Mother Used to Say*® and *More Momilies*®. Her most recent book was the collection *I Shudder at Your Touch: Tales of Sex and Horror.*

In addition, she served as editor for the Plume American Women Writers series, presenting long out-of-print fiction in a uniform format, and she was first an editor, then a columnist for the *Washington Post Book World.*